If You Believe the Soldiers

If You Believe the Soldiers

ALEXANDER CORDELL

DOUBLEDAY & COMPANY, INC.

GARDEN CITY, NEW YORK

1974

ISBN: 0-385-09612-7
Library of Congress Catalog Card Number 73–13277
Copyright © 1973 by Alexander Cordell
All Rights Reserved
Printed in the United States of America
First Edition in the United States of America

For Alun Evans

If you believe the doctors,
nothing is wholesome; if
you believe the theologians,
nothing is innocent; if
you believe the soldiers,
nothing is safe.

LORD SALISBURY

If You Believe the Soldiers

CHAPTER 1

I first met Hallie at Hatherley; even the names were gently coinci-
dental. Ironically, it was Moira, my wife, who invited her to come
there to meet me. In retrospect, I would rather have met her anywhere but at Hatherley, which I loved; it was an invasion of its
sanctity.

Here, in the house of my parents and three generations before
them, were the long summers of my childhood; fishing with my
father on sultry summer afternoons, tennis, swimming, and mad
chases over the Big Field after butterfly specimens—the straw-
boatered adolescent on half-term from Eton.

Ancient, seemingly indestructible, Hatherley had survived the
blood-bath of the First World War, when it lost many of its sons,
and had defied the indiscriminate bombing of the Second. Its huge
poplars still waved down the Woking lanes; its woods, guarded by
the Mole River, were hazed with blue now that spring had come
again. Here, it was claimed, was always heard the first cuckoo in
the area of Woking; here the kingfishers flashed their colours down
the little brook that sang to the mill. Hatherley, for me, was classically perfect—a house unchanged until the coming of Moira: perhaps it was a tribute to her strength of character that only she could
have changed it.

The house with its eight acres was born in the manner of the
period; my father increased the family fortune by big legal cases
abroad. He read to me religious tracts every Sunday evening, shot
grouse in Scotland, and possessed a mistress in London called Fifi.
His Jewish conservatism contrasted with my mother's liberal ma-

11

ternalism, which extended to the housemaids. With one of these, Dolly Barber, I was in love at the age of fourteen; she was two years older, and ought to have known better, according to my mother. She had black hair and wet, red lips, I recall, and dandruff on her shoulders. And I got her in the wood shed with the light out, and Cook stood on a brick and peeped through the window, and later reported us. Dolly was discharged and sent to her mother with a letter, while I sat in sweating terror, listening to my father's footsteps mounting the stairs to my bedroom. But it was worth it. Next to Sharps' Creamy Toffee, Dolly Barber was the sweetest thing that had then happened to me.

Originally, the Goldstein fortune (my father had changed our name to Seaton by deed poll) had been battered out of the Gold Coast, where finger-amputation was the standard punishment for leaving one's place of work without permission, but Hatherley had managed to absorb such unpleasantries and none of this affected the liberalism I had learned from my mother. The house, for me, was an oasis of peace and love (including that of Dolly Barber) until the advent of Moira twenty years later and, more recently, the arrival of Hallie.

Marriage to Moira, the daughter of a Connemara gipsy landowner, had brought the sherry parties. With my mother dead and my father practising in Stuttgart, the place was invaded most weekends by blue-jowled men of tweed who barked over whisky about hunting and the Market, while their shagged-out, nasal wives planned the working-class vote through meals-on-wheels and a now politically conscious W.I. All this, plus fanatical bridge, was Moira's world, and she swept through it with the gusto of the horsed beggar, receiving the approbation of the Woking executive set, the Master of the local hunt, and the tributes of one lover after another.

It was a far cry from the white breast of little Dolly Barber, who was my first real descent into the moral abyss, before I met Hallie.

Following Moira's invitation, Hallie had come to Hatherley with Anthony Hargreaves, now head of Brander's Moral Guidance Council—scarcely a diplomatic choice, I considered. She had been given a double bedroom with him by a mischievous Moira, and accepted it without protest. And, when I came in from London after a hard day at the Ministry, she was sitting at the lounge window where my mother used to sit, staring over the Big Field beyond the drive. I saw her the moment I stopped the car, and did not bother to garage it. For she was like a ghost of the past sitting there in her long, white dress, unmoving. The party was already going with a swing, I remember, with Marsella, Moira's hunting friend, the centre of attraction; there were some beautiful women in the room, but only Hallie attracted me. I paused before her, holding my briefcase against my stomach, now an indiscretion.

"Good evening," I said.

If she replied, I did not hear her.

It was her eyes. They drifted over me in slow assessment, seeming to dance with an inner merriment. There was a reason for this, of course, and I should have been aware of it. She was beautiful, but scarcely pretty. White lace at her throat enhanced the dark sheen of her flawless skin. Her hands and feet were tiny; she was a woman in miniature. Then Hargreaves, coming up, cried, "Ah, here you are, Mark . . . !" and was instantly pushed aside by Marsella, who cried, gin in hand:

"Oh, no you don't, Tony, this is mine." And she swung to the guests, shouting in her raucous voice, "Mark, this is Hallie Fitzgeralt, the five-foot model of the Courval Salon, where we now buy our clothes. Hallie, my pet, this is Mark Seaton, the new Director of Contracts in his Ministry and the master of beautiful Hatherley," and she added, "Look out, Moira, she's got him!"

She had.

Making love to Hallie Fitzgeralt, I discovered later, was like swimming in a jar of warm honey. But there was more to it than the intensity of my physical relief; she was like a balm—freedom from my immense and awful loneliness.

And if Moira, in the coming weeks, knew of our affair she made no visible sign. She could have had me back with the touch of her hand, but doubtless, with more lovers than she could at present conveniently handle, she was glad to be free of me.

For my part I never really loved Hallie. After the nightmares and the savage, sweating dreams that reached out from my youth, she was a woman in which to hide in the absence of my wife.

Later, with the guests gone, Moira said, "She's a pretty wee thing that Hallie, ye know. She's a Jewess, says Marsella—d'you realise that?"

I paused at the lounge door on my way to bed. She was lying on a settee with her shoes off and a large gin, moving with accentuated indolence.

"No," I answered. "I did not know."

She said at nothing, "You could do worse than a return to the tribe of Israel, you know—God knows why you ever married out of it."

"Good night," I said.

It was forgivable—she was a little drunk, of course.

CHAPTER 2

A group of lounging blackshirt guards were outside the Ministry of Building when I came out of it some weeks later. It was just over a month since Brander's military coup, I remember, during which time my friendship with Hallie had flourished, much to the disgust of Anthony Hargreaves, who plainly considered her his property. Certainly, it was surprising that Hallie seemed to prefer me to him, for he was twenty years my junior, extremely goodlooking, and his position as head of Moral Guidance was a glamorous comparison, in prospects, to my desultory position as Director of Contracts.

Brander's blackshirts stood unmoving before me—the usual attempt at silent intimidation, and I stood on the steps of the Ministry with my hands in my pockets until Security Jones, our hall porter, came down and cleared them. One said:

"What about his pass, then?"

"He's the Director of Contracts," replied Security Jones, bulging with open hostility. "Make way if you know what's good for you."

I doubted the wisdom of it. Later, at the first opportunity, they would doubtless see to the pair of us. With my briefcase under my arm I walked down to the Cenotaph: there Sam, my taxi, was waiting.

"Bond Street, please," I said.

"The Courval Salon on Thursdays," said Sam, and drove away. Knowledge of my movements over the past ten years was one of Sam's indulgences; he had been quick to appreciate my change of venue on Thursdays over the past month, though as far as Moira knew, I was still sleeping at the Reform Club.

"Same time tomorrow morning, Mr. Seaton?" he asked now.

"Unless I telephone the kiosk earlier, and it's not what you think."

"Of course not," said Sam.

A few minor fires were still burning in the city. Although the coup was supposed to be over and Brander's victory complete, there were still occurring spasmodic attacks upon his authority. The Admiralty, for instance, was still smouldering from the Unionist assault the night before last, although they had been repelled with terrifying losses by Brander's storm troopers. And the wind was acrid with smoke as I opened the taxi door outside the Courval Salon. An old Centurion tank clanked past me towards Piccadilly where a workers' demonstration was due to be held that night, and there were a lot of blackshirts on the streets, always a sign of impending Trade Union sabotage. I stared about me at the growing dusk as I rang the bell of the salon.

"Ah, Mark—I'm glad you could come," cried Hallie.

"Scarcely, a comparison with the eminent Hargreaves?"

"Do we have to talk about him?"

Dressed in a white gown she looked charming; white enhanced her figure—tiny, yet beautifully proportioned; her dark hair was lying loosely on her shoulders.

I saw her against an avenue of naked plastic models who displayed their limbs in caricatures of death; witless victims of a shattering bomb, their hands protecting their faces as if in horror. And Hallie led the way through these puppets. Tomorrow, she informed me, they would have new clothes on, for things were becoming more normal after the Brander coup—even the Paris fashions were starting to come in. Moira, I reflected dully, would be delighted; she spent a lot of my money at Courval's—mainly on items modelled by Hallie, perhaps a minor act of revenge: yet, even if she knew of our affair, I thought, she was scarcely in a position to mention it.

A monstrous and ornate grandfather clock was guarding the doors to the flat upstairs, and it was ticking like a time-bomb. Sweat sprang to my face and I closed my eyes.

"I'm sorry," said Hallie, pausing to stop its pendulum. "I really should have remembered. Are . . . are you all right?" She touched my arm.

"Perfectly."

"Poor Mark." On tiptoe, she kissed my face.

To have apologised yet again for this weakness would have soiled the solemnity of Monsieur Courval's personal morgue, which had to be entered to get to Hallie.

In the serenity of the flat above I held her, smiling within my induced oblivion. Thoughtfully, she took off her watch and laid it on the dressing-table, yet its faint ticking held me with rooted force.

"Mark, Mark!" she said.

But I only really heard the ticking of the watch.

Unaccountably, in the midst of this love-making I kept remembering the face of Moira: some sweetness seemed to be reaching out its arms to me from the early days of our marriage: even in Hallie's sighs I heard the sounds of Moira. Now, lying in the bed with Hallie's hand in mine, I wondered if Moira would be at Hatherley this coming weekend, and if she might receive a gesture of love with patience: if a new refinement and mutual respect might even now be built between us. Then I remembered Henry Shearer and decided that this weekend she would probably be away somewhere with him. Vaguely I wondered how Kate, Shearer's wife, managed to put up with his blatant infidelity: one of the most beautiful women in London, she had so far managed to ignore the growing scandals that pestered me in the office. And Su-len? Su-len, I decided, would be as passively Oriental as ever; sitting at the window where Hallie had sat, awaiting the sound of my car at the end of the drive. She never asked where I had been when away at night: for an adopted fifteen-year-old she was surprisingly diplomatic about my nightly disappearances, and the Chinese are a notably curious race. As if detecting an infidelity, Hallie asked, "What are you thinking?"

I did not answer immediately, for I had begun to think about Bishop Forsward whom Colonel Brander's Triumvirate had recently arrested for criticism of his regime. Amazingly, as if reading my thoughts, Hallie said suddenly, "If they shoot that bishop there's going to be trouble, you know."

"Forsward, the South African?"

"The only churchman with the guts to speak out."

I grunted. "If they do shoot him he won't be the last—go to sleep, forget it all."

She sat up, resting on an elbow beside me. Her face, in that blue light was that of an albino; white, aesthetic, with puddles of darkness for eyes. Her voice was disdainful. "Forget it? Is that all we can do? Brander's thugs have been arresting and killing for weeks. What are they doing about it in the ministries?"

"There is nothing anybody can do, and you know it."

"You've only got to go into the street and the blackshirts whistle —you try being a woman these days. One day I'll spit in their faces."

"I'd confine that to the bedroom, if I were you."

"All last night they were out after the Union Apprentices—just boys. They were shooting them half the night—and you Londoners go to bed and sleep."

"It won't last—you don't know Londoners."

I was a little surprised at her. Until now I had considered her as a surprisingly intelligent model: it was a sort of pathological madness for anyone to criticise Brander. There was more to Hallie than superficially appeared, but I was wishing her to the devil; I desperately needed sleep. Warming to her subject, she said "What about the children, Mark? Do you want your Su-len to grow up under Brander's Fascism? Joe's an adult, but what about young Su-len?"

"What about her?" Exhaustion was claiming me. I was drooping, and she was wide awake. Ironically I reflected on the disparity between our ages—the old fool in the young bed; vaguely I wondered what Moira was doing.

Hallie replied, "Yes, what about her? Can you really insist that she drops her nationality and becomes British in the Brander state?" I scarcely heard her; I was listening to distant guns.

"I am not insisting that she becomes British. On the contrary, I encourage her in everything Chinese—she attends the Woking School of Afro-Asian Studies—I even talk to her in Cantonese."

"What does she look like?"

I groaned. "Oh, Hallie, at this time of night?"

She pulled me over to face her. "Haven't I the right? You say you're in love with me, but I know practically nothing about you. You let me find out about your son Joe, and you've only once mentioned Su-len—what's she like?"

"She has black hair and slanted eyes."

"So have most Chinese."

"God Almighty!" I sat up, fumbling for a cigarette.

The moon was sitting in the window, I remember, and in that light I saw her face. By some trick of the moonlight it was strangely darker, and her hair, in shadow, was as black as Su-len's. Indeed, she was at once incredibly like Su-len; then the moon faded, and the vision vanished.

"How long have you had her, Mark?"

"Su? About twelve years—she was three when we adopted her."

"In England?"

"No—Malaya. I was on a tour of the East for the Ministry, lecturing on computerised bills of quantities . . . look, do we have to? It's getting very late . . ."

"Tell me." She was intent, unmoving.

I said, "Well, I was called to Kuala Lumpur to arbitrate on a contractual dispute near Kajang—nothing at all to do with the Ministry. There was a big muck-shifting contract—airfield clearance—I found her wandering around the site."

"And you picked her up and brought her home?"

"Not immediately. In one of the hutment clearings a blade-grader unearthed an old Japanese bomb, and the contractor called me over. To my astonishment, it was ticking."

She opened wide eyes at me. I continued: "This was my work after the war, remember? And I recognised its type immediately. It was far too big to blow in situ—there were hundreds of native huts around, I decided to disarm it."

She nodded, unspeaking.

19

"Well, I sent down to First Aid for a stethoscope and got out the jeep's tools. Somebody found me a ratchet-chain and I took the top off the thing. There was nothing complicated about it—a simple clock mechanism, or I wouldn't have attempted it."

"And Su-len?"

"I remembered her probably because she was the youngest child there—after I'd got the clock out the villagers wandered back—you know how kids stand and stare. I spoke to her in Tamil, but she didn't understand, and the head man told me she was Chinese, and had only been in the village a week. Somebody passing through must have dumped her on the road near by. He said he thought she was Tangar, from the Pearl River delta—aboriginal extraction, she was nearly as dark as a Negress . . ."

"But why did you take her away from there?"

I said, "After I'd disarmed the bomb I called a tractor driver in and told him to hitch it up, drag it off the site and bury it somewhere. Then I went back to the jeep, got in it and drove away. I hadn't got a quarter of a mile before there was an explosion—the bloody thing had gone up with everybody standing round it."

"Oh, God."

"It was the simplest booby-trap in the world, and I fell for it—a dud clockwork bomb linked by chain to a live one ten yards away; when the dud was moved the real one went up. It decimated the village; forty people were killed and nearly a hundred wounded —the tractor was blown to pieces, its shrapnel hit the surrounding compounds. The only child survivor was Su-len. Because I'd made a fuss of her she had followed my jeep down the road."

"And this saved her."

I nodded. "But she was badly shocked." The ticking began in my head again. I added, "I killed them as surely as if I'd shot them up —sodding around with a Jap alarm clock and forgetting to isolate a first-stage booby. It was unforgivable."

"And Su-len's part of the guilt complex?" Hallie stared at me.

"I suppose so. I telephoned Moira from Singapore and she agreed to the adoption—it wasn't easy, you know; children are precious in the East."

"So Moira brought her up?"

"No, I did. After the initial excitement of the adoption, Moira grew less and less interested in her. But she was Chinese, and entitled to her heritage. I had been educated in China and had never quite lost my links, so I taught her the language—Cantonese, since she obviously came from the south. Embarrassingly, since Moira's set are anti-social, as Su-len got older her skin grew darker—proof indeed that she was Tangar."

"So she became Mark's personal property!"

"I wouldn't put it like that."

"Based on a pygmalion theme?"

I replied, "That could be thought unkind."

"It was meant to be. I'm already tired of this particular specimen." The gunfire, I recall, was becoming louder.

"Hallie, don't be ridiculous!"

She stretched beside me with artless grace, her hands in my hair. "Ridiculous, perhaps, but keep her safe at Hatherley while you make love to me, for I don't intend to share."

Turning my face to hers, she asked with her eyes.

"I doubt if I can," I said.

"Ah, now! That's what Tony Hargreaves said."

"What did Hargreaves say?"

"That if I took Mark Seaton as a lover I'd be applying for compassionate assistance to the Civil Service Clerical Association."

"One up to Hargreaves," I said. "Most of the juniors are under fifty and better at this than me."

"Are all Directors as ineffectual?"

"Count yourself lucky—you ought to be in bed with Anstruther."

She put a finger under her chin, looking pert. "Anstruther? Is he the old bluffer I met at Hatherley?"

"Possibly."

The mention of Hatherley had stilled me.

I closed my eyes, remembering Moira.

In Hallie's gusty breathing I still remembered Moira.

$\bullet \quad \bullet \quad \bullet \quad \bullet \quad \bullet$

Just after midnight the bedside telephone rang. Hallie groaned, switching on the light, then handed me the receiver. "It's for you, Mark." She didn't sound surprised.

"At this time of night!" Unaccountably, I expected to hear Moira's voice, but Anthony Hargreaves said:

"Doubtless that's you, Mark." I merely stuttered reply; I was half asleep and he had the edge on me, saying, "Sorry to break up the heavy romance, but how soon can you get back to the office?"

I said, "How long have you been head of my Department?"

"Just as you like, or would you prefer to speak to your Permanent Secretary?"

"You're a bastard, Hargreaves."

"Of course. I'll send a car round for you at once—and be careful how you come—the Union Apprentices are on the streets again."

I slammed down the receiver, and Hallie said, eyes closed, "Do you really have to go, darling?" It almost sounded legitimate, the way she said it.

"I do. This bed sleeps three, apparently, but Hargreaves wouldn't be on to me unless it was something important." I dressed swiftly. "And keep the door locked, there's trouble in the city."

Hargreaves, in the event, was understating the case.

The staff car he sent me had to make diversions around Brander's road blocks even to reach Leicester Square, and this took us right into the fighting. Here whole blocks of buildings were ablaze. My driver shouted, "Union Apprentices, sir. They got over from the Waterloo area last night—no road block on Hungerford Bridge, and they've been bombing everything in sight. You heard the radio?"

I said I had not.

"Only kids—the blackshirts are into them with anti-tank guns— my mate said he's never seen anything like it."

Neither had I, and I inwardly cursed him for taking us east when he could have struck south for Constitution Hill and got through to Whitehall that way. Later, the underground newspapers reported that a thousand boys had ambushed a company of blackshirts in Lambeth, killed and wounded most of them, and faded away into the city streets before a battalion could be organised against them.

Silencing the blackshirt machine-gunners in Duncannon Street, they had fought their way around the National Gallery and funnelled into Irving Street, and here the Scots Guards met them head on, firing into their packed ranks until overwhelmed by numbers. Yelling their Union battle cry, eight hundred of the youngsters burst into Leicester Square, drunk with success, firing at everything that moved, and on the grass of the Square eighty last-stand blackshirts were massacred. Then began a systematic bombing of the buildings, and on the top of the Odeon the Union flag was hoisted. But now, with dawn, they were penned by Brander's storm-troopers within the Square, and here they were selling their lives with blood. For the crack National Guard was into them, battering their way into the buildings, and the fighting was hand-to-hand.

It was as if a curtain of fire had dropped around us. One moment the night was peaceful, save for a few desultory shots, next we were in the midst of bedlam. Now that the Brander tanks had come up behind us, reinforcements to the National Fifth Task Force parachutists, brought by armoured cars from their camp in Green Park, were racing down the pavements, swerving to the Apprentice snipers. Ambulances were wailing, fire-engines hopelessly trapped in the jam of traffic in all entries to the Square. Tracer-fire was tearing through the soft-skinned vehicles before us while behind us barked the heavy guns of the tanks, battering at the upper storeys of the buildings where the young Unionists were flinging down their hand-grenades and spraying the jammed columns with incendiaries. And a flame-thrower, forcing a path through the traffic, was pumping liquid flame through the windows about us; rocket-launchers, the little two-pounders, were showering their cone-charges against the walls, blowing down the external façades to expose the defenders within. At an average age of sixteen, the boys fought it out, their ranks stiffened by young black patrials from the ghettos of Notting Hill, and their bodies shrank and withered against a backcloth of flame. Then a plastic grenade hit the roof of our car, rolled off and exploded behind us in a shattering of glass.

"Christ Almighty," said my driver.

"We'd better try it on foot," I said. "You're a bloody idiot for getting us into this." Opening the doors, we ducked out and ran, seeking cover from the bullets. An old Centurion tank was nosing through the cars behind us, lock-skidding its tracks in a zig-zag approach, barging everything aside, and I threw myself flat as its big gun billowed flame in a deafening concussion; turning, I saw the stone façades of the Odeon topple and crash down, instantly exposing the Unionist snipers against the flames. Screams rose above the crackling flames as many of the boys jumped to their deaths. And the Nationals sprayed them mercilessly with automatic tracer even as they fell, jerking their limbs with the impact of the bullets. Little groups of the insurgents, tottering out of entrances with their clothes ablaze, were instantly shot down. The street about me was now crammed with infantry, for Brander's headquarters had realised the extent of the Unionist threat, and crack Civilian Riot Control troops had joined the Nationals and blackshirt forces: in time, as usual for the summary executions.

Fear, contained until now by the astonishing speed of events, swept over me. Before me the street was being raked with machine-gun fire; behind me petrol tanks were exploding in mushrooms of flame. At first I ran blindly, ducking to the ricochets, crying aloud to the crashing of the tank guns. But, on the edge of the fighting, I grew cooler, lying in the shelter of a wall while the advancing infantry leaped over me. Suddenly the noises of the battle grew ragged and died into spasmodic thumps; long bursts of shooting announcing the execution of the young Unionists as they streamed from their cover to surrender.

I had long since lost my staff car driver and ran down Whitcomb Street into Pall Mall, which was almost completely deserted. But in Trafalgar Square dishevelled men and boys, captured earlier, were being herded into army trucks by the National Guard, the élite of the School of Infantry. These were fulfilling the old promise by the military reactionaries, and the mass execution of known shop stewards and Union Commanders was now taking place in obscure detention camps. Silent under the rifle butts these prisoners went: ragged patrials, the refuse of an earlier battle, were loading the Apprentices' dead into carts and pulling them away to the suburbs.

With a few other civilians I was stopped at the Charles I statue —this road block had been up since the beginning of the Brander coup. The blackshirts waved me on after a glance at my official pass.

A ludicrous comparison to the dramatic events I had just witnessed, I now walked up Whitehall to my Ministry in my pin-stripes with my briefcase under my arm. A great deal had happened, I reflected, since Bull Brander came to power. Yet his military coup, ostensibly over in a week, was still engaged, a month later, in the bloody aftermath of its initial victory—the massacre of the insurgent elements of the defeated unions.

Colonel Brander, unofficially known as Bull Brander, had become a legendary hero during the Irish troubles of the 'seventies, capturing public imagination and support by his verve, fearlessness and bloody repression of the warring factions after Whitelaw had failed with peaceful methods. With brutal thoroughness Brander had waged a campaign in Northern Ireland without consideration of religious or political belief and installed there a caretaker government based predominantly on Protestant influence. And Brander, a product of the New Army, had long advocated a similar repression of the malaise of concerted violence at home; contending that the only absolute danger to the established order was a crystallising of extremist aims.

Further, he had injected a new assurance into a fading army élite, which, until his appearance, had restricted its military operations to the polemics of the officers' messes. His revolutionary methods and operational handbooks abandoned defence of the Realm for defence of the State, for he claimed that the danger lay within, not without: concentrating on the suppression of public disorder, he indicted the Unions for their growing violence in picketing. Under the slogan of *Britain for the Right*, he created a new, political soldier, an army of bachelors in the tradition of Plato, separated by indoctrination from civilian ideas and standards. Working on the premise that it was impossible to use an army of civilians against the civil population, he built a small but specialist New Army unattached to civilian services and independent of anything but military authority.

Brander, arriving as he did in a Britain of Rightist principles and belief, gathered with ease to his ranks the older reactionary officers and politicians. Claiming on his many television appearances that he offered protection to business and a guarantee of industrial peace; the financiers supported him and the Government applauded him. Men feared him; women were fascinated by his charm and good looks.

The coup itself coincided with the temporary abduction from Downing Street of the aged Prime Minister, Paul Whiting-Jones, who sent Enoch Powell into political oblivion—poetic justice for Powell's similar treatment of Heath. This operation was conducted smoothly and with an efficiency born of months of planning in army headquarters; Whiting-Jones was visited at home by senior officers, informed that he was under protective arrest and taken into the country while the staff of Number Ten worked for three days at the point of a gun. Claiming that the Prime Minister's disappearance was a military responsibility since the police had failed in his protection, Brander led a nation-wide search under declaration of martial law. Gratitude to the new junta was widespread in the Press when Whiting-Jones was found; those newspapers who suggested at political connivance were instantly shut down and their presses dismantled; the *Daily Worker* (now retitled again) went this way. With Whiting-Jones's return a second member of the Brander Triumvirate arose—the homosexual Air Vice-Marshal Boland, who grounded the Air Force during the military operations. With four-fifths of the army in barracks awaiting orders that never arrived, Brander moved his Nationals and blackshirts into the streets, spearheading them with paratroopers and small but highly trained S.A.S. columns, against the civil population. He captured immediately the usual focal points of control—the television stations, Fleet Street, the central banks. Particularly, the television and radio media were given a taste of the ruthlessness to come, scores of trainees, producers and directors—even actors at work on the set at Lime Grove

—being executed on flimsy allegations of Marxism; it was a bloodbath from which the media's small element of the intellectual Left never recovered in Brander's time.

Now, the nerve-centres secure, the Triumvirate's infantry radiated; mobile columns raced north and south; parachutist regiments were dropped in Wales and in the mountains of Scotland, attacking the unprepared local governments. Within a week all major towns and cities were moderately secure, and the population believed, through the broadcasts of the traitor, Whiting-Jones, that Brander's every action, however ruthless, was in the public interest. On the tenth day of the coup the Royal Family, until then confined for their safety, were quietly gathered up and spirited away to Paris. Buckingham Palace became the military junta headquarters.

Disenchanted with the two great political parties of the 'seventies, the arrogance, ineptitude and wrangling, the voters, as always when apathetic, had drifted inevitably into the Fascism of which Wilson had warned. But if the general public knew of the mass execution of intellectuals and faithful politicians, the brutal interrogations of the underground cellars, it made no visible sign. Britain, at last, had returned to an era of prosperity and peace. And it was from the ranks of the New Army that a new spectre rose—the *Vaporiser*—a small body of pseudo-citizen police formed for the investigation of suspected activists in local government and the Civil Service—ever the buffer between State and the public. Some of its representatives, I pondered, might even now be awaiting me at the Ministry of Building, and it wouldn't be just for sleeping with Hallie.

Security Jones had a right to look jaded at three o'clock in the morning.

"They're up in Room 127, sir," said he.

"What's all this about?"

"Search me, sir, they're pulling everybody in."

And in the corridor of the second floor I met Hargreaves's intimate smile, "How's our Hallie?"

It was not his knowledge of the affair that I feared, but its official recognition. If Hargreaves didn't actually preach the virtue of celibacy himself, he was still the official head of Moral Guidance, Brander's new anti-permissive purge department: a defection from approved standards might be used against me. I said now, "What the hell's going on here?"

"Pure routine, Mark. Just act naturally, you're not in the red."

"That doesn't particularly bother me."

His eyes danced as he pulled on his cigarette. "I shouldn't be too hostile, if I were you."

I pushed past him. "The unions would be interested in that—I've just come from Trafalgar Square. Do we need mass killing to keep your lot in power?"

He put his hands into his pockets, smiling down at me. "What else do you expect of the army? It was the unions, you know, who began this infantile brawling."

"And it will be the unions who will end it—where's this bloody room?"

Bill Waring and Pud Benedict were standing outside the door, staring aimlessly down at the Cenotaph, and I wondered what the Foreign Office was doing there. Benedict I liked immensely; he could be tepid, but was an inscrutable diplomatist, and behind his projection of intellectual vacuity lay a razoring brain. Waring was new to the Service; I had got to know him through maintenance of the foreign embassies. Of quiet calm, he could erupt into fierce anger. Turning, he filled his pipe, glowering about him, saying:

"Good morning, Seaton. Don't tell me they're also sorting out the technical directorates."

I answered, bitterly, "They're shooting shop stewards now, why not quantity surveyors?" and Benedict added:

"They'd all be dead if the architects had their way." He patted his portly stomach. "But why me? I'm a very small cog in affairs of state."

"Do you know what they're after?" I asked him, and Waring replied:

"If it's a renewal of official vows—and I suspect that it is—they're getting nothing from me. I don't intend to serve a bunch of mentally enclosed military blockheads. Christ, what a country!"

Benedict said, and I was surprised, "It's an assembly of witches —a midnight frolic to stop us getting together. But, personally, I don't care much who seizes power as long as I continue to draw my salary."

"It's a time for cool heads, Waring," and I told them what Hargreaves said.

"Hargreaves," Waring replied, "is a political pimp. If I think this lot are a shower of military bastards, I reserve the right to say so."

Johanson of Intelligence greeted us, strange bedfellows at that time of the morning, and said heavily, pipe in mouth, "I don't know what the hell's happening here, but unless we make a stand we're going to be sunk. You've heard the military have taken over my department, I suppose?"

"Taken over Intelligence, Jo? You can't mean it!" Waring was aghast.

"Now God help us in the cut and thrust; there isn't a glimmer of intelligence from Brander down, and I've just sent a note to the Foreign Office expressing it."

"Really?" ejaculated Benedict. "I don't know if that's diplomacy."

"We've had too much diplomacy," said Johanson. "I'm for making a stand. Oppose them at every turn, every action—it's the only way. All right, a few of us go under, but there's others coming on." He smiled with slow charm. "Like you, Seaton; I'm with you. I can't think how Intelligence can help, but I'm with you all the way. I've just seen your latest directive on suppression of departmental corruption—hit them with the bucket, man; it's where the public money lies that you'll find them active."

They spoke more but I did not hear them, for I was watching the departmental heads collecting in the corridor. Then a young brigadier called me into the room, gesturing to a chair before him. A bulky sergeant of the Argyll and Sutherland Highlanders, recently reformed by Brander, shut the door behind us.

"I see you are the Director of Contracts," said the brigadier.

I nodded, and he added, "I won't waste your time, Mr. Seaton.

The military caretaker government has sent instructions that all department representatives are immediately to be interviewed, and we make no apology for the time of the morning." He raised his face to mine. "Certain posts are to be abolished, others filled by military personnel." He leaned forward, scrutinising a paper. "In your particular case, Mr. Cheriton, the Minister of Building, has recommended that you be substantiated in post so there's no complication here. Are you prepared to serve?" He folded his hands, regarding me.

"This is a temporary measure?" I asked.

"The post?"

"No, the caretaker government."

"You disapprove of it?"

I sat back. "As a civilian I naturally reject military autonomy."

"As a civilian you should have ensured there was no necessity for it. But I think I can assure you that we will last only for as long as required."

"What does that mean?"

His face flushed and he tapped quietly on the desk with his pen. "Your attitude's a little hostile, isn't it?"

"No, businesslike. You asked me a question and I'll give you my answer, but not without certain inquiries."

Sighing, he replied, "The Triumvirate will be in power all the time civil disorder exists, Seaton—make no mistake on that." He tossed the paper towards me. It was, as Waring had guessed, a simple reaffirmation of loyalty; I signed it and tossed it back. "Let's hope so; some of your cures for social ills I'm finding a little excessive."

He rose. "If the workers challenge the authority of the law then they must take the consequences."

"Like Bishop Forsward? If my memory serves me, you arrested him for advocating a return to free elections; I wouldn't have thought that much of a challenge to law and order."

He opened the door for me. "Like you, Mr. Seaton, he was particularly irritating in his reactionary views. The fact that he's a bishop won't save him; we all have our roles, and I suggest you stick to yours as Director of Contracts."

"We'll have to see," I said.

It was the last word, but scarcely satisfying.

It was politically inadvisable to return to Hallie so I spent the night in the office, and the next few nights as well. Somebody of foresight had actually provided beds.

Hargreaves, whom I met in the communal dormitory, was clearly delighted.

"Sleep well," he said.

I wondered, unhappily, what Moira might be doing.

CHAPTER 3

It was exactly a week later, another Thursday; the telephone rang as I came into the office. Miss Carrington, my secretary, said, "Good morning, Mr. Seaton. Could you come over to Sir Stanley's office right away?"

"At this time of the morning? The streets aren't aired."

"They are over here," said she.

When I got to Room 303, Carrie and Stan Waters were together at the desk like anarchists huddled over a bomb. I liked and respected Stan Waters; he was a blue-blooded civil servant who did his job without complaint; now he raised his great, cadaverous face to mine.

"We're in trouble, Mark."

"So I gather."

Carrie, large and angular, was trembling, I noticed, though she had done this before when in close proximity with trousers: they were an unnerving duet. Stan said, "The usual thing—a late tender —the Severnside Project. And speed is the essence of this one—the Minister's announcing acceptance in the House this afternoon." He handed me a list of the competing building contractors—Messrs Ranklyt Thommasson, the late tender, was entered on the form in red ink.

I asked, "Who opened the tender box?"

Stan replied, "I did—with Harmsworth, the Minister's latest P.A. There were seven offers. Then Mr. Fiddler, my new E.O., brought in this late one."

"Fiddler?" I groaned. "God! The Press are going to love it. How long have you had him?"

"Fiddler? Only a couple of weeks. He seems a nice young chap."

"What's wrong, then?"

Carrie said, "After the seven tenders were listed—and before Mr. Fiddler brought in the late one, Mr. Harmsworth made a telephone call."

"Did he now! Who to?"

"Ostensibly to Mr. Cheriton, the Minister. Later, however, Sir Stanley discovered that he wasn't speaking to him at all, but to Mr. Fiddler."

"Oh, Christ." To Stan I said, "But you were in the room when he made the call? Surely . . ."

He stared at me with his large, watery eyes. "Well, actually . . ."

"Don't tell me you left the tender board with the box open!"

"I . . . I had to. You see, since my operation . . . I was only in the toilet for a moment or two . . ."

"Long enough for Harmsworth to make a call while you were away?" I thought: we'll all be the laughing stock of the Ministry. The coming scandal, with the Minister involved, was bad enough, and heads, including mine, would roll—all because Stan Waters couldn't hold his water. I asked, "You didn't hear him make the call then?" Stan shook his head dolefully, and I said:

"Then, how do you know Harmsworth was arranging things with Fiddler?"

Carrie said, faintly, "Sir Stanley, it would save an awful lot of time, if . . ."

He sighed and opened a drawer in his desk: a tiny tape-recorder was in there. I said, "Oh no!—don't tell me you bugged the phone!"

His eyes were suddenly defiant. "Why not? Brander's got us all wired up, monitored and photographed, hasn't he?"

"Do we have to descend to his level?"

"It's the only way you keep ahead of the swine!"

"Easy, Stan," I said. We glared at each other, and Carrie said:

"To summarise this, Mr. Seaton—the tape makes it clear. When Mr. Harmsworth knew the amount of the lowest tender he telephoned Extension 290—Mr. Fiddler's extension—and reported the lowest figure, all the time making out that he was talking to

33

Mr. Cheriton, the Minister—in case Sir Stanley was listening. Obviously, he was speaking in code for Fiddler's benefit. Mr. Fiddler then entered a still lower figure on a pre-signed offer form, sealed it in an envelope, initialled it as a late tender, stamped in time of receipt, and brought it in to Sir Stanley as a normal late arrival; this allowed the Severnside contract to be awarded, incorrectly, to Ranklyt Thommasson."

"Which was once the Minister's firm," said Stan. "When he took office he passed it over to his brother-in-law; I've checked this."

"Better play me that tape," I said, and wandered to the window, staring down at Whitehall. A young Asian girl, the image of my lovely Su-len, was standing at the Cenotaph; Chinese, too, by her movements, for the Japanese have a slovenly gait. Su-len would be at Hatherley, I reflected, when I got home tonight. The tape played on, a complete indictment. I said, "We'll have to have this Mr. Fiddler in, won't we?" and Carrie called on the intercom.

A pallid, ineffectual youth entered apprehensively. Carrie said, instantly, "Would you care to sit down, Mr. Fiddler?"

He did so; his knuckles white on the arm of the chair, and looked at me with the look I have seen in the eyes of a calf swaying on the road to the slaughterhouse. I began, "I suppose you know why you're here, Mr. Fiddler."

He lowered his pale face.

"We have a recording of a conversation you had this morning with Mr. Harmsworth. You haven't left me much of an alternative, have you?"

He said, suddenly defiant, "I want to see Mr. Cheriton, sir; I'm not saying anything until I've seen Mr. Cheriton."

"What has the Minister to do with it?"

Terror struck his face and he swallowed deep in his throat. "I mean, Mr. Harmsworth, sir—that's right—Mr. Harmsworth."

"That's easy." Picking up the telephone I dialled the extension, and said, "Harmsworth, is that you? This is Seaton here. I've got a Mr. Fiddler, of Finance in Stan Waters's office—Room 303, and I'd like to talk to you about the late tender on the Severnside Project. Can you come over at once?"

"Willingly. Actually, Mark, I did want a word with you, anyway —about the new upper limits on term contracts."

And he didn't even catch a breath.

This is the stuff of which big men are made; the unshakeable, incorruptible representatives of the people, always with us.

But Harmsworth did not come as promised, and every time I telephoned they said he was in with Cheriton. Now I was wondering, as I left the office for lunch with Hallie, how I could bring the corruption to light without using the official channels, for taking on my Minister meant taking on Brander; it wasn't an entertaining prospect.

I was actually on the pavement outside the Ministry when Security Jones came running, gasping, down the steps. "Just caught sight of you, Mr. Seaton. A lady's been on the telephone—she wouldn't go through to your office. Will you please ring Surbiton 3043 at half-past one today?"

"Didn't she say who she was?"

"Wouldn't give a name, sir. But she said it was important—sounded distressed, sir."

I nodded and took a bus to the Strand, reflecting that it didn't sound much like Moira.

It was a stimulus to my fading ego to watch the effect Hallie had upon the males, so every other week I took her to lunch. Now she fairly glowed at the white-clothed table of the Savoy, like some native beauty straight from a sun-drenched beach; the waiters, preceded by silver, stalked about us with professional interest; she looked delightful.

"You look tired, Mark."

"So would you if you'd been sleeping in the office."

"You still haven't been home?"

"Actually, the emergency ends today. God knows what's happening in Hatherley. The lines are still down to Woking."

"Won't Moira be there?"

"I doubt it. In spring, Moira's fancy lightly turns to little Henry Shearer; she keeps big Johnny Hampshire for the winter months."

"Johnny Hampshire?"

"It doesn't really matter." I played with my soup.

"You still love Moira, don't you?"

"Of course. I've never denied it."

"Yet you make love to me. It does rather make me into a substitute for relief—scarcely flattering, you know."

"I'm sorry."

"Is that the best you can do?"

Reaching out, I caught her hand. She was wearing a white, pleated spring dress, and her broad-rimmed hat was a mirror to the blackness of her hair; she was beautiful, and a passing woman gave her a chilling glance, the proof of it. I said, "An onlooker unversed in the incongruities of love would be quite confounded—petite and lovely model from the Courval Salon and plump, balding senior civil servant. We're an odd pair."

"You are the odd one."

"Oh, no! It's perfectly possible for a man to love two women simultaneously; you are beautiful, and you are young. In you I discover my lost youth, but what do you see in me?"

"Put it down to a deep, affectionate concern."

"There must be more to it than that."

She smiled whimsically, her head on one side. "Young women often become deeply involved with men twice their age, haven't you heard?"

"And that won't do either."

She snapped open her handbag, searching it furiously. "Do I have to give my every reason for letting you make love to me? Many men would think the opportunity more than enough."

"Many others might wonder what you were up to."

"Oh, God, what a lunch. I'd better go."

We sat, unspeaking. Hallie was pale, her dark eyes raising uncertainly at me over the table, I said, "I'm sorry. I'm being a pig; forgive me."

"You're worried about something, aren't you?"

I nodded, and she asked, "Would it help if you told me about it?

Even if Tony Hargreaves always restricted his official duties to his office?"

"This is bigger than Tony Hargreaves." I told her about Cheriton's attempt at fraudulent conversion of public funds, and she said:

"Surely you aren't going to pursue it?"

"Of course—what else can I do?"

"But your own Minister!"

"Why should he get away with it? I've got Harmsworth sewn up —Cheriton's the next obvious step."

"Are you forgetting he was personally appointed by Brander?"

"What difference does that make?"

She sniffed, moving testily. "Thank God for the purists, but you won't get any medals for exposing ministerial dishonesty—can't you keep it at Harmsworth's level?"

"Of course not. If I raise it at all, and I intend to, I've got to bring Cheriton into it."

"How much is involved?"

"About two hundred thousand."

She whistled softly. "And you've got absolute proof of corruption?"

"I've got the tape-recording in a safe place and I've checked on the firm Ranklyt Thommasson. Before the Brander appointment Cheriton was its managing director, now it's run by his brother-in-law. Incidentally, Harmsworth's a major shareholder, so they collect it every way."

"Much of this goes on?"

"People have been winking at it since the halcyon days of the 'seventies."

Four blackshirt officers were dining at the next table and they fingered Hallie with their eyes and the brooding intent of the hunting male. Hallie, in the event, could have handled all four of them: You, too, Hargreaves once drily observed, can have a forty-inch chest, but never the potential of my little Hallie. I reflected dully that life would be rare indeed if the blackshirts turned their attentions to me. She said, glancing at them:

"So you've reported it?"

37

I nodded.

"It's suicide."

"Don't rate me too highly."

"Have you considered Sir Stanley Waters's position?"

"Carrie says he's scared to death."

"So am I." After the waiter had served her she sat back, smiling, and said, "I don't understand why I should be in love with you; you are not an attractive man, you are twice my age. Also, at times you are very stupid. Anybody can be a mule, and you'll be the first Director to go up the chimney."

"Let's hope the cause is worth it. The public pays me well to stop this kind of caper."

"Men like you have been burned in Spain and the public didn't raise an eye."

"It's a comforting thought." I glanced at my watch. "Just remembered—I've got a call to make."

One of the blackshirts, a young major, rose and went to Hallie's table the moment I was in the foyer; they talked with surprising verve, I thought.

In the telephone booth, I said, "This is Mark Seaton here. I was asked to phone this number."

"Ah, Mr. Seaton—thank you for calling. This is Verity Waring speaking. Have you seen anything of Bill over the last couple of days?"

"Hasn't he been home, then?"

"No. That's why I'm ringing around."

I said, "The last time I saw him was with Pud Benedict—have you been on to him? Your husband isn't my department, Mrs. Waring."

"I tried Mr. Benedict first—he hasn't seen him since the night interview at the office, and he's been home since then. It's two nights now—I can't get a thing out of his office."

"What did his secretary say?"

"That he's away for a few days."

"Isn't that enough?"

"No. Bill just doesn't go off like that without a word."

"You've told Benedict all this?"

"Yes, and he's getting on to Security."

"I must say it's a little odd . . ." It was banal, but I had to say something, for I was remembering Waring's talent for indiscretion, and wondered how he got on that night with the young brigadier. His wife suddenly said:

"Oh God, Mr. Seaton, I'm worried to death . . ."

I replied, "Look, there's bound to be a simple explanation—people don't just disappear . . ." I instantly regretted it; I wasn't doing very well. She answered:

"They do these days . . ." I heard the monitor click out.

Hallie was awaiting me in the lounge with the coffee. I said, "I've got to get back at once—Bill Waring's disappeared . . ."

"He won't be the last at your rate of progression. Who is he, anyway?"

It was surprisingly cold, and I remembered it. Pecking her cheek, I said, "I'll give you a ring when I get back from Hatherley."

"Give my love to Su-len," she said. I left her, to return to the office.

I was surprised to find Benedict at his desk at two o'clock, and said on the phone, "Benedict, this is Seaton. I've just been speaking to Waring's wife . . ." The monitor instantly clicked, and he interjected, saying:

"We might as well have it officially recorded, I suppose. News of him has just come through—he's been found dead in the sea off Sidmouth."

"Good God!"

"A boating accident, apparently." Benedict's voice was flat. I cried:

"But what the devil was he doing in Sidmouth?"

"Don't ask me. According to his brother he had no interest in boats, but who knows what these days—anything happens. You knew, of course, that he's been up twice before Kish?"

"No, I didn't."

"And that he told our brigadier friend just what he thought of him? Our bachelor army has an amazing ability to produce departmental casualties . . ."

"Goodbye, sir," I said.

Sitting there at my desk I was seized with a sudden, overwhelming depression and a growing sense of approaching disaster.

For no obvious reason I began to recall the Civil Service of my youth when, uncomplicated by the high-level decisions and political aura of Director status, I lived in Basingstoke on a housing estate, semi-detached, with a very different Moira.

It was before I returned to Hatherley, and there was a road-sweeper living alone in one of the council houses near by; he was enduring such loneliness that he would arrive every morning outside our house and await my car-horn goodbye to Moira as I swung out of the drive, in the mistaken belief that I was signalling to him. Moira, of course, would still be abed, but wet or fine, my friend would be there. Beaming, he would hammer his broom on his barrow for the one bright moment of his day.

Thus, it became imperative to me that I should never be too early for him, or too late, lest I should somehow miss him, and despoil his pleasure. For there had grown between us an unspoken friendship based solely on a gesture, and it lasted three years. And, when he died, he left ten pounds in his will to 'the young man who is my friend, Mark Andrew Seaton, who lives on the corner'. He had got my name from a newspaper, apparently.

Within the growing complication of my life, the coming confrontations—these were quite inevitable—the rise of militarism in my country, my rejection by Moira and the degrading association with Hallie, half my age, it had suddenly become apparent to me that my car-horn friendship with an unnamed old man was my only experience of absolute love in a world of inhumanity.

I had the ten-pound note in my hands when Carrie came in.

"That for me, sir?"

I managed a smile.

I could have wept for Verity Waring; if only for her loneliness.

CHAPTER 4

For the past two years, since Whiting-Jones had seized power from Powell, Commissioner Kish of the Departmental Investigation had been circling over the ministries like a bird of prey. The early bravura of the staff restaurant—'You know what bloody Kish can do'—had died on the rack of redundancy and what Kish actually did. Civil servants with known liberal tendencies were interviewed by him and summarily dismissed; the more outspoken of the upper grades—men like Waring—disappeared: an assignation with his Investigation Section usually meant the opening of a secret file on the interviewee, the starting point of which was invariably the telephone monitor, for it was from the telephone that most of the reactionary information was obtained.

Ostensibly, Kish had been enlisted by Brander for a legitimate duty—the hearing of departmental complaints. With the Civil Service unions outlawed, Whitleyism destroyed, there was nobody left for the private individual to appeal to except the underground Press, and this Brander wanted to avoid. Ombudsmen like Kish obtained for the Triumvirate additional information on individuals.

But Civil Service complaints were not confined to the Ministries. Brander had covered some ground in his short term of office. With food prices still rocketing since entry into the Common Market (they were now two and a half times those of the early 'seventies) and the cost of living index going higher every month, Brander imposed a wage freeze on all salaries save those of top executives and army personnel. Hours of work were increased to a national average of fifty a week; holidays for the lower paid were cut to ten days a year. The effect of this was a Stock Exchange bonanza, and foreign investment was pouring into the country, whose finances were now controlled by what was virtually a banking dictatorship. Even in the years when Powell held office, the mortgage rate of interest lending was raised to just under three hundred per cent of the initial loan with the built-in clause that the children of the mortgagee would continue to pay: second mortgages were available from the big financial houses at fifty per cent; third and fourth mortgages were half as much again.

With Parliament in permanent recess, Brander passed swingeing laws, such as a ban on overtime working. No worker in receipt of less than three thousand pounds a year was allowed to possess a car; every business employing more than fifty people would house and maintain a political commissar for advice and guidance in a government role.

With the unemployment figure now approaching two and a quarter million, Brander set up military cadres for the institutional training of the young in return for extra food—a new militarism based on the excuse of the communistic threat. Government narks were appearing in public houses and places of worship: a meeting of more than six was forbidden in the public interest. Strikes were outlawed; the Euthanasia Bill was under consideration within a fortnight of the Fascists' seizure of power. Corporal and capital punishment were returned; attempts to reform the dying unions were now punishable by death. The four freedoms, said Benedict, are being stolen so quickly that you can even watch them dissolve. This he actually said on the telephone to me, a crass but brave idiocy; a second later the monitor clicked in.

But the tragedy did not end there. It was rumoured from the Treasury that the fifty million pounds set up by the Tories in the 'seventies for assistance to foreign prospectors had now been increased overnight to four times this amount; the parcelling up of Britain for sale to American gas, oil and heavy industrial interests was now in full flood as government and private financiers were given free reign, and the Department of Trade increased its licences to foreign speculators in search of our mineral wealth. According to Nigel Kinson, who was in a position to know, the Americans alone now owned just under forty-eight per cent of the British economy.

With the nation in a ferment of unrest, with a simmering anarchy threatening to explode into street violence and the higher echelons of the Civil Service growing in criticism, Brander saw the need for men like Commissioner Kish, the new political ombudsmen of his junta.

And I was quite aware that, if I persisted in my departmental complaint against my Minister of Building, I would very soon be called before Kish for an official hearing.

This happened sooner than I expected.

Carrie came into the office: her hair, as usual, was untidy; indeed, her continual state of inelegance was part of her charm—for the six years she had been my secretary I had never seen her in any dress that didn't look shop-soiled. Tall, constantly screwing her hands, she scarcely inspired confidence, but I wouldn't have exchanged her for all the sex amazons in the Ministry of Building.

There were times when I pitied Miss Carrington. She lived in Balham with an invalid mother, to whom she was devoted, but this devotion often encroached upon her efficiency: certainly, I was under no illusion as to who would take a back seat if ever it came to a choice between Mother and me. Once, I recall, I saw Carrie in the Strand, bending over another woman's pram. The longing in her eyes was such that I never forgot it, but then, the Civil Service, even under Brander, was a hive of potential but disappointed mothers.

In more generous moments I would like to have seen Carrie with a baby in her arms. But now she was adopting an air of frigidity; plainly not a woman to be tampered with.

"What's wrong now?" I asked, sorting papers.

She wandered about, clutching at her dress. "Do you mind if I speak plainly, sir?"

"I've little option," I replied, "you invariably do."

"I think you're being outrageously silly about this Cheriton business."

"Do you?"

"I know things are different these days—also I know the truth of your allegations. But this is your own Minister."

"Well?" I stared up at her.

She faltered. "Couldn't you tone it down a bit? The Civil Service isn't what it used to be, but really . . ."

"Sit down," I said.

She did so, glaring at me. Bespectacled efficiency might have robbed her of human contact, but it had bequeathed to her an independent mind. One day such women are mother figures, worried about the weight of the particular executive or the randy philanderings of his junior staff; next moment they are harridans. She said, up on her dignity, "I mean, do you have to handle it with a sledge-hammer? Reporting your own Minister to Departmental Investigation, it's unheard of!"

"Don't shirk it, Carrie—we both know the truth. The pair of them are corrupt."

Her face was pale. "But, even if they are, do you have to wash dirty linen in public? This could be privately dealt with. You know very well that Mr. Anstruther would settle it out of court, as it were—that's the job of a Permanent Secretary."

"And what would you advise if it were a couple of clerical officers doing the fiddling?"

"Then it would be your level and your duty to deal with it as you thought fit, but . . ."

"Send them to prison, I suppose? But no prison for the Minister of Building and his crooked P.A."

She lowered her face. "You make me sound terrible, putting it like that."

"Is there any other way to put it?"

"People like Sir Stanley Waters, the old breed, would know how to handle it."

It was out. Sweat sprang to her face and she sighed, eyes closed.

"It's the public, first and last, that we're supposed to serve, Carrie. I don't care if it's the Prime Minister—if he's corrupt he must stand to account before the people. They pay me thirty-two thousand a year to keep my Department clean."

"But . . . this terrible man Kish, sir . . ."

I turned to her. There was a sadness in her face, a strange projection that could have been love.

"It's the chance I take." I picked up some papers.

She said, face averted, "This . . . this is really why I've come . . . You see, I'm not very truthful, am I? I don't really care a lot about the Minister." She added, "Disgraceful, isn't it?"

A silence came and we shared it, then she said, "Does . . . does your wife know about it all?"

"No, Carrie."

Her face was suddenly alive. "I mean, a trouble shared . . ."

"No, she wouldn't understand it. I share it mainly with you."

I will remember her standing there.

"Thank you, Mr. Seaton."

A telephone jangled between us, and I lifted it. "Seaton."

A voice said, "This is Worsely of the Legal Department, sir. You recall your complaint to Investigation about a ministerial tendering procedure? I am to tell you that the Kish Commission will be sitting at nine-thirty next Wednesday, to hear this complaint. Can you attend?"

I covered the mouthpiece and said to Carrie, "Am I free next Wednesday at nine-thirty?"

She closed her eyes at the ceiling, picking the diary out of the air.

"Yes, sir," she said.

"Enter me for the Kish Commission." To Worsely I said, "Yes, I'll be there."

"Do you require legal representation, Mr. Seaton?"

"I don't, but perhaps Cheriton does."

"Goodbye, sir."

I replaced the receiver.

My heart was thumping as I went back to the window. There were a lot of people in Whitehall for that time of day, especially around the Cenotaph.

"Oh, by the way, sir," said Carrie, "Miss Hallie telephoned. I rather think she was hoping you'd be free this evening."

"Thank you," I said.

She left me very quietly.

45

CHAPTER 5

On the evening Bolo Mombara, Brander's new minister of Patrials, was murdered in my house, I telephoned Sam, my taxi, with the intention of catching the five-forty to Woking, for Moira had rung me to come home early.

Actually, it was inconvenient, for apart from my preparations for my interview with the Kish Commission, now twice delayed, things were frantic in the Department. A contract had gone wrong in Aldershot, the roofs of six married quarters had blown off in Fleet and an embassy had been burned down in Djakarta, which was fast becoming a habit. A main grade quantity surveyor was flying out to assess the damage, for which I hoped the Indonesians would pay; in the event, they didn't.

Often I wondered at the wisdom of keeping these establishments going, for they were now useless diplomatically; hotbeds of espionage which were doing their best, like international sport, to destroy *détente*. Israel was an example. Since the Russo-Arab victory we were steadfastly maintaining a consulate in Jerusalem at a cost of half a million a year, yet the State was now basically Arab. Since the defeat of Israel and the ensuing blood-bath (while the rest of the world looked on and did nothing) the Jewish population had been reduced to less than four hundred thousands. It was much the same in Peking since the Chinese conquest of India, which, for the first time in its history was beginning to eat: one man and a boy were wandering gilded rooms, which doubtless would soon be burned down again by Mao's successor, who seemed dedicated to the role of burning foreign embassies. Only in Greece and America, and others with neo-Fascist governments like ours, did our assets appear safe.

"'Evening, Mr. Seaton." Sam, my taxi, was awaiting me near the Cenotaph, as usual. "Bond Street?"

"You've got the date wrong," I replied. "It's a Friday—the five-forty from Waterloo, and make it snappy."

He glanced at his watch. "Gawd, I'm a magician."

Down the Whitehall diversion I noticed a young couple kissing on the pavement: the girl was small and slim, Scandinavian in type; the boy was a rag-bagged weed. Intellectuality, I reflected, must be the key to it, for most young males of this generation appeared to have difficulty in standing upright. But virility, as Marsella Besford claims, comes in many garbs—like the ninety-year-old fakir of Johore she cited—he who begat triplets at the eighth attempt in sixteen hours without food or water, though you can't believe everything that comes out of Marsella.

The girl, for size and beauty, reminded me of Su-len.

Now, as we flew along, I watched the drab disarray of home-going Londoners, like thin lines of dirty washing which once were gay with summer. Bare-footed urchins were playing at the top of Scotland Yard, now the Divisional Blackshirt headquarters, with its dreaded interrogation cellars. Storm troopers still patrolled the Admiralty Arch, an administrative stupidity because all the buildings were flattened after the last Unionist attacks. Downing Street, I noticed, had suffered badly; the S.A.S. had shown incredible violence here when opposed by the Household Cavalry just before Brander's attempt to detain the Queen: the road had been cordoned off and the railings against which the Chancellor was executed, the moderate Will Chevalier, were still hung with faded flowers, put there by his constituency.

Parliament Square was deserted of cars, for the House was still in recess, and I pondered on Brander's foolishness in keeping it closed so long. In the main the people accepted a temporary desertion of the hub of what they once called democracy, but this was going too far: such, I reflected, are the elemental errors of ineffective rule—an inability to assess the people's mood: the arrogance of

47

the Heath administration that put it out of touch with the man in the street; the total failure of Wilson's to provide the basic requirements of socialism to a working class sick of a ruling élite. As a result we were now the peasants of Europe.

Red light from burning warehouses along the right bank of the Thames reflected dully as we approached Westminster Bridge; white craft, unmoored by patrials, drifted down-river pursued by river police; squat barges with rotting cargoes aboard raked the muddy shores as if in sullen anger.

But, in mid-river was anchored the giant ocean barge of the homosexual Air Chief Marshal Boland, one of his first purchases since coming to power, and beyond it, ablaze with light, was the once Royal Yacht, now the home of Colonel Brander when not in official residence in the Palace. Guarded by a squadron of river police, it sat in illumined beauty, its role of a hospital ship still unfulfilled despite the casualties London had suffered from Brander's attacks to the carnage of the Blitz.

Apart from the gaiety of the yacht's floodlit decks, a sense of utter dreariness and defeat pervaded the place. And yet, inexplicably, for all the absence of panache, there continued to exist in London's atmosphere an electrical field of expectancy and courage that had always charged the batteries of the city: a phenomenon of polarity in concert with the days of the bombing was returning; it was in the air, the sounds, the very smells of London, and I wondered if Brander realised it.

God help him if he didn't.

Beth, the flower-seller, an apt symbol of such defiance, was standing at her barrow outside County Hall. Unavailingly, the young constables and the Brander police cajoled and threatened, trying to move her on. One of the stable institutions of London, even Brander couldn't shift her, which was understandable, for Hitler couldn't. Her mass of fat had defied the Blitz. She had given two of her three sons to the bayonet charges of Arras in 1940, and she was proud, she once told me, that they died in the Guards. Seeing her, Sam called over his shoulder:

"Flowers on Friday, sir—shall I stop?"

"If you please."

Out on the pavement Beth actually opened her arms to me. "Hallo, sir—got good roses today, Mr. Seaton."

"Give me a dozen, Beth."

Traffic fumes and roar enveloped us, sullying her purity. I watched her plump, red hands working with swift beauty. Suddenly, pulling out a spotted, red handkerchief, she wiped her florid face. "God, ain't it hot! Where you been? I ain't seen you lately, 'ave I?"

"Been pretty busy."

"With this lot?" She jerked her thumb towards the river. "The sooner you shift them the better." Her hands paused on the roses now. "One of those taddy fellas—a blackshirt—comes down here last Monday. 'Missus,' says he, 'you'd better move on or we'll be takin' you in.' The bloody cheek of it. 'You ain't shifting me, young man,' I says, 'I'll write to my M.P. Mondays and Fridays is my pitch —I got it signed and sealed by the London County Council, and you can go and tell that to your Brander.' The cheek of it, Mr. Seaton— no more'n a kid he was. I was selling flowers 'ere before he was weaned."

I said, "Make it quick, Beth, or you'll get us pinched."

"What we want is the Liberals back—I always voted Liberal, ye know."

"They're all as bad as each other, Beth, take it from me."

She held the roses against her. "I mean, it ain't a free country no more, is it? It weren't the same under the old aristocracy now, was it? And her Majesty the Queen gone, and all that. You know the Queen Mother bought flowers from me during the bombing? I tell you—the incendiaries were landing in the bloody river, and she comes up to me . . ."

"Yes, Beth, you told me."

"Move on, indeed! And even the tea don't taste the same, either —you noticed that? It's the French, you know." She wrapped the roses with deft fat fingers. "Never did trust the French. Ten pounds —special price to you, Mr. Seaton."

I gave her a hundred and fifty Euro-francs, the new equivalent, and she took it with a sniff, stuffing it into her apron pocket, then turned and shouted at the home-going crowds, "Flowers for the Queen, gents—buy a rose for the Queen, lady?"

"Goodbye, Beth," I said.

Yes, I reflected, if Brander didn't watch it, he was due for trouble, and probably sooner than even I expected.

Now, back in the taxi, I shouted at Sam, "No, I'm taking them home, I don't want them dropped into Bond Street!"

For Moira's hands, I remembered, possessed the same grace, and the marvellous symmetry as Beth's, when arranging red roses.

The taxi sped on. Behind us Big Ben, wrong for the first time since I could remember, tolled half-past five—six minutes slow, according to my watch, and Sam nodded his head. It was a frightening situation.

"I know," I called, "you've got four minutes."

"If we can get through this bloody lot," said he, and slowed to a stop.

The black patrials were coming in from Southwark, their internment area, for the nightly street-cleaning which once was done by machines. They came in batches of five hundred; men, women and children festooned with brooms and brushes, and hauling garbage carts. It was open knowledge that their living conditions were appalling—Bolo Mombara, their recently appointed Minister, was always complaining to Brander, to no purpose. And it was in their defence that Nigel Kinson later fell from grace: the *Vaporiser*, according to his wife, who eventually committed suicide, collected him at two o'clock in the morning.

The legal barriers of the early 'seventies had now been swept aside; with or without passports, providing they were properly attested, the blacks were welcomed in after Brander seized power. But the massive initial immigration of these and the Pakawa Asians had dropped to a trickle once the ghetto conditions and restrictions were learned. Working under the batons of the blackshirts, living as Class 3 citizens with the attendant curfew passes, ration cards, stop-identity checks and nightly reporting to blackshirt headquarters, the patrials sent secret messages abroad, and the inflow stopped. Now they were being brought in by force; we were back as Benedict declared, to the slave shipments of Bristol, though this time they came roped together, instead of chained.

The clock had been put back a century.

I caught the train to Woking with only seconds to spare.

A Celt cannot afford to look drab. Dark-skinned and black-haired Moira, my Connemara beauty, was aware that such beauty can soon attain to grossness. Therefore she wore her Courval Salon clothes with grace, selecting them with care, discounting cost; she attended the most expensive beauty salons; her perfumes were faint but exotic; as she grew older her colours grew brighter. She possessed two lovers who were practically alight—Henry Shearer and Johnny Hampshire. Now she breezed towards me in the hall, face up to be kissed, and said, "For God's sake, Mark—what time d'ye call this? You know we've got a party on." It was basic Connemara Irish.

"I came as soon as I could—they're burning the embassies again, and you pinched the car, remember?"

Ezra came and took my coat. Moira's stake in racism, he was the new cult of the blackamoor, the latest rage that drove her up to town.

I said, at my whisky, "By the way, I met Kate and Henry Shearer on the train—they had Hargreaves with them."

"Hargreaves, Hargreaves . . . ?" She looked dismayed, and Ezra said, passing us, "He's that friend o' Miss Hallie, the model—remember, ma'am?"

She knew quite well, of course; she was only making the point. I thumbed idly through *The Times*. It was still a newspaper but scarcely a thunderer. "Who else is coming?"

Moira was staring into her gin. "Claud and Marsella, of course, the Besford daughters, Pud Benedict—I knew you'd want him; Cotteril and Adam Steen—quite a few others."

"Strange, Pud never mentioned it, and I rang him today. Has Joe been on yet?"

"Joe?" She lowered her glass.

"Didn't he say he'd drop in this weekend?"

She opened her arms in empty disgust. "Oh no, Mark! *Mary and Joseph*—we haven't got room for fifty shop stewards!"

"He probably won't come, but why this party at all?"

"Because I'll give ye three guesses on the guest of honour."

"Bull Brander."

Ezra arrived in the lounge now, strangled by a captain's tunic of red and gold braid, looking like a bandmaster, and he cried in his cracked falsetto, "You know what time Mr. Mombara's arrivin', ma'am? 'Cause Mamie's asking in the kitchen." He drifted away, not waiting for a reply.

It turned me. "Mister who, for heaven's sake?"

She was contented. "Mr. Bolo Mombara, the Minister of Patrials." She pirouetted, smiling over her shoulder.

I put down my glass. "Mo, you can't mean it!"

"Aye, sure I do. It'll leave 'em stunned in Woking, ye know."

"You invited Mombara, and he accepted?" I paused, watching her. "Come on, who put you up to it?"

"Henry, but he was only tryin' to help with the list—what's wrong?"

"Of all the stupid idiots!"

"Faith, can I do anything right?"

"Remind me to check the guests for hand-grenades. It might make an impression on Woking, but the housing estate won't like it."

"It could bring us trouble?"

"Not if we board up the windows. Mo, why do you listen to fools like Shearer? Mombara's hot company politically—he's looking for any platform these days. You've got important people coming and the Press will love it. He'll probably arrive in an armoured car."

"Now it's becomin' attractive."

Ezra, appearing from nowhere, said, "Don't worry, Mr. Mark, sir. Bolo, ole Bolo'll quieten 'em down." He wheezed and patted his skinny chest. "They'm a lot o' pesky niggers, I reckon, rioting that way."

It was stage black man, for Ez had once been an actor, but it was this very division, I often reflected, that contributed to the defeat of Black Power. Black freedom was dying, and people like Ezra were the butchers. The crammed slavers that shimmered in African waters, sunk for insurance by vicious Bristol traders, were the monuments of a lost ideal. Black men everywhere were the contributors to their own, terrifying subjugation.

"You'd better start changing," said Moira, "not walk around drinking—they'll soon be here."

"And Henry Shearer's another bad selection."

"Because you don't like him, I suppose."

I said, "Because he's basically immoral, and you know it. That last thing of his was sheer perversion . . ."

"And Brander himself went to the first night."

"But nobody of note has been since. *Act of Love* runs right across the party line—Benedict saw it and nearly fell out of his seat."

"It's a work of art, ye fool."

"It's the product of a sick mind. The whole troika, from Brander down, is basically immoral, but every movement from the Right begins with purity and vigilantes. Let Shearer take you to town, if you like, but don't invite him here."

She made a face and began slapping things about. "God, if I listened to you we'd never get two for a vicarage tea-party." Snatching up the flowers I had brought her she shoved them against Ezra. "Put those in water."

Even as she glared at me I could have taken her into my arms.

An analysis of our situation might have accused me of self-pity, and this was probably correct, but in Moira's absolute rejection of me I knew a vacuum in which I wandered, devoid of warmth, and no Hallie in the world could fill it. Within this silence was the migraine, the tremblings and sweating weaknesses. Drugs, alcohol, merely caricatured my isolation, bringing the impossibility of outside communication, a fraud of death. Only Moira, as once she did, could obliterate my terror of the approaching detonation; within her arms there was protection against the white blaze of the gelignite. The back-fire of a car, a quarrying explosion, the sound of thunder, even a dropped plate could paralyse my consciousness

53

into a shell-shocked haze—extending in time the process of annihilation, like a man being methodically chopped, squared, trimmed and wired within the sequences of a mechanical baler.

Moira's early companionship, now lost to me, was more than physical redemption; the sounds of her, her gaiety and forceful personality had once surrounded me with artless friends, and a joyous sense of belonging.

Once, I remember, when we were newly married, we were walking on a beach in moonlight—it isn't important where it was—and, as if called by a voice, she stopped and turned me into her arms.

"Mark," she said, "I want a child."

"But, you said . . ."

"Mark, please, *please* . . ."

There was nothing in my world then but sand and sea, and Moira. Now, in the lounge of Hatherley, I put my hands to my face.

On my way up to my room I began to think about Henry Shearer; it would be easier for everybody, I reflected—even Moira—if he were to die.

In these days it was unusual to find defectors in such high places. Brander, of course, ran a harem of mistresses—even Whiting-Jones was escort to the young and beautiful Countess Devernon, while Air Chief Marshal Boland, the third of the Triumvirate, was an acknowledged pervert. And Press leaks about the roistering and blatant immorality of the new top-crust political soldiers were proliferating at the very time that the Triumvirate publicity machine was projecting, through Moral Guidance, a higher moral tone.

Before the Brander coup, the B.B.C., for all its claimed idealism from its lofty-minded executive, had been giving us the sexual act pictorially, when all good children were supposed to be in bed, but, with the advent of Brander, was again confining itself to its dreary repetitions of the accepted classics of the middle-class institutions —Royalty historicals, Dickens and the Brontës.

Actually, Shearer's defection was a personal disappointment. I'd have staked my life on his integrity, if only because he had been in

Auschwitz, and, like me, was a Jew, but his new *Act of Love* had all the trappings of a prostituted artist—unforgivable from such an articulate composer. It was a contribution to the top-level permissiveness, and I despised him for it.

It was not so much because he was sleeping with my wife—my delicious Moira was an ardent adulteress; it was because he was tainting the lives of the young, like Su-len. Amazingly, he was getting away with it.

I undressed slowly at my bedroom window that overlooked the drive, considering the possibility that somebody in service to Cheriton might have even suggested to Shearer the invitation to so dangerous a guest as Mombara. The last thing I wanted, at such a sensitive time, was doubtful political connections—the moral ones with Hallie were dangerous enough. I had come out of the shower and was sitting on the bed in my dressing-gown, contemplating this, when a faint tap came on the door.

"Come in."

It was Su-len.

There was about this child an individualism that brought me to nostalgic peace; she alone could invade the untenanted areas of my mind. And, now she was growing to womanhood, she was becoming the representative of an era I had lost. Standing there in her white gown, with her black hair and near-black skin of the primitive Tangar clan, she brought to me the garlic reek of the Chinese sea-board villages which were once my home.

I immediately showed my disinterest by turning my back on her. Wandering to the window, I said:

"Aren't you supposed to be in bed?"

In Cantonese, she replied, "Yes, but it is much too early. Moira sent me to bed because she does not want me. Besides, have you forgotten that it is Friday?"

"What's significant about that?" I began to fix my tie in the mirror.

"It is the full moon—and therefore the first day of the Festival of the Hungry Ghosts, according to the Chinese calendar."

"Then your calendar is wrong."

Closing the door behind her, she slowly entered the room, obviously aware that I had forbidden her to be there. She said:

"Last month, when I reminded you of the festival, you promised to take me down to the river to the little fishing lodge, to have my supper with the little innocents—don't you remember?"

Knowing I could see her in the mirror, she drew her gown closer about her. Her face, small and high-cheeked, was also that of a woman; many such aboriginal children are child-bearing at the age of twelve. I replied in Chinese, "I am sorry, but I do not recall it."

"Also, you said we would buy shrimps from the fishmonger in Woking—even shrimps out of a tin would do, you said, as long as we kept the festival. You said we would wait until Mamie went out, then fry rice-balls in the kitchen—surely you remember this?"

"See sense, Su. Did I know about this party?"

"You did not even read the letter I wrote to you. Look, this one." She held it out to me. "This envelope is not opened. I found it in the coat that smells of tobacco."

"I am sorry, but my life is a busy one."

"When you are away my life is empty."

"Please turn your back, I want to put my trousers on."

"It isn't necessary. Many times I have seen you with your trousers off. The souls of the drowned people are walking tonight, and they will not have food."

I thought she was going to cry, but she straightened when Moira yelled from the landing, "Mark, hurry yourself, the Besfords are comin' up the drive!"

Su-len said, "Grown-up people are always forgetting . . ."

"Did ye hear me, Mark?" shouted Moira.

"All right," said Su-len, "I will go alone. I have made the coloured lantern and I have some rice for boiling . . ."

I turned. "You will not. I forbid you to go to the river after dark." Pulling on my dinner jacket, I added, "You are becoming a nuisance. Go back to bed."

The door came open then and Moira swept in, saying, "Mark, have ye no conception of time? Another couple of minutes and the big black fella'll be here." Suddenly, seeing Su-len behind the door, she shouted, "Ah, this is the trouble, come on, out! You're supposed to be in bed, not high-mindin' it with your father—*out!*"

At the door Su-len turned and looked at me.

I would have liked to have kissed her good night, but the Chinese do not kiss in public.

Somebody was blowing a hunting horn coming up the drive, a disgusting noise, and I guessed it was Marsella.

The Besfords were a tribal clan with ramifications all over the county, and Marsella was their high priestess; their money had come by theft, following reparations in Ireland after the vicious repressions of the '98 Rebellion. Since then the Besfords, like other pseudo-Irish gentry, had lived in England off their Irish estates, watching the successive blood feuds which they had created. Their men were of military bearing, virile in bed and the field; their women wore flat hats and tweed. Often, I had speculated about the Besford entries in the Data Bank begun by Heath, for a lot of people had gone under since the census of 1971, now a basis of police information.

Rumour had it that, in the seventeenth century, one of the Besfords was born with the face of a fox; a tiny, misshapen creature being fed on a bottle in an attic in Mortgay Manor. But the squireens got to hear of it, and in their cups they dragged him out and put him to the chase. The hounds got him south of Wexford town, and tore him to pieces. Marsella was no fool: Claud, though a teetotaller when they married, coached her to restrain her alcoholism and became addicted in the process. Only a man of Claud's nonentity could arrive at a party on a chestnut hunter; his impotence was stamped on his face. He was in hunting pink; Marsella and her three daughters, Portia, Alicia and Gertrude, were dressed in the habit of nuns, the latest craze. And the stable yard was suddenly alive with stamping, tossing hacks; smart beaux, the parasites of wealth, clustered around Ezra's tray of punch, yelling above Marsella's horn-blasts with excited vacuity. Then Claud started blowing it, and I took him inside if only to stop him. I liked Claud; his family was charming.

"Marsella's on form," I said, pouring him a drink. "How's she behaving?"

He sighed, "You know Marsella."

The place was rapidly filling with cocktail thunder; Claud said, chinlessly, "Caught her out in the Dorchester last month. Heard she was in town and phoned her suite. Old Randy Soones answered."

"What's wrong with that?"

"It was four o'clock in the morning." He gulped at the whisky. "Good heavens, look what's coming."

Kate and Henry Shearer had arrived; she, inches the taller, of monarchical grace in a crimson gown, glided from a knot of women while he followed in her train. Claud said, "Now I know why Henry can't get up in the morning. By the way, have you seen his opera?"

The guests were jostling about us now, shouting for drinks. I said, "What I've heard is enough."

"Perverted rubbish. Pimps and pansies flouncing around in feathers. Marsella and I were in the front stalls—nearly got entangled with mating couples. What the devil is Tony Hargreaves and his Moral Guidance doing?"

"Performing operations on art of political taint. Shearer flourishes in official indignation, but it comes under the banner of social freedom. For this we can thank the Ali Babas—Brander, Boland and Whiting-Jones, every one corrupt."

Claud glanced about him. "Steady Mark, for God's sake."

I said, "Shearer sickens me; his erotomania is political sorcery—he's merely kissed the rear of the Establishment, but it won't last for ever."

"Excuse me," said Claud.

It needed nerve to stand the pace, of course. Alone, I watched the young set flooding in from the drive.

In their new plastic power-zoota suits they came, the young males brass-buttoned to the throat and stiff with Fascism, yet hollow-chested, wasted by wealth. The girls, ever the congenital victors, thrived like amazons on the new delinquency. All entered at once, hairy primates in search of food; bright-clawed and greedy

at the sight of the loaded tables, shrieking their latest jargons, pushing, shoving amid the protests of the serving matrons who supplied
the latest colours in pyjamas, working on Moira's premise that once
you lift your face you go into crimson. Old and elegant Cotteril was
talking in a corner to Adam Steen; beside them was fat little Benedict, friend of the murdered Waring. I straightened as Kate Shearer
waved from the crowd and came towards me.

"Good evening, Mark."

It seemed appropriate to bow to her. She said, smiling beautifully, "Moira certainly knows how to throw a party. Isn't it good to
see them enjoying themselves?" I presumed she meant the young
people, but she was looking at her husband and Moira; he was holding her hands, smiling into her face.

"I am glad you could come, Kate," I said.

Despite the drum of conversation, there was a silence between
us, and she looked at me, shrugging vacantly, as if in excuse for such
blatant infidelity. "What are we going to do about it, Mark?"

I stared at my glass. "I really don't know."

"Does Moira love him?"

"I doubt it."

Her eyes were filled with an inner serenity; her features were
classically perfect, her skin flawless: it was astonishing to me how
such a woman could tolerate the degeneration of Henry Shearer.
She said, "Do you think they're happy?"

"I doubt that, too."

"Would . . . would you release her if they wanted to marry?"

"I hadn't really considered it."

She said, "You see, I can't bear the adultery—not for my own
interests, but for theirs. Henry's marvellously gifted—I don't always
agree with every aspect of his work, of course—but I've ceased to
be of any real use to him. This hiding about in hotels is so bad for
both of them."

"You love him, don't you?"

She said, faintly, a break in her voice, "It seems beyond the
realms of love." She gestured emptily. "Ridiculous, isn't it—really?
When you weigh him up, he's a funny little man."

"I'm sorry, Kate."

She touched my hand and drifted away, saying, "Try to be kind to Moira; like Henry, she must be terribly unhappy."

I made a mental note to leave my footprints on Henry Shearer.

On my way over to Pud Benedict, Hargreaves joined me, smiling as usual.

"Good party, Seaton!"

"Trust Moira."

"Seen our Hallie lately?"

"Thank God you're not in the Diplomatic Service."

"It's the price you pay for taking her off me. Is she well, my dark lovely creature?"

Hargreaves was a political opportunist; according to Anstruther he got the Moral Guidance Council for sending the chairman of the T.U.C. to prison under Carr's Industrial Relations Bill in the time of Whiting-Jones, but fell from grace after a scandal in a Vorster arms transaction: under Brander, naturally, he had hit front rank. Benedict said he was corrupt, so I got the two of them together for kicks. Adam Steen, beside Benedict, greeted him with impeccable charm, "Ah, Mr. Hargreaves, how's Moral Guidance going?"

"As well as can be expected with Shearers in the vicinity."

"You can keep the Shearers," replied Adam, "I've got a Kish."

Benedict said, "Does Kish affect the Board of Trade? I thought he was mainly hunting in my Department. According to my P.A. he opened a cupboard in the staff toilet and a Kish fell out with a tape-recorder. It's a new lavatorial high fidelity, they say, working on sonic booms."

"How's poor old Stan Waters doing, Mark?" asked Adam sincerely. "Isn't he the recording expert?"

"We haven't seen him lately," Hargreaves replied. "They tell me he's through the first investigation, but castration actually occurs during Phase Two, it appears. They bring in a patrial with a knife, and Kish plays an aria from Shearer's *Celestial Eunuch* on a trumpet during the butchery—did you realise he played the trumpet, Seaton?"

Benedict said, "I'd have thought that pretty indelicate from any-

60

body but you, Hargreaves," and added, to me, "How's your complaint against Cheriton moving?"

"It isn't. It's an inquiry into me."

"Really?" said Hargreaves, and arched an eye. "Let's pray you stand the pry, old chap. Anyway, there's always the Staff Side appeal if you're unjustly treated, or think you are," and Benedict replied:

"Justice used to be a fact—within reason. Now we've got the likes of you and the Shearers—I'd have jailed him for that *Act of Love* thing."

Hargreaves replied, "So *you* don't approve of Henry Shearer now—Colonel Brander wouldn't like that—he adored the play."

"It was basically anti-Semitic—that's why he got away with it." Benedict was in belligerent mood, and I was uneasy. He added, "The fact that it's also pornographic is almost beside the point."

Hargreaves said, his eyes dancing, "Oh, come, sir—you're not accusing our Prime Minister of disliking the Jews? Aren't you forgetting that Shearer was in Auschwitz? You can't accuse him of everything."

"I accuse him of heralding a pogrom," said Benedict. "By God, he might be the thief of public standards, Hargreaves, but you're the Fagin. It's because of people like you that Seaton, here, is being investigated when he should be publicly applauded." He groaned and wiped his sweating face, adding, "God knows what I'm doing here, anyway, it's dangerous enough in the office." He moved away.

Hargreaves said, his hand on my shoulder, "A pogrom, eh? I hadn't thought of that. Good gracious, Seaton, if they start that you'll certainly have to watch it, won't you!"

He knew I was a Jew, of course: in his capacity in Moral Guidance he had access to everybody's file. Reaching Benedict, I said: "It's pretty hot in here, sir—are you all right?"

He replied, glowering after Hargreaves, "It might not be diplomacy, Seaton, but that man's a bastard, and don't you trust him."

It had never been my intention.

．　　．　　．　　．　　．

Moira's parties possessed a virtue all of their own; the women were as beautiful as the men physically indifferent, but Bolo Mombara, like Hargreaves, was an exception. Nor had his years in successive British prisons done much to reduce his girth, I reflected, as I stood in the ceremonial aisle of applause to greet him, pestered by an intuition of coming disaster.

Principles might be in tatters, I thought, but it only needed one dedicated revolutionary with a gun . . . I looked around the little sea of painted faces: it was an era of self-immolation when it could have been one of glory. These, the children of the rich, were Class 1 citizens under the Brander Triumvirate, yet demented lemmings set on a course of self-destruction. Hunting, shooting, they schemed for the easy jobs in their fathers' cartels, the scampish remains of a vanished heroism that once knew how to die straight out of university. Once the protestors of the Vietnam Atrocity, they had turned their heritage into moral corruption. Marsella, apart from them now, whispered into my ear, "How on earth did he get to the top?"

"He's shot all the others," said Shearer beside me. "You must admit it was a bit of a coup getting him here, Mark."

I didn't reply because I was looking above the heads of the crowd towards the landing beyond the stairs; here an apparition in white had moved. In one hand it carried a burning joss-stick; in the other it held a Chinese lantern.

"What are you doing out of bed?"

Su-len was standing within the folds of the landing curtain. I added, "Tonight is important to your mother, yet you continue to be a pest."

"Somebody has followed you, Papa," she whispered.

Hargreaves came with indolent self-assurance. "Well, well, well!" He leaned against the banister, hands in pockets, regarding us. "It's a truly astonishing house, Seaton. A black patrial plus bodyguard in the lounge and little Oriental ladies wandering around in nightgowns."

I said, "There is trouble between us. Tonight, she says, is the Festival of the Hungry Ghosts, and we have to put up with Mombara."

But he wasn't listening. Bending towards Su-len, he asked, "By your looks you are Hoklo?"

She straightened, her face up, "I am Tangar."

"Of the Boat People from the Pearl River? Why didn't I know about you before?" Reaching out, he gently took her lantern, smiling into its wavering light. "What is your name?"

"Su-len."

I said, "Your Council knows: you are not too well informed."

He ignored it. "Dear me, Seaton, you're a rum one. Surely she's old enough to be down with the party? Or is she kept under glass?"

I said to Su-len, in Chinese, "Bed at once!"

Hargreaves lit a cigarette, watching her retreating figure in the flame of the lighter. "By George, you kept her quiet. Where does she fit in? I mean, isn't it a pretty captive environment?"

"I wasn't aware that we had to advertise her."

"You even speak Chinese to her—an almost perfect female of the species."

"It isn't original, Hargreaves, it's been said before."

"And does wife Moira assist in the process of grooming, or is it a Seaton patent?"

I lied, "She's on the census return, and legally adopted—all is perfectly in order."

"I wasn't suggesting that a thing's out of place." He regarded me with an understanding smile; it was infuriating. I said, "Have you children, Hargreaves?"

"Not that I'm aware of, though I haven't asked Hallie lately."

"Then you wouldn't know it, but the sanctity between father and an adopted daughter is a very personal relationship."

"Undoubtedly."

"It's simpler than your bloody computers and you'll find nothing about it in the history of genetics. When I want a woman I go to Bond Street."

"So I gather."

"So this cosy dialogue is getting us nowhere. Shall we go downstairs to hear Mombara talk?"

"One thing's sure, she doesn't carry explosives in her bra," said Hargreaves, reflectively.

CHAPTER 6

Johnny Hampshire, Moira's winter string, was doing up his face in the mirror as I called in on my way to the lounge.

"Good evening, Mr. Seaton."

Actually, I quite liked Johnny: he always accorded me scrupulous respect, doubtless as reward for the favours granted him by Moira. And there was a new theory afloat in the mating game, apparently—colour and smell were linked: so Johnny was putting red under his arms and gold behind his ears as I arrived. His naked chest was covered with beads, his dyed, coiffeured hair was lying on his broad, brown shoulders. Pursing his lips now, he painted them with care, standing back to examine the effect.

"Does it taste?" I asked, going past him to the toilet.

He said, double bass, "You don't approve of this, do you, Mr. Seaton?"

"It doesn't actually overwhelm me; even I subscribe to additional hair in the mating season."

"Good gracious, what conceit!"

"Don't underrate us, we're better than you think," I said, otherwise engaged. Grinning, he straightened to his full height of six-feet-four. His left ear, I noticed with joy, was heavily thickened; I smelled bruised grass and mud, and heard the bawdy language of the scrum. According to Benedict, who followed Wokington, he was an absolute bastard in the ruck.

Mombara, when I reached him, was turning out some pretty vitriolic stuff. It was happening exactly as I had feared; he had found a public platform.

He cried, his arms up, "Unity is being constructed between minority groups that will defy aggression from any quarter of the world! Given self-government and not the oppression of this military junta, the black patrials of Britain would not only serve this country but guard her—a standing army against the creeping paralysis of Communism which threatens to engulf us." He had the place on the tips of his fingers, and knew it. "Are there reporters here?"

Hands were raised in the lounge; undoubtedly the underground Press, and Mombara shouted, "Then go back to your editors and tell them this—Bolo Mombara accuses Brander of neo-Fascism. He has proved this by his brutal methods of seizing power, and his violence against the labouring population; his treatment of patrial labour is outrageous. My countrymen run the transport of this country, nurse in its hospitals, collect its refuse. And they are penned, as a reward, in Class 3 housing. They are slaves in a country that fought to free slaves—the ciphers of a dictatorship that founds its roots in the Monday Club and the racism of South Africa! And you here tonight are responsible for this, for you fed the conditions that brought this junta to power!"

The initial silence of astonishment was now split by furious discord; men bawled insults, women abuse, and the younger set began to jostle towards the chair on which he was standing, but he yelled:

"We are denied contraceptives to keep down our birth-rate, so our slums are now breeding-grounds of cheap labour. If plague comes to those doss-houses you call Central Patrial Control, it will spread to you whites—we are dying in hundreds from endemic fevers." His black face bulged with anger; the purple scars of tribal wounding shone vividly on his cheeks, and he shouted, "If I speak sedition, then let it be reported. This could be the country of a dream, for black as well as white, but you sold it out to bring Brander to power, so I tell you this. Enoch Powell warned of the rise of the black man here, and we will prove him right. For if you are prepared to watch Britain destroyed by this Triumvirate, we are not. We will take the streets against this Saturnalia!"

Strangely, all were silent, as if in disbelief at the effrontery: such a speech could only end in internment. I looked around, anxious to see the effect on Benedict, but could not find him. Instead, beyond the french doors that led to the garden, I saw Su-len, and she raised a hand to me. As Mombara began again I slipped through a knot of people and opened the doors.

"Su, for God's sake," I whispered.

For reply, she seized my hand, dragging at me. "Come on. Papa, *come on!*"

Spellbound, I obeyed, going with her across the lawn. It seemed an escape into cleanness. The air was sweet and warm, blowing from the Mole River, and we went hand-in-hand down to the stile on the edge of the Big Field. Here panting, I looked back, seeing the blaze of the lounge, the white shirt-fronts, the coloured dresses.

"Come on!"

The wood beyond, I remember, was shafted with moonlight; the river flashed quicksilver brilliance through the scarecrows of trees. On its bank we stopped and Su-len darted around, uncovering a hidden saucepan, and this she cleaned with grass; I built stones, she found sticks and leaves, and ran down to the edge of the river for water, chattering all the time in furious, unintelligible Chinese. Her very excitement was having an elemental effect upon me: the sounds of the night, the swirling river, the darkness of her face was making the moments timeless. At once I was of China again, marvellously alive in my own country.

She struck matches; the fire blazed red on her face as she knelt, piling on leaves, then set the saucepan upon the stones, which is the way the land-locked Tangar cook. Fevered with excitement, she cried, "You see this fire?"

I nodded, watching her.

"The flames are made by the wand of the son of Chuan, minister to the Yellow Emperor . . ." She passed her fingers through the flame. "See how he leaps to burn, but my hand is untouched. Look, even the little hairs are not eaten with the heat!" She held it out to me. "I am not burned because Chuan has pleasure in me, the Tangar!"

I took her hand; it was hot from the fire, and trembling. She

66

cried, "Isn't this better than listening to the black man?" She tossed me a tin of shrimps and an opener, and I set it upon a stone between my knees. She cried, "One day we will leave this stinking old place and go to Kwangtung, and the rest of the world—old Moira, Mamie and Ezra we will put into pig-baskets and drop into the Han River."

"Do not talk like that about your mother," I said, pointing.

She squatted on her haunches, instantly arrogant. "She is not my mother, neither are you my father."

"You are a child," I said, "and should have respect for elders."

Now she squatted in the leaves before me, her hands appealing. "You think I am a child, but I am a woman. I am nearly sixteen by the Chinese calendar. My body speaks that I could make a baby, and if I had one I would smell him all over for the baby-smell, like the Tangar women." She held her breasts, saying in Chinese now, "Look for yourself, these can make milk. Perhaps I could make a boy-baby, if I would find a husband to lie with me—a first-time baby . . ." She snapped her fingers before my face. "Tip tip, I say, *tip tip!* I would have a one-hour labour like the little prawns." She held herself. "You are a man and you do not know. Why won't you take me back to the sea? In the Pearl River with the big junks I would be a woman."

I had no words for her. She said, "I wait, and you do not come, and when you do, you do not speak to me." Reaching out, she touched my face. "Do not be silent with me now, please?"

I spoke the old language to please her. "I am silent because my stomach is empty."

A trembling excitement seized her. "Listen, then, do you hear the wind crying? Let us go out for snapper in the China Sea, through the straits of Amoy where the big junks run. Oh, be a friend, Mark, play the sea-game like the Amoy urchins! I shall take the tiller and you will cast the nets like Old Man!" She made a bow of her hands above her head, and cried, "Snapper, snapper, grouper, snake-fish! *Wheeeah!*" She caught my hands, pulling me to my feet. "Do you hear them shouting from the sea?" Thrusting me away, she began to dance in a circle around the fire, then knelt, snatching

67

up the tin I had opened; on her haunches now, coolie-style, she began to stir the water in the saucepan and poured in rice and shrimps. "See how the rice is whirling in pain and the little shrimps are crying in the scalding. *Tin Hau!* Are these shrimps?" She cursed vividly in Cantonese. "You are snapper-belly shrimps, half eaten! Off Swatow in the summer tides, we catch you ten inches long!" Leaping up, she drew me back to the fire. "They are not really cooked, but the ghosts will not know. Oh, thank you, Mark, thank you for coming!"

Still chattering gutturally, she took the saucepan off the fire, strained off the water with a leaf and placed the pan before me, saying, "I give this food to the Taoist priest and he will bless it and put it in a lantern for the souls of those who are drowned, then none shall enter our house." Eyes wide, she stared up at me in the firelight.

I repeated, "None shall enter our house."

Lifting the pan she emptied it into the coloured lantern; I followed her down to the river's edge and there she knelt again, saying, "On the beach of Chuk Chu Wan I have built an image of the King of Hell, also three hands above a cone of dumplings made of flour and spinach, and a pig's head with buttons for eyes. Eat and stay in hell, but do not enter our house." She looked at me over her shoulder.

"Do not enter our house," I said.

She pushed the lantern on to the surface of the river and rose, her arms about my waist; together we watched it float into the moonlight.

Su-len turned to me, saying, "Good, all the ghosts are fed, and we have kept the custom. Will you now make love to me?"

In her arms I smelled the sweet-sour durian, the stinking-smell fruit that pervades Malaya: I stood outside myself, the *doppelganger* of another age; twelve years dropped away and she stared down at the bomb, aged three.

"Mark!" I was instantly back with her.

Now she was a woman in her demands, her fingers moving swiftly on the buttons of her gown; her hair was coarse and crinkled under my hands.

"Get the children out of here," I said. The Malayan sun was glistening in my eyes.

Head Man said, "Him too big to pull away, mister." He was ragged and thin; his eyes, heavily-lidded, moved opaquely in his pock-marked face. "Him Japanese, eh?"

Now Su-len sought me; the grass was damp with night-dew; the river beside us sparkled and sang; and still the children stared down at the bomb; a voice answered, "Yes, Mr. Seaton . . ."

"Can you get the tractor up here?"

"And pull him away?"

"Why not?"

"The ground is wet, him spin wheels."

"We can't just leave the bloody thing—look, I told you to get everybody away from here, Head Man."

"Him not go bang some thirty years, perhaps," he replied. "One time we get two like this. English officer come and take off top."

"I bet." The coloured lantern was a speck of light on the river . . .

I remember that the tractor driver came with his bag of tools, and there came to me then the old, sad song of the bomb-happies; the eerie note that bridges the insulators between terror and relief, and the casing of the bomb was slippery under my hands, with sweat. And I saw in Su-len's face the face of the bomb, and the light of the sun in the blackness of the wrenching fear was the light on the Mole River at Hatherley. First the eyes of the peering child I saw, aged three, then the face of a girl, and this was Su-len. I put out my hands to hold a child, and found it was a woman, and kissed the face of Su-len and found it was a child. Sweat ran down my fingers as I forced them into the bomb.

I sought her in that wavering light. I heard her gusty breathing in the sounds of the river; her lips were warm on my face and she was whispering in guttural Cantonese words I did not understand while the rain beat down, running in silvered torrents from the thatch of mango leaves and rattan, and thunder bellowed and re-verberated along the swamped road to Kajang. It seemed fruitless that I should be kneeling here, busting a 250 kilo Jap H3 when I could be safe in Kuala Lumpur. The wrench jammed on the casing bolts, rusted with the years of damp, and I cursed my stupidity, for they were anti-clockwise, and the moment the head moved the sod began to tick. I waited in sweat and unheard gasps for the slow-motion fracturing of the steel: the riveting, upward splitting of the casing that exposed the picric explosives on fire within, and it enveloped me, as in the arms of Su-len. It snatched me into suspension, an explosion of pain. As if disembodied, I flew in light, and this was the light of the Malayan sun . . . the mating of bomb and bomb-defuser in that slow second of agony when the detonators glow, the A.S.A. ignites the fulminate, and the face is blown apart. I heard Su-len say:

"Mark, I love you. Mark, I love you."

"You done it, mister?" said Head Man.

"Yes, I think so." I rose, standing above the bomb with the alarm-clock mechanism in my hands. "You bloody Jap," I said.

Su-len said, "Do not leave me."

I once read about a man who went to a cinema and interfered with a child.

"Do not leave me, Mark," said Su-len.

"God Almighty," I whispered.

"We tow him out now, sir?" asked the tractor driver.

"Yes, get a chain round it and dump it somewhere—better bury it."

I threw away the alarm clock and got back into the jeep. The little Chinese girl they called Su-len regarded me with quiet, brown eyes.

"Goodbye," I said, and ruffled her hair.

We were well down the road to Kajang, the jeep and I, when the thing went up. Forty people died, mainly children, and the tractor was blown to pieces—shrapnel from it killed people in surrounding compounds. I'd seen some things in my time in bomb-disposal, but nothing as bad as that. The only survivor was Su-len. Because I had made a fuss of her she had followed my jeep down the road . . .

Su-len said now, laughing in my face, "What are you talking about, Mark? You are here with me, you are not in Malaya!" Her arms, lithe and strong, were about me. "And you are not Moira's no more, you belong to me!"

Hargreaves did not speak, but I knew that somebody was there; then I saw him in the light of the moon, and heard him say above the rushing of the river, "Yes, indeed; Seaton, the sanctity between father and adopted daughter is a very personal relationship, isn't it? Get back to the house, man, Mombara's been shot."

Mombara was still lying on the carpet of the lounge when I got there; women were shrieking, Moira was hysterical, with Marsella and Kate holding her down, and the bodyguard had lined up the men around the walls; Mrs. Mombara was upon her knees beside her husband, wailing some tribal chant. I looked around the room for Shearer, but could not find him.

Never have I seen a man bleed so much, and the mess of it had a curious effect upon me; I actually felt faint, pushing through the shocked people towards the garden. Hargreaves, following me, said softly:

"What with one thing and another, your life's becoming complicated, old chap."

I did not reply, and he said, "It was organised, of course. Bolo Mombara was bound to drop some time—and where better than here, in this house, to discredit you!"

"You can't mean it!"

He lit another of his eternal cigarettes, exhaling noisily. "Oh yes, I do, since you insist on becoming so damnably important. I take it that your wife invited him—did anyone put her up to it?"

After a silence, he asked, "Shearer?"

I wandered away, and he followed me, saying softly, "We're all going to need some pretty firm alibis, you know, but I can't think yours will be so very valuable."

I replied, "I went for a walk along the river—what's wrong with that?"

He stared at me, then smiled. "What's wrong? Don't you know? The child was naked, Seaton!"

Later, in the lounge, he said quietly, "Wouldn't it be best, in view of what has happened, to drop your ridiculous charge against Cheriton?"

CHAPTER 7

I did not appear before the Kish Commission until nearly six weeks after lodging my complaint against Cheriton and Harmsworth, both of whom continued to show me the utmost respect in our dealings: it was as if they happily knew the outcome of what they considered a very frivolous affair.

It was unnerving to have the interview constantly cancelled—according to Kish he was engaged in obtaining outstanding evidence. Further, Stan Waters and Carrie had both been examined by the Commission; the former twice, and with terrifying effect. His unexplained temporary suspension from duty was followed by his nervous breakdown, and his doctor forbade my request to visit him at home. But Carrie, on the other hand, was lavish in her praise of the Commission's fairness, and Kish's personal charm.

"They are completely unbiased," said she. "It was obvious to me that all they're after is the truth. I really can't think what went wrong for Sir Stanley."

"I have a faint idea," I replied.

She was instantly hostile. "Well, I speak as I find. As far as I'm concerned the dreadful stories one hears about Mr. Kish are quite slanderous."

"I'll let you know at lunchtime," I said, and glanced at my watch. Now that the interview was imminent, I knew a mounting dread, adding, "According to some Kish has interviewed he has a magnificent talent for manipulation—one against the other."

"Oh, really, sir, that's most unfair." But at the door she said, more kindly, "Good luck, sir."

I took the lift to the ground floor and crossed Whitehall to the new Treasury building.

"Your name, please?"

"Mark Andrew Seaton."

"Age?"

I said, "You've got it in front of you."

Commissioner Kish raised his round, benign face to mine, removed his pince-nez spectacles, and smiled around the semi-circular mahogany table at his companions either side of him. He said, gently, "Mr. Seaton, it will not assist your case if you act discourteously . . ."

"My case?"

He spread his podgy hands. "The case of Seaton versus Mr. Cheriton and Mr. Harmsworth. Are you not here with the request that this Commission should examine an allegation of corrupt practice against these two gentlemen?"

"For which reason they ought to be present, surely?"

"The procedure of this Commission you will leave to me, sir. You are married, I see. Children?"

I sighed. "My son, Joseph, is twenty-one: Su-len, our adopted Chinese daughter, is nearly sixteen."

"Su-len?" This from a big, gingery man on Kish's right: his face, on a bird, would have ripped and torn. The other members smiled up: Kish clasped his little hands, beaming. "Her name is beautiful, Mr. Seaton. What does it mean?"

"Water lily."

"How very lovely." He glanced down at his papers. "According to Mr. Hargreaves of the Moral Guidance Council, she is advanced for her age."

"She is, but I don't see what that has to do with Cheriton's attempt to defraud the public."

He nodded, unmoved. "We will discuss this . . . this defrauding, as you call it, in my time, not yours. I see that you entered the Civil Service at twenty-five in the administrative class: later, you qualified as a quantity surveyor. Now you are Director of Contracts." He looked up. "Admirable progress. Why take a chance on throwing it all away?"

"Because I'm a public servant."

"Commendable, but surely a little trite? Has it nothing at all to do with Mr. Cheriton's politics—as a member of our Triumvirate?"

"It's confined to his attempt to swindle the public."

He gazed at me, expressionless. "Your remark is actionable, you realise this?"

I nodded. "Then let Cheriton sue and justice will be served that much quicker."

"Justice will be served here, Seaton, have no doubt," he murmured, and said to the man on his left, "When you are ready, Dr. Schreiber," and this man rose and said, bloodlessly, "When was your last medical check, Seaton?"

"I don't remember."

"The Secretariat does. Your health demands another examination; earlier administrations were undeniably lax."

"Compared with this one I wouldn't call it a fault."

He smiled faintly. "You were in bomb-disposal during the early post-war years, I see. This work can have a traumatic effect on the mind."

I replied, "It depends upon the individual."

He turned to Kish. "It is possible for a man engaged on bomb-disposal to suffer the same delayed action as the devices he defuses. Military hospitals, indeed, still have patients from war service who broke down later in life, suffering from a megalomania known as bomb-happiness—you've heard of this, Seaton?"

I said, "Can we call Mr. Cheriton and get on with the business in hand?"

"Self-exaltation is not an uncommon element in this unhappy condition, as the Commission might already have noticed? As to Mr. Cheriton being called, I may say that while it is your right to make allegations, Seaton, it is also right for the Commission to adjudicate on your mental condition at the time you make them. The very nature of your medical history demands examination."

"What does that mean?"

74

"That it is in your own interests to prove that you are now free of the illness that has diluted your responsibility in the past."

I thought: you are a proliferation of obscene bastards. I will lay you under a bomb and you can look up into its electronics and the ribbed yellow and red of its explosive picric, which is like the mouth of a cat. And you will wonder, as I did, if it is heat-reactive, mechanical or photo-electric; and, when you trip the automatic in error and the ticking begins, your bowels, like mine, will turn to water. I heard a voice say:

"Sunray, Sunray . . . ?"

"Christ, she's away. Can you hear her?"

"Like Big Ben. You're down eight feet, Mark, you'll have to switch her out."

"Get the hose down. I'm doing this girl."

"You can't—it'll take you fifty seconds to get clear, and she'll blow in thirty. Take it slowly. The cut-out is behind the mainstage detonator. Get your bridger in—watch bare wires. The terminals should be over to the left if she's Mark III . . ."

I began to shiver. Sweat trickled down my face and I wiped it into my hair. Kish, watching me closely, said, kindly, "Are you all right, Mr. Seaton?"

I nodded.

"You have gone pale." He looked about him. "It is very close in here. Would you care for a glass of water?"

A voice in the room said, "Are you a Jew, Seaton?"

I turned to it, and Kish interjected, "We are not concerned with this witness's nationality; please withdraw that question."

Clearly, as if he was standing at the table before me, I heard the voice of Vidor, who said:

"Listen, Mark, you've *got* to bridge her; I'm sitting up here as well, you know—I'm in this, too." His voice went fainter. "Don't panic over there—just keep recording. We think she's a Mark III but there's a scar on the identity plate, and it could be Mark II. If she isn't, she'll blow in seconds from now, unless Seaton bridges the cut-out, and . . ."

Dr. Schreiber said, "I've always been interested in the quality of mind, the necessary training, the ingenuity necessary to invent such devices. In the Mine Research Laboratory at Farnham, psychology plays a major role—the ability to deduce exactly what the reaction of a potential disarmer might be under conditions of stress. Some panic under actuation-tick; some are tuned by the sound to a point of sensitivity when they are at their most efficient, though later they may cry. Others accept the challenge and sweat it out, a few do nothing when the ticking begins, except sit, awaiting death." He stared about him. "Do you know that live statistics were drawn up by German Intelligence? They were based on experiments carried out on selected victims ranging from frump to intellectual—to determine human reaction resultant upon 'Speak'. This is a condition imposed upon the mind when an explosive device assumes a paranormal process—it answers back—it gives a rebuke, in fact, to the disarmer's attempted interference in its role of destruction." He turned to Kish. "The results, Commissioner, were shattering. Steel, you see, is tongueless—it makes no sound. And so, the ticking—the endowment of speech—to an inarticulate object is one of the most terrifying phenomena in Nature; it cuts deeply into the human subconscious. And the actual pitch and regulation of the ticking is important, too—irregular beats correspond to emotional agitation, and this affects the skill of the potential disarmer." He consulted his notes, adding, "It was conclusively proved that, as a result of the experiments mentioned, some forty-two per cent of those subjected suffered immediate mental damage; a few were actually deranged, but others endured ill-effects much later in their lives. May I suggest, sir, that Mr. Seaton is such a patient?"

Kish said, "Thank you, Dr. Schreiber." He turned to me. "I think you'll agree, Seaton, that the psychologist's theories are brilliant."

"He was taught in the right place," I said.

None appeared to hear this, and Kish said, "Well, you've made the charges and apparently intend to enforce them, so I suggest we go into recess; however, before we do so, be so good as to name your witnesses."

I replied, "Sir Stanley Waters, Miss Carrington, my secretary; Mr. Anstruther, my Permanent Secretary, Mr. Fiddler, with whom

76

Harmsworth was in liaison, and, of course, Mr. Cheriton and Mr. Harmsworth."

He raised an expressionless face. "Are they likely to give evidence against themselves?"

"Cheriton will give evidence, on oath, that his firm, managed by one of his relatives, is entered on the Ministry List of Contractors in the name of Ranklyt Thommasson."

Kish nodded, writing, then said, "This opening session of the inquiry might have proved a little . . . exacting, Seaton, but I will see to it that evidence is taken in an impartial manner. So, in your own interests, may I remind you that the recorded tape—the one Sir Stanley Waters took of the alleged conversation between Mr. Harmsworth and Mr. Fiddler . . . might prove of value to your case?"

"I haven't overlooked it."

"Good, good." He rose, gathering up his papers. "The secretary will please arrange for a tape-recorder to be available at our future meetings."

"Yes, sir," said he.

They were all, quite suddenly, motionless, staring at me as men might stare at the pegged body of a sacrificial savage, awaiting the raking horn, and scream.

"Thank you, Seaton. We will call you again," said Kish.

A workman entered carrying an old, large school clock; this he proceeded to fix on the wall behind me. It began to tick in my head even as I watched it.

"Yes, indeed, we will call you again," said Kish.

I met Carrie outside my office. "The Permanent Secretary is waiting to see you sir," she said.

"Ask him to come in," I put my hat and umbrella in the stand.

James Anstruther came from a string of highly placed theologians: rumour had it that he was directly descended from Latimer; he, who with Master Ridley, lit a torch to enlighten England. Also, he was a non-functional member of a family of Press tycoons. His brother was a dean, his cousin a deacon; he had an uncle running a Greek Orthodox mission in Cyprus, his male secretary was a Welsh druid; strangely enough, I trusted Anstruther. Now he entered my office, a perfectly-mannered, Kiplingesque, elongated gnome. "How did you get on with Kish?"

I sat down, too. "He taught me that we're governed by scientific materialism."

"But the Prime Minister thinks the world of him."

"From what I've heard of Brander I'm not surprised."

He lit a cigarette, smiling. "You know, Mark, one day the Triumvirate's going to be interested in you—you don't exactly wrap things up. Actually, Kish telephoned me. You were honest and they liked that, but they complained of your rudeness."

"The man's practically Buddha—where the hell do they get their people from?"

He shrugged. "They're the sad invention of the times. Orwell anticipated them."

"Yes, from the wrong side of the fence. These are Fascists. To claim that a left-wing dictatorship will govern us in 1984 was the neurosis of a man short of creative ideas."

"Dear me, the *Vaporiser* wouldn't like to hear you say things like that."

"In due course it might. Where does democracy stand? I was in with Kish an hour and Cheriton's name was scarcely mentioned."

"Then why did they sit?"

"To inquire into me."

He gestured impatiently. "Come, Mark, don't be ridiculous."

"To inquire into me," I repeated. "Macarthyism run by the Greek colonels."

"Really, you do make the most startling allegations." He played with his cigarette, torn by honour. "To . . . to admit the colour of any administration is fruitless. As servants of the Crown we must serve the Communists if they come to power."

"Right. Now tell me where you stand in this business."

He got up and wandered about. "If you're forcing investigation of a tender-board error, then I'm behind you. But if you're making unsubstantiated attacks on our Minister's character, then count me out."

"And if I prove his attempt to defraud the public?"

He gestured. "Even then I'd urge you to be more moderate. Saints should sometimes look the other way in the public interest."

"Christ, you're as bad as the rest of them."

"Assess me as you wish. It's easy to be a bull in a china shop."

"That makes you as bad as Cheriton."

He ignored it, saying, "Heads will roll, yours, too—the ramifications could be boundless . . ."

"But cheap at two hundred thousand, James. I knew a junior who went to the wall for eight and sixpence."

He smiled indulgently. "But the juniors always die alone, don't they? Your executions insist on taking place before the vulgar crowd."

I said, "The Service isn't what it was, is it? The seniors I knew in the old days used to go under hand-in-hand."

He went to the door. "Unofficially, I admire your action, Mark; officially I reject it. The great thing today is to stay submerged."

"I doubt if Latimer would approve."

It stopped him in his tracks, then he smiled and opened the door. Carrie, standing there, said to me, "Sorry to intrude, sir, but there've been several calls for you. Will you be in this afternoon?"

"I will not. I'm dead, gone out, or had a baby—you can tell that to your charming Kish, and in any damned order you please."

Come to think of it, I had always preferred Master Ridley.

CHAPTER 8

The most unusual aspect of the Kish investigation, I now considered, was that no mention had yet been made about the death of Bolo Mombara in my house, although the newspapers were full of it. Doubtless, they were keeping this for the next meeting, when the name of Su-len would surely arise—indeed, she might even be called to give evidence.

I badly wanted to save her this frightening experience, with all its fearful innuendo. Added to this was my realisation that I was now on the defensive: in the face of this complication, my need to prove the guilt of Cheriton and Harmsworth was now secondary; I had to protect Su-len.

It was about three weeks later. As I came into the office the telephone rang. It was Dr. Leyton of Public Research, I didn't like Leyton; he suffered from spots, and his breath was bad. He said, "Ah, Mr. Seaton, I want to talk to you about the junior lavatory pedestals."

"Good heavens."

"My research people tell me the children are sitting three-eighths of an inch too low."

"Really?"

"It's important. There's a medically accepted posture, you know; jack-knifing can lead to serious internal complications."

I said, "But is there any real compulsion to make contact with the seat? I mean, couldn't you issue a directive for everybody under ten to sit on tiptoe?"

"Don't trifle with me, Director; it's a big financial commitment. A quarter of a million pedestals might have to be changed."

"But they've been on the things since Queen Victoria."

He said, reflectively, "I suppose it's Finance, really."

"Of course it's Finance. If Stan Waters's department agrees I'll issue the running contract."

"Then, since this is three-cornered, could we both pop over to see him?"

"When Stan gets back, Leyton—I'm very busy now."

"But he's back."

"No!"

"Yes, he is—he started again yesterday."

"Then why the devil don't people tell me these things?" I rooted around in my tray, but there was nothing about it there. I said, "I'll meet you in his office straightaway," and Leyton, strangely, replied:

"I'll give you a few minutes to talk to him first."

I wondered, of course, how such a thing had missed Carrie; at that moment she came in, saying:

"There's a frightfully big post, Mr. Seaton—and piles of Press cuttings still about that dreadful Mombara business—I suggest you don't bother reading them." She began slapping things down into the trays.

"I don't intend to—not now, anyway. I'm meeting Dr. Leyton in Finance; he's complaining about the height of the junior lavatory pedestals."

"Is he? Actually, I stand on mine." I was a little surprised. She added, "It's men like Leyton who give birth to this inordinate rubbish. And the Press are being absolutely vile about Mombara. Surely they can't get away with such slanted opinions?"

"This is what comes of taking an evening stroll with one's adopted daughter."

"I'm very sorry, Mr. Seaton." She hesitated. "How's your wife taking it?"

"As an occupational hazard—after all, it isn't every day that one gets a Cabinet Minister shot dead in the lounge."

"That's a little bitter."

I didn't answer this, and she added, "Incidentally, Miss Hallie phoned twice yesterday. She eventually said that it's all right for next weekend. Does that . . . mean anything to you?" She glanced down at her fingers, then seized her diary, and said quickly, "And you've got a busy week, you know, sir; there's the first meeting of the Bayswater Underpass contract at eleven, so you can't stay long with Dr. Leyton—unless you get somebody else to take the chair?"

"Get young Collins on to it—he's good on roads."

"It's over a million, sir—it's really your level."

"Then why the hell didn't you say so?"

Her face snapped up. "It's entered in your diary!"

"No, it is not!" I got up, wandering about. "And, while we're at it, why wasn't I told that Stan Waters was back?"

She stared at me. "Is he . . . ?"

"Of course. He's been back days—the only friend I've got in the building, and I don't even know . . ."

Somewhere outside a pneumatic hammer was thumping; it seemed to fill the office. Basically, of course, Carrie's trouble was her mother—all her mental mishaps could be attributed to this, but even in my anger I pitied her. If love and sacrifice, I pondered, could be weighed like coal, they would raise enough energy to run a private hell. Now Carrie's arms were about me and I faintly heard her say, "Oh, God . . . Mr. Seaton . . ." and sweat, my old enemy, began to run in cold streams over my body, for Hendriks was an amazing sight when we got him out of the clay—he was six-feet-one when he went down the hole and under three feet long when we pulled the tarpaulin over him, and any time now the telephone bell would ring and call me for the second meeting with the Kish Commission. It was all right playing the merry facetious with people like Leyton, but people like Kish were facts, and I badly wanted to keep Su-len out of it—after all, I hadn't done anything to her, as far as I knew—but quite obviously somebody was feeding the Brander Press. A pain had been growing in my head since Mombara's assassination; a ticking like that of a bomb, and in the *window* . . .

. . . *weakness,* and Colonel Vidor said, "Come on, come on, Seaton, get on with it, we haven't got all day—if you're that bloody scared of it I'll come down and do it myself . . ." and I shouted at Carrie, who was trembling before me:

"Look, there's nothing in here about the Bayswater Underpass —no, don't sidetrack me, see for yourself!" I flapped the pages of the diary at her. She said:

"In your *desk* diary, Mr. Seaton—I can't enter appointments in that one—you keep it in your pocket!"

"It was the same with Stan Waters—you deliberately keep certain information from me!"

The sun, I recall, was of strickening brilliance, glowing on her red dress, and I remembered a splinter of light ramming down through my cocked boots: my feet were up in the air and my hair was in water and I could smell the 808 explosive, and the thing was beating like a hammer against my sweating face while I worked on the coned head: tick-tock, tick-tock, *tick-tock*, and Moira said, "What the devil were you doing with her down at the river, anyway? Honestly, Mark, if I didn't know you better . . ." She switched on the bedroom light and it scorched the retinae of my eyes, flashing on the bomb-casing in the blackness ten feet down. The room began to shake with the thudding of the pneumatic hammer, blomp, blomp, *blomp,* and I cried to Carrie, "Can you get somebody to throw some sacking over the hole, for Christ's sake? I can't see a thing with the torch." She was messing around with a chair now, her mouth jarring open and closed, but making no sound, and I kicked the chair out of her hands, sending it spinning; Vidor said through the intercom:

"What the hell's wrong with you today, Mark? You've got enough light down there for a searchlight tattoo—for heaven's sake stop talking and get on with it." But the one Hendriks did under Balham Tube Station was an incendiary, too. It didn't go up when the ticking stopped—there was no explosive release, no shattering into nothingness; it merely glowed and slowly fried him. I saw the earth-compacting hammer leaping in a big man's hands, and Carrie suddenly cried out and ran to the office window, slamming it shut. I was lying against the wall, I remember, watching her in a mist as she rattled the telephone, shouting, "Yes, I *am* speaking for the Director of Contracts—get on to the contractor in the road and tell him to stop that noise, there's somebody ill in here."

We waited. She was leaning over the desk, panting, her hand to her chest. Lying still, I stared at her, slowly bringing her into focus. A minute passed, I suppose, then another: the hammer stopped. Swaying, I climbed to my feet, and said, "It was Hendriks. He really was a dreadful sight. I had to go down and get him out. He was small, like a doll."

"I know, I know, Mr. Seaton."

"We had to hose it first, of course, to kill the fire. And they kept taking temperature readings before they sent me down."

"Please, Mr. Seaton . . ." Running for the chair, she put it before me, her hands reaching out for me as I backed away. "Oh, you're so ill . . . why doesn't your wife . . . ?"

"You leave my wife out of this," I said.

The telephone rang then, and she snatched it up, standing there with her hand over the receiver. I managed to get to the desk and there supported myself, saying:

"Don't you want this bloody job, then?"

Her face was blank. "I . . . I beg your pardon, sir . . . ?"

"What grade are you?"

Replacing the receiver, she said, straightening, "I . . . I think I'd better go, Mr. Seaton."

"Oh no, you don't—you'll answer my question. If you find yourself inhibited, or whatever you damned females are from time to time, then take a holiday with a man and your mother with you, but don't you lie to me to cover your bloody inefficiency!" Snatching up the desk diary I flung it at her, and although she tried to avoid it, it struck her in the face. "There's nothing in there about the Bayswater Underpass, is there?"

"No, sir."

"And you knew about Stan Waters, too, didn't you?"

"Yes, sir."

"That's better. You're like the rest of your secretarial class; the less you have to do the more inefficient you get—Vidor was the only exception—he'd never ask you to touch one he couldn't do himself. Did you ever meet him?"

She replied, her eyes closed, "No, but I've heard you speak of him many times. Are . . . are you feeling better?"

"Much better."

She put the chair behind me and pulled me down upon it, then hurried to my desk and opened a drawer; taking out two pills she ran to the lavatory and returned with water. Obediently, I took the pills. She stood behind the chair.

"There now, there now," she said, her face against mine.

After a few moments she went to the door, and said, "Will there be anything else, Mr. Seaton?"

I put my head in my hands, and replied, "Yes, there is. I've just remembered, I've got a meeting of the Bayswater Underpass—I saw it entered in my diary."

"No you haven't, sir—I've put Mr. Collins on to it—it's above his financial level, but he's good on roads. Have you forgotten you're due to meet Dr. Leyton in Sir Stanley's office any time now?" She glanced at her watch. "You'll have to hurry, sir, if you're going to be with the Permanent Secretary for an early lunch. Would you like me to come with you to Sir Stanley?"

"No, I'm all right now, thank you."

She was leaning against the door now; vaguely, I recalled that she had given me some pills; it was good having Carrie about when these little breakdowns occurred, for she took them calmly: a contrast to Moira who ran around shouting for Ezra and telephoning the doctor.

"Thanks, Carrie," I said, and she was instantly embarrassed.

Her hair, I remember, was untidy.

When I got to Room 303 I knocked and entered: the door was very heavy under my hands.

Stan was hanging behind it by his braces, his head awry, his face black and contorted. To complete the obscenity, his trousers had come down and were hanging around his feet.

Leyton followed me into the room as if part of the play, staring up at the body. I climbed on a chair and cut the braces from the fanlight over the door.

"God, how horrible," he said.

We laid Stan on the floor of his office and I covered his face with my coat. I was still kneeling with his hand in mine when the police began fussing about me. Security Jones said, his hand on my shoulder:

"Fond of 'im, wasn't you, sir?"

I nodded.

"Any idea why he did it, Mr. Seaton?" asked a detective.

I looked up. "Of course. He was being investigated; this, to him, was a reflection upon his honour. He didn't stop to consider that it was routine in a police state."

"Easy, sir," said Security Jones, glancing about him.

"He was ill, of course," said somebody.

I got up. "Have it your own way."

A blackshirt officer watched me as I went through the door.

Carrie, unsuspecting, was awaiting me in my office; she said, "Glad you've returned, sir—I was just about to ring you. A call has just come through from the secretary of the Kish Commission . . ." Her face flushed, I noticed; she added, "They were due to interview Sir Stanley, it appears, but he hasn't come in this morning." She smiled gently. "They are hoping you'll take his place—good to bring it to a head, Mr. Seaton."

I nodded.

She inquired, anxiously, "But not if you feel unwell—I mentioned . . ."

"I'm perfectly well now," I said. "When do they want me?"

"Within the next half an hour."

Whoever was responsible for this particular operation, I thought, was timing it with artistry.

CHAPTER 9

"Your name, please," said Kish.

I replied, "Andrew Mark Seaton."

The shorthand writer said, "If you please, Mr. Chairman, that is not the same order of Christian names submitted by the interviewee previously," and Kish raised his puckered face, smiled brightly about him at the other four members, and said to me, "You are in light mood this morning?"

I answered, "Variety can lend colour to farcical proceedings. I've nothing to lose."

"We'll try to remedy that in due course, Seaton. Meanwhile accept the condolences of the Commission on the death of Sir Stanley, your friend. I am also to inform you that Mr. Fiddler of his Finance Branch, whom you were going to call in evidence, has disappeared from his home. Did you know this?"

I shook my head. Kish said, "Every effort is being made to find him, naturally, but his absence considerably weakens your case. Incidentally, since you intend to call Mr. James Anstruther, your Permanent Secretary, may I ask if you discussed your allegations with him before you brought this complaint?"

"I did."

"And what did he advise?" He peered at me.

"That I shouldn't pursue it."

"Why not?"

"I'm not prepared to quote him."

"I can well imagine."

A man sitting on Kish's extreme left, rose, and said, "Mr. Seaton,

I'm the Assistant Director of Public Prosecutions. I'd like to point out that the only witness who can actually support you in your allegations is Miss Carrington, a very junior grade—considered by some to be a potentially biased witness." He folded his hands before him. "I ask you to listen to me, in your own interests. You're seeking a confrontation not only with your Minister, but with the Triumvirate—do you realise this? The Prime Minister himself cannot stand aside in the face of your charge of ministerial corruption." He cleared his throat portentously. "No doubt you're an expert in contract law, but this, though based on common law, won't avail you when dealing with legal professionals. If you lose this case, and I'm certain you will, your resignation from the Civil Service will be automatic; Mr. Cheriton and his junior may take action against you; who could blame them? This could lead to heavy damages, even prison, and pension loss. Do you see the dangers?"

"Of course."

"You don't appear to, so it becomes my duty to give you one last chance to withdraw your groundless charges."

I had watched him during this oratorical nonsense, and I think it was his self-assurance which angered me most. Coercion would follow, of course. Mention would soon be made of Mombara's death, if this failed; blackmail would come with questions about Su-len. Violence itself might be employed in the end. Benedict once said, I recall, that the lost causes of today are the midwives of tomorrow; the embryo of the absolutist State. I was becoming uneasy, but said, "What do you want me to do?"

All were instantly attentive. Kish smiled, saying, "Just make a simple statement withdrawing your charge, Mr. Seaton—a clarifying record, so I can close this ridiculous case and we can all go home."

I nodded, and he added, snapping his fingers, "Clerk, prepare to take this down." I said:

"Public funds are involved here and I'm a public servant. At the end of it, it is the people who will judge me, not this Commission. So, I insist that this inquiry—if that's what you call it—continues. I demand the attendance of Cheriton and Harmsworth; I ask for examination of the tender-board procedure, and investigation into the true identity of the firm Ranklyt Thommasson, and its directorships."

They relaxed, visibly dejected—all except Kish, who grinned wryly, rubbed his chin, and said, "By God, Seaton, I give you credit. We will now move to the next item on the agenda—the shooting to death of Mr. Bolo Mombara in your house on June the Second."

I rose, crying, "I object. Mombara's death is a police case. How can it be on this Commission's agenda?"

"Objection noted," said he. "The Public Prosecutor will continue."

The Prosecutor said, "Before I call Mr. Cheriton and Mr. Harmsworth to defend themselves, I would like to record that the recent case of the Crown versus Lord Wentorth is scarcely parallel to this one."

"Then why raise this case law?" asked Kish, blankly.

"Only to define that Lord Wentorth's traitorous behaviour was not based, as first thought, on an attempt to gain political advantage—this has been inferred in the case of Mr. Seaton—but because he suffered a slow decline in moral standards."

Kish looked vague. "It's entertaining, but scarcely relevant. Mr. Seaton is not accused of treason."

"Agreed, sir. I am only trying to establish that, as in the case of Lord Wentorth, a man can suffer diminution of responsibility." The Prosecutor smiled about him. "In this particular instance, you'll recall, his lordship became attracted to a young girl."

Kish observed with disinterest, "Such a friendship need not necessarily be dishonourable."

"Exactly. This was Wentorth's defence."

I got up. "What has this to do with the hearing of my complaint?"

Kish said, over-speaking me, "Mr. Prosecutor, I am at a complete loss as to what you're getting at. Seaton's moral standards are not on trial."

"Later, it was proved that Wentorth slept with the child."

Kish sighed, saying, "Look, I've been patient. Will you please get on with the essence of the case. I'm not the least interested in your case law or who slept with who, majors or minors. Do you agree, Seaton?"

I shrugged, turning away, and he continued. "Can you yourself see a parallel between your life and that of Lord Wentorth, lately convicted of treason?"

I shook my head, but he must have seen I was trembling. The Prosecutor said:

"At the time Mr. Bolo Mombara was murdered you were absent from your house, Seaton?"

"Yes." The clock on the wall behind me began to tick in my head.

"Where were you?"

Before I could reply, a small man to the right of Kish rose, and said, "Mr. Seaton, I am the Government's official Press representative. As you know, this case is causing tremendous official interest, and is now being reported in the newspapers . . ."

"It is being twisted by the newspapers," I said, but he continued:

"According to Mr. Anthony Hargreaves, who happened to be at your house on that night, he actually saw you on the river bank—minutes after Mombara had been shot—with your adopted Chinese daughter?"

"That's correct."

Kish spread his hands. "He took his daughter for a walk by the river. What's wrong with that?"

The Press man said, "Isn't it a strange thing for a host to leave his guests at such an hour—it was eleven o'clock—for a nocturnal meeting with a child?"

Kish brought his fist down on to the table. "How dare you! Withdraw that." He glared about him. "The inference is monstrous, and it will not be recorded here. A father has a perfect right to walk alone with a child of the house." He rustled his papers while the Prosecutor looked disconsolate, and added, "I'll not have Mr. Seaton's honour traduced. Even if the parties are unrelated, as in this particular case, there must be no speculation on the possibility of intimacy. Were this to pass then many would stand condemned."

He looked about him, licking his lips. "Though I must agree that in the more . . . more personalised moments of my life, I . . ."

The room swelled with laughter; men thumped their papers, stamped their feet. Holding up his hand for silence, Kish said, "It's only necessary to record, I think, that when the Minister of Patrials was murdered by a high velocity rifle fired from the garden, Mr. Seaton, whose guest he was, was otherwise engaged." He peered at me. "Shall we leave it at that?"

"Yes," I said.

"Doubtless with some relief?" He smiled, his eyes twinkling. The Prosecutor leaped up. "May I call the child as a witness, sir?"

"You shall not. She is a minor, and I'll not have her distressed." There was silence, save for the clock, and he added, "However, if, at a later date I consider her testimony needful, no doubt Mr. Seaton would be the first to agree . . . ?" He removed his spectacles, and gazed at me. "Yes, Mr. Seaton . . . ?"

I nodded.

"Now to get on with your complaint. Call Mr. James Anstruther."

The Commission Clerk shouted, "Mr. James Anstruther!"

I thought: I shouldn't, of course, have left her off the census return. At the time, however, there seemed no reason to register her; as an Oriental, she didn't come under the Racist Bill, one of Whiting-Jones's earlier successes. Now I began to wonder if the Race Programmer would have boggled at her inclusion, as it had boggled, apparently, when Pargeter, Hargreaves's friend, had made a hole in the Overseas Aid card and paid himself sixteen thousand pounds a year into the Bank of Uganda. The Public Prosecutor had asked for the death penalty, and got it, though it was general knowledge at the Bar (who were all doing it) that he had a much larger amount in a Swiss bank. So Pargeter was hanged—presumably on the endearing financial ethic that you can rape our women but must never steal our money.

I was sorry for Pargeter's wife: she was a local commandant in the Girl Guides, a movement now banned—a charming woman who lived in a tent in her mansion in Bryanston Square and sat on an

Elsan in the middle of the hall—unreservedly an out-of-doors person.

As Benedict remarked at the time, there are often conclusive reasons why men like Pargeter go wrong.

Assignations with Chinese waifs can have the same effect, I was finding. Being parent to the likes of Su-len was like tiptoeing on bare feet through a world of tin-tacks.

"Are you asleep, Mr. Seaton?" asked Kish.

I was very much awake.

Anstruther entered, and didn't glance my way; coldly efficient in bearing and intent, he took his seat, and Kish said, "You are James Charles Anstruther, Permanent Secretary to the Minister of Building, against whom Seaton is making complaint?"

It was a mouthful and Anstruther just sat, not bothering to reply. Kish, obviously disconcerted, said, "Please give an assessment of Seaton's character."

"It's beyond reproach."

"Rephrase that, because, if it's true, he's the only man in the world so blessed."

"His character's excellent; that's why he's in the post."

"But lacking in tact, I believe? Didn't you once record that?"

James crossed his thin legs. "I might have added that he doesn't tolerate fools."

"Fools exist in your Department, Mr. Anstruther?"

"We have our share."

"You also have liberals, I understand—even Socialists."

James nodded. "As far as I know we still have a free vote."

"Seaton, for one, has some radical views?"

"Perhaps. I know that he carries a sticker in the back of his car, which says, 'Don't blame me, I didn't vote for anybody'."

The Prosecutor interjected, "The Architectural Division has complained about his attitude to them, do you know this?"

"Yes, he doesn't like architects—few quantity surveyors do. Come to that, he doesn't like administrators, either."

"But you yourself are an administrator."

"That's because when I came out of University my father didn't know where to put me—the Church and Sandhurst happened to be full."

James gazed around the room, and Kish said sharply, "It's almost an ecstasy of self-mutilation, isn't it, Mr. Anstruther? You're not here to be flippant with this Commission, you know. Please answer this. Do you support this man in his allegation?"

"No, I don't."

Kish leaned back in his seat. "Tell us why."

"Because the wise civil servant should know where to draw the line—it's irresponsible of Seaton to wash these facts in public."

Baffled, I leaned forward, intent; Kish said, "So, in essence, you believe the charges to be accurate."

"Oh, yes—Seaton's right, without a doubt—I know him. He's cursed with a legal mind. It's a positive attempt to defraud, or he wouldn't speak out."

There was a long silence, and Kish said, "Let's have this clear, Anstruther. You are confirming that, in your view, your Minister attempted to convert public funds to his own use?"

"Yes." James added, "Harmsworth too, of course."

"You realise the importance of what you are saying—that you are now equally responsible, in the slander, with Seaton?"

"I do."

Kish, momentarily lost for words, said, "But a few minutes ago, in this very room, you said you didn't support him in his charge of corruption!"

"For the last few minutes I've been in here, Mr. Kish."

All faces swept up; motionless. James added, while I held my breath, "In some circumstances one overlooks a degree of corruption, and this is such a case. But, if Seaton insists upon a confrontation, then he is entitled to have Cheriton and Harmsworth face him and deny his accusations. Alternatively, they can sue for slander and take their damages in court—if any."

I thought, in the following silence, By God, Anstruther, they don't pay people like you in multiples of thirty. As if hearing this, Kish said:

"Mr. Anstruther, your vacillation and obvious disrespect for this Commission will be notified to the proper quarter. You may go."

James rose, smiling at me, saying, "You were right, Mark—moderation's worth a fight. In this neo-Fascism we will lean on the public —one can't stay submerged if these are the dirty standards."

I've seen careers end in worse ways.

Latimer, at least, would have approved.

CHAPTER 10

They brought in Colonel Paul Vidor next, my old C.O. from the post-war days of the bomb-happies. Paul was older, of course, but hadn't changed a great deal: still the ice-cold, imperturbable bomb-buster, undersized but aristocratic in bearing, though I thought his new monocle was a little out of character. Dr. Schreiber began this session by saying:

"Colonel Vidor, we understand that you commanded a bomb-disposal unit during the last war, and continued its activities well into the post-war years—clearing dangerous objects in built-up areas?"

Paul nodded, and Schreiber added, "Do you recognise the man before you as Mark Seaton, who worked under you as a junior officer?"

"Yes."

"The work was dangerous?" asked Schreiber.

Paul shrugged. "Sometimes, but a lot of it was routine. Beach mines, for example, can usually be exploded *in situ*."

"But the men under you suffered many ailments, due to nervous strain?"

"The usual, with mine-busting—skin rashes, boils. But don't over-estimate this—young men get a lot of this, anyway."

"Mental breakdowns?"

"Sometimes. The job isn't a nice one, you know. Every so often somebody would find a bomb in the vicinity of important buildings —hospitals, and suchlike, and these just had to be disarmed: you couldn't put a few rings of cordtex around those and run away." He sighed, plainly bored.

Schreiber said, "Will you describe the general problems in mine and bomb-disarming for this tribunal, but do err on grounds of simplicity."

Paul answered, "It varied, according to the type of bomb, of course. Some you could just haul out with a pulley-block and gantry, and a car. Others, more virulent, had to be carefully handled. Usually, we'd dig a hole down beside the thing and get a chap alongside it. After he'd taken off the cover-plate and removed the detonators, we'd get a steam hose into it and steam out the bulk explosive."

"You make it sound simple."

"If it isn't, the chances are you won't know about it." Paul added, "At times, of course, we found certain devices built in, and it came a little more difficult."

"Booby-traps?"

"That's the layman's term for it—heat-transmitters that forbade the use of steam—temperature gauges that triggered them up, anti-handling devices, electrical circuits, centring bottles, acid cracks and clock-mechanism." He raised his eyes to the clock ticking on the wall above me and gave me a sudden wink. "Take your pick, eh, Seaton?"

Kish said, "Was Mr. Seaton an able officer?"

"He was as good as the next."

"Did he also suffer from nervous complaints?"

"Of course—he was pretty browned off at times."

Schreiber interjected, "The Commissioner didn't mean that. Did Seaton show any nervous reaction to the dangerous nature of the work involved?"

Paul replied, "He was often depressed, of course, but this happened to us all—and he was inclined to be emotional, but that was normal."

"Emotional?" asked Kish.

"Yes, emotional. Many bomb-disposal people—good men—work on the edge of tears. What do you want me to say—that he ran amok?"

"I do not want you to say anything but the truth, Colonel Vidor," said Kish. "But it is important to this tribunal that we know the effect of such work on Mr. Seaton's youth. I've heard it said, for instance, that men constantly employed on hazardous work are often more apt to seek the company of women. Is this a fact?"

"Good God, yes—they were boys for the girls!" Paul was plainly delighted.

"Seaton in particular?" asked Schreiber.

"What's that supposed to mean?"

Dr. Schreiber said, carefully, "Isn't it true that the charms of women have a soothing effect upon men on the verge of serious neurosis? I mean, are you aware that this officer, in particular, spent much of his spare time in the company of the opposite sex?"

"Oh, yes," said Paul. "He was better-looking than me in those days—usually he beat me to it."

"Please don't be light with this Commission," said Kish. "You are expected to give plain and accurate answers."

"So what the hell do you want me to say, then, that he was a sexual maniac?" Kish ignored the outburst: Schreiber said, "You quarrelled often?"

"Of course. We were at each other's throats half the bloody time —what do you expect?"

Schreiber said, "Think carefully, Colonel Vidor. Did Mr. Seaton, to your knowledge, suffer from bomb-rapture?"

"We all got a bit of that."

"Can you define the state?"

I interrupted, "I can, because I'm the expert here. Bomb-rapture usually begins with insomnia; this is followed by near-suicidal depression. Fear, which causes all this, is replaced with ecstasy—you can even hum a happy tune while listening to the ticking. And the ticking of the clock mechanism becomes the rhythm of a song—like this bastard you have put on the wall behind me."

Kish said, with a sigh, "Mr. Seaton, I really must remind you . . ."

I continued, "You don't sweat a lot with bomb-rapture, for you live in the delusion that bombs are your friends. Six feet down a hole, with your head in water, you can wrap one in your arms while it merrily talks to you—people have even been known to go to sleep." I paused and smiled at Schreiber, adding, "But permanent damage can be caused if the hallucination isn't soon arrested—that is out of the medical text-book." I pointed at the table. "In there—my personal file—are the findings of the medical boards who interviewed me on the three occasions I was taken to mental homes—the last time by force. Go on, read them, and put an end to this bloody nonsense so we can get on to Cheriton's corruption. In there you'll find three certificates stating my sanity, and I doubt if there's anybody in this room who can boast of one."

Kish adopted an expression of pained vacuity, and said, "Are you indeed in possession of these certificates, Dr. Schreiber?"

I smiled about me with cheerful ingratiation, and Schreiber, moving uneasily, replied, "Mr. Chairman, in point of fact . . ." He emptied his hands at Kish, who replied:

"Because, if you are, may I congratulate you on the handling of this case to date, and ask you to withdraw." He turned to me. "And, before we adjourn for lunch, Mr. Seaton—bearing in mind, of course, that you are the only sane person in the room—do you intend to continue these slanderous accusations?"

"Of course."

"Then be it on your head."

He gave Schreiber a look to kill, snatched up his papers, and swept out.

I went for a drink in the Strand. When I returned to the office, Carrie was absent, and a busty, highly-peroxided, miniature amazon was sitting at her desk.

I paused instantly. "Who are you?"

"Gloria Henderson, sir."

"Where's Miss Carrington?"

"Took ill, sir. Either that or her mother, sir—I wasn't here, but they said a man came to fetch her."

"When?"

"About an hour ago, sir, they said. I'm from the typing pool, till she gets back . . ."

I was disturbed, and said, "Didn't Miss Carrington leave a message for me?"

Her small, fat hands began to turn over the trays. "Might be something on your desk, sir."

I almost ran into my room: nothing there. Everything on my desk was meticulously in place; somebody, it appeared—and this wasn't Carrie, because she accepted my untidiness—had been having a clear up. I pressed the bell and the amazon came in.

"Have you touched this desk?" I asked.

She made an accentuated gesture of innocence. "Oh no, sir!"

"Have there been any calls while I've been away?"

She rushed back into her room and peered at a scrap of paper. "You've got to phone the Secretary, sir." Returning, she stood to bulging attention before me.

"Who?"

"The permanent one, sir," she said, in abject bewilderment, and I pitied her, asking, "Was it Mr. Anstruther, the Permanent Secretary?"

It brought her to life. Pointing at me, she shouted, "That's 'im!"

"Get him straightaway, please."

"Oh, Gawd."

"No—wait. I'll speak to Personnel first."

Misery was on her face. I said, "No need to be so scared, Miss Henderson—I've got a daughter at home only a little younger than you."

She visibly relaxed. "Oh, yes, I've been reading about her in the papers. She's Chinese, ain't she?"

I nodded, eyes closed, and said, "Better get me Personnel—look, get me the extension and I'll do it."

This we managed between us, and a voice said, "Personnel here, Mr. Grey."

I said into the phone, "Mr. Grey—we haven't met—this is Mark Seaton, Director of Contracts. Do you know what's happened to Miss Carrington, my secretary?"

"In what respect, sir?"

"I've a replacement here from the typing pool—it appears that Miss Carrington was taken ill before lunch."

"Hold on, sir." I could hear him flapping pages, then he said, "Sorry to keep you. No, we've had no sick report from her, or anything like that."

"Has she applied for compassionate leave? She has a very sick mother."

"Ah, now, that'll be another department, sir, and I'm afraid Mr. Fraser hasn't returned from lunch."

"God Almighty."

I slammed down the receiver, glancing at my watch. It was half-past two: doubtless Anstruther would be back from lunch, even if most of the Personnel juniors weren't. His secretary said, "I'll put you through, sir," and James ejaculated:

"Mark! You're still in one piece?"

I swung my chair to the window. "Fractured, but whole—what about you?"

"Ah, now! It isn't usual to arrest Permanent Secretaries for indiscretions against Kish, but I wouldn't take long odds on you."

"It's not me I'm worried about—I reckon they've collected Carrie."

"Detained for interrogation? Haven't they informed you?"

"Well, no, nothing so official, but a replacement's in post, and it's not like Carrie to go off without a word."

"I see."

He was plainly uninterested; there was a pause, then he asked:

"How did Vidor's testimony go?"

"It degenerated into an attempt to prove insanity." I told him about the certificates, and he said, "Listen, Mark, there's more opposition than you think. Adam Steen served with Cheriton some twenty years ago—they were in Supplies Board together; he says the man's always been open to suggestions. In fact, there was one minor scandal of stores selling in the 'fifties when Cheriton got away by the skin of his teeth."

I said, "I hope you realise this thing's monitored."

"All the better, let's dissipate the heat. And Benedict's got an appointment this evening with the Foreign Secretary."

"But he's a Brander man."

"Of course. That's exactly what we want—to get it to Brander. But wait for the best bit of all—Fiddler has confessed."

"What!" I stared at the receiver.

"The civil police had him; he was being taken under escort to the *Vaporiser,* and managed to get away."

"Who did he talk to?"

"Johanson, in Intelligence."

"You mean he spilled the beans?"

"Completely."

"I wouldn't be in his shoes, or Johanson's come to that. Does Jo realise the dangers?"

"If he doesn't, who does? He immediately got on to Benedict."

"What happens now?"

"We wait."

I said, "That's the most dangerous part of all. What are the chances of a properly constituted trial for slander?"

"None at all. The more guilty they are the less chance of them taking action. It's got to be a Crown prosecution—unless in the meantime we can force Cheriton's resignation; this is what Pud Benedict's going after."

"Thank God for you, James."

"And I still think you're wrong. God knows how I manage to mix myself up with you purity drive surveyors."

I heard the monitor cut a moment before I replaced the receiver.

For a long time I sat at my desk staring at the telephone. James was only a couple of floors down; he could just as easily have sent for me and talked privately. Undoubtedly he was speaking for the benefit of the monitor, and I wondered how much truth there was in any of it. Perhaps he was taking a calculated risk, but whoever's risk it was, I had most to lose.

I rang for Carrie, completely forgetting, and Miss Henderson came in.

I said, "I'm going away for the weekend and hope to be in about ten on Monday morning."

"Won't you call me Gloria, sir?"

"If you insist."

"Can I get you at 'ome if required, sir?"

She was adenoidal and had obviously been undernourished in childhood. And I cursed the system that continued to relegate these youngsters to near-poverty—this time the typing pool—while the Architectural Division, for example, was rampant with straight-line administrators who worked in cubism while roofs blew off and top executives of industry drew salaries under false pretences and worked the Expenses racket. Now I caught a fleeting vision of a basement flat in Holland Park, and Gloria sharing it with three other girls; a frying-pan on a stained gas stove and limp nylons hanging above it. I said, gently, "No, Gloria, I shall not be at home."

"But you'll leave an address, sir?"

I shook my head. "No, no address."

She smiled slowly, exposing large frontal teeth. "Goin' to see a lady, sir?"

"Yes."

Now she entered my life with the instinctive perception of another paramour, and slowly closed one eye at me. "I get it, sir."

"I expect you do."

The telephone rang and I lifted the receiver. "Seaton."

A voice said, "Mark—Johanson of Intelligence here—Anstruther's just been on to me. I understand you've applied for Miss Carrington, your secretary, to be a witness for you at the next session of the Kish Commission?"

"That's right."

"They've beaten you to it, man. They collected her an hour ago."

"What for?" I was bolt upright.

"Isn't it obvious? I think you'll find, when she does appear, that her testimony might not be as reliable as you expected."

"Is . . . is she in any danger?"

"Not immediately; but she could be if she doesn't prove resilient."

"For God's sake—can't we do something about it?"

"You make the suggestions."

"But this is your department!"

"I've bigger fish to fry, Seaton—I wouldn't be ringing you now, but Anstruther thought you ought to know."

"But what about Carrie?"

"The grade's too low—goodbye."

For a long time I sat at my desk, thinking furiously, my head in my hands. The telephone rang again and again, and I made a few decisions automatically, for I could not drive Carrie from my mind; the possibility that they might harm her brought me to an inner coldness. Then, just before five o'clock, the phone rang again, and Carrie said:

"Mr. Seaton . . . ?"

"Carrie!"

"I . . . I just want to tell you that my mother's ill . . . I had to come home straightaway, and I'll be back as soon . . ."

"Where are you? Carrie, listen, it's important. I've got to know who took you from the office."

She hesitated, and I knew somebody was with her. She was breathing heavily, as if under stress. She said, "Please, Mr. Seaton —I'm all right, really I am. I'll . . . I'll be back in a couple of days."

"Are you at home?"

"Not now . . ."

"Aren't you at home with your mother . . . ?"

"Oh, God," she said, and the line went dead.

I had to get out of this, so I telephoned Hallie; she had the bright idea that we might visit North Wales for the weekend, but I was scarcely in the mood for travelling. But, as I considered earlier, a weekend with Hallie anywhere was a safer political bet than being alone at Hatherley with Su-len at a time like this.

As I went to the door Gloria appeared and made a faint clucking noise out of the corner of her mouth; it was reasonable, for I had bred the familiarity, so I gave her a smile, knowing that soon it would end.

The earthy humanity of the typing pool, in terms of charm, had no advantages at all over the martinet formality of the secretarial college, and Carrie.

Sam, my taxi, was waiting near the Cenotaph.

"Bond Street," I said.

His round face appeared on the glass partition. "But it ain't Thursday, Mr. Seaton!"

"Bond Street!" I shouted, "and not so much talk about it!"

"Christ!" said Sam.

The whisky at Hallie's, I reflected, might dilute this agonising worry over Carrie.

CHAPTER 11

It was significant that in between my sessions with the Kish Commission I was now accompanied, on and off, by a certain Mr. Flowers, who had the ability to become a part of my official life and yet never actually enter it. I would see Mr. Flowers on street corners and sitting in restaurants, watching me with Hallie; I would leave her flat in the morning and he would be strolling down Bond Street. I had even seen him in the corridors of the Ministry, and he invariably greeted me with affable concern for my health.

"Morning, Mr. Seaton. How are you?"

I tried ignoring him, but this didn't work; Mr. Flowers was always there.

His name belied him, for he was well over six feet, more than sixteen stone, as he once informed me, and his near-bald, bullet-shaped head was decorated by a pair of professional cauliflowered ears; caused, so he said, by collecting the head-smashes while coming in with the right cross.

Now he said in his light, fighter's voice, "You all right then, Mr. Seaton?"

"Yes, thank you, Mr. Flowers."

We sat together on the bare seat in the mausoleum of the Treasury Hall, awaiting yet another command from the Kish Commission, and Mr. Flowers leaned confidentially towards me, whispering hoarsely, "Not often I 'ave to see to a gentleman, y'know. 'Flowers,' I always say, 'you can always tell a real gentleman'."

"Thank you."

"Now, if you was to try to get away—mitch it, like—then I'd 'ave to stop you. But I only ever use the force necessary, this is why I'm here—very delicate. If a fella comes awkward, then he has to 'ave it, as the saying goes, and there's no two ways. But if a chap comes quiet, like you, then there is nobody tender'n me, Alf Flowers." He nudged me. "I was hitting up the heavyweight title once, y'know."

"Really."

I sensed in him the companionship of one who, like me, had ended his career. He said, confidingly, "I like people, y'know, sir. You'd never believe it, but I'm very partial to people. I've spent all me life knockin' 'em about—even these days I have to bring 'em in line, so to speak—but I'm very, very fond of people."

A voice shouted, "Call Mr. Seaton!" But Mr. Flowers, steeped in humanity, regarded me, unhearing, with the warm eyes of friendship. "Mind," said he, "it ain't up to me to say so, sir, but you 'ave to watch this bloody lot." He jerked his thumb at the Commission door. "Inside that room they're real gentlemen, but once they get you outside they can be real sods—beggin' your pardon for the language. Take it from me, it's best to agree with 'em, then it won't come inconvenient for either of us. I mean, who wants to beat up a nice gentleman?"

"I take the point, Mr. Flowers."

"Because, if there's anything I can't abide, it's violence. You know, I'd be real upset if I 'ad to work you over, you being a dignitary of the Church, an' all that."

"I'm in the Civil Service, actually, Mr. Flowers."

He looked morose. "I ain't never done a dignitary of the Civil Service."

"Let's hope you never have reason."

"Call Mr. Seaton!" bellowed the hall porter, his head around the door, and Mr. Flowers, raked from his reverie, gripped me and hauled me to my feet, crying, "Now get in there—come on, get in there, or you're goin' to bloody 'ave it."

He opened the door and the semi-circular table faced me again.

Kish said, "The tribunal will remember that Sir Stanley Waters took the unusual step of making a tape-recording of a conversation between Mr. Harmsworth and another person at the time of the

Severnside Project tender board. He turned to me. "You realise, of course, that this isn't admissible evidence in a court of law, Mr. Seaton?"

"I do."

"You have this tape-recording with you this morning, as agreed?"

"Yes, it is here."

"Please give it to the clerk, so it can be played back. The short-hand typist will make a record of the tape, that it may stand as a visual statement, countersigned by all present."

"Yes, sir," said she, and waited, pencil poised; the tape hissed through the recorder. We waited.

We waited, looking at each other. The clock ticked on heavily. Kish sighed, and said to the clerk, "Have you got that thing properly adjusted, man?"

"Yes, sir."

"And you're playing the correct side?"

"Oh, yes, sir."

Minutes passed; sweat was gathering on my face. The tape ran out. Kish said, "You obviously didn't have the correct side, did you? Turn the damned thing round and try again."

The clerk turned it over, and switched on. Even as the tape hissed through I realised what was happening. Under stress one can make unendurable mistakes—it was quite simple—they had rubbed it off. I bowed my head: Stan Waters had died for nothing. The recorder clicked. Kish moved impatiently, saying, "You know, Seaton, this Commission's being very patient with you—did you bring the right tape?"

"Yes."

"But this one's a blank."

"It was all right when I brought it in here."

He glared at me. "That's impertinent!" He added, tersely, "We'd better have your last witness in and put an end to this extraordinary business. Call Miss Carrington."

Carrie entered with the expression of a woman lost. It could have been her tears, or even a minor stroke from fright, but even from a distance her face appeared to be bruised. With a blackshirt standing behind her, she sat down, lowered her eyes and clenched her hands in her lap. The Prosecutor rose, and said:

"Miss Carrington, the tribunal realises that you are ill, so may I suggest that the clerk reads the statement you have made and signed?"

She nodded, and the clerk read from a paper, "On the morning of May the fourth Sir Stanley Waters called me to his office to witness the opening of the tender box by himself and Mr. Harmsworth. During the listing of the offers, Mr. Fiddler of the Finance Branch brought in a late tender delivery by hand. This offer was also listed; the correct procedure was followed in every instance. I did not see the tender figures."

Kish said, "One question, Miss Carrington. You were not officially a member of the tender board—why did Sir Stanley call you in?"

Carrie lifted her face to mine, saying flatly, "He . . . he wasn't well, sir. He said he wanted an independent witness from the Contracts Section."

"I see. And did Mr. Harmsworth, to your knowledge, make a telephone call from Sir Stanley's office?"

She put her hand to her face, staring at me. "No, sir."

"Did you, at any time, see a tape-recording which Sir Stanley is alleged to have made of a telephone conversation between Mr. Harmsworth and Mr. Fiddler in respect of this contract?"

She lowered her head. "No, sir."

"Right, Miss Carrington, you may go."

I watched her; she was moving awkwardly, like a woman in splints; it was obvious that she had been badly beaten. At the door, she turned again and looked at me. I said:

"It's all right, Carrie—it's all right . . ."

Certainly, her mother, at the age of seventy-five, and ill, was a possible candidate for Brander's Euthanasia Bill.

I remembered that they had arrested Bishop Forsward, the darling of the people, for suggesting on a television programme that free elections should be reintroduced. If they could do this to a man like Bishop Forsward, God knows what they would do to Carrie.

The door closed behind her, and Kish immediately began:

"Mr. Seaton, while before this Commission you have protested at unfair treatment. You've repeated slanderous accusations against your own Minister, indulged in rhetoric, made false statements, yet I have put up with this because I realise that you are ill. Sir Stanley Waters, your main witness, has committed suicide—unable to continue the farce. Mr. Fiddler, a prime mover in the case according to you, ran away—the deduction is obvious. Mr. Anstruther, although managing to be disrespectful to me, didn't bring a single fact to your aid. Miss Carrington, you've just heard, refutes your allegation of incorrect tendering procedure." He lifted the tape. "And now this—just another element in the fantasy of hatred for your Minister which you have built in your mind; something clearly based on your political disagreement."

I tried to speak, but he waved me into silence, saying, "As I've said before, Seaton, you are ill—the medical evidence before me substantiates this. Indeed, I would say that you've been ill for a very long time, and been unaware of it. But since these proceedings should show absolute impartiality, Dr. Schreiber recommends that, although plainly unfit to do so, you should be given a final opportunity to make a statement. I do hope that it will take the form of a withdrawal of your unfounded charges against two innocent people. If you do this, I will recommend your early retirement on the grounds of ill-health with full pension rights; if you don't, I can't be responsible for the decision of this tribunal."

I got to my feet, and he glanced at me peremptorily, saying, "I beg you to be brief."

I said, "While before this court I've been the accused rather than the accuser: at no time has Cheriton been called to answer my charges, yet I have served the public in important posts for over twenty years." They began to talk among themselves, shuffling papers. I shouted, "May I continue, please?"

Kish, reading his notes, nodded, saying, "Of course. Freedom of speech is your right under the law."

I said, "Since Brander seized power, venality is an accepted fact; it now exists in every rank in the Civil Service, including Ministers. His junta has zoned people and housing—racism is flourishing. People like you, Kish, have built a data bank of information comparable with that of National Socialism. The military dictatorship has disbanded the Unions and murdered or imprisoned its leaders—even the Service, which you say you serve, is one where defecting shop stewards compete for the favour of the higher grades . . ." I faltered: it was wrong, ineffectual, and they began to talk again, laughing softly between themselves, as at a private joke. I said, "Cheriton and Harmsworth are guilty of an attempt to defraud, and you know it; the Press, which has been misreporting this case, knows it. The people know it, and what is most important of all, you do, too. Aren't you aware that Fiddler has confessed to Johanson? Get Johanson here!"

Kish said, turning to me with a smile, "Come, will this diatribe go on much longer . . . ?"

I shouted, "You're flourishing now, but the day this country decides that you and Brander are rotten, they'll take to the streets . . ."

Kish glanced up; the smile had left his face. "You've spoken sedition, Seaton, d'you realise it?"

I sat down, longing for words of meaning and importance; aware that I had made an undignified mess of it.

There was no profound silence. Kish rustled his papers with a majestic flourish, handed a note to the clerk, and said, "Please give that to the gentleman waiting outside the door." Turning to me, he cleared his throat noisily, and added, "Mark Andrew Seaton, it becomes increasingly clear that your mental state demands care and attention. It is in your own interests that I place you in protective custody—you must be aware of the hostile public reaction to this case. But, should you at any time be prepared to withdraw your allegations, we will interview you again." He beamed at me, polishing his spectacles. "The rest will do you good; you are suspended from your duties until notified to the contrary."

Mr. Flowers was awaiting me in the Treasury Hall, and he said, taking my arm, "Be good enough to step this way, sir. We don't want no trouble with a nice gentleman now, do we?"

I expected to be left alone with my future and my braces.

I couldn't have been more mistaken.

CHAPTER 12

A car was awaiting us outside the Treasury Hall and Flowers pushed me into it. Behind its heavily-curtained windows I could not see where the driver was taking us but judged, by sound and direction, that we stopped in the vicinity of Charing Cross, the *Vaporiser* Interrogation Centre. Rather like the German of the 'thirties who knew that people 'went up the chimney' in the concentration camps, and did nothing about it, so the transient population of Charing Cross discreetly referred to these old air-raid vaults as New Army Headquarters, mindless of the faint underground thuds, the distant shrieks. Foolishly, even as I entered the little office with its three lounging blackshirt guards, it never occurred to me that I was in any particular danger.

Flowers said, reading from a paper, "Seaton, Mark Andrew. Investigation; hostile witness."

Normally I would have taken issue with this, but one guard, beginning to write, asked, "Post?"

"Recently Director of Contracts. The Cheriton business." I was a little surprised at the normality of his speech. The guard commander said, smiling: "Can't break him, eh?" Frowning now, he went on writing.

These were the blackshirt thugs of the New Army élite: scum that comes to the top of the brew, their predecessors spawned in the apprenticeships of the Crumlin Road and Long Kesh. Distantly I heard Flowers say, "The Kish Commission couldn't."

The guard commander, still writing, said, "Take off your clothes."

"I beg your pardon?" It was weak to the point of embarrassment, even in retrospect. He glared up.

"I said, take off your clothes."

"You'll have to do it," I replied, and ducked, came up and swung my fist at Flowers's jaw. I do not remember the blow landing or Flowers even touching me, but when I opened my eyes I was naked on the floor and my clothes were strewn around me. One of the blackshirts emptied the remnants of a jug of water over my face.

"Get up."

The room slanted about me, the electric light danced in my eyes. Flowers said, helping me to my feet, "Now, you know what I told yer, sir—remember? We don't want no trouble. They always 'as to take off their clothes, y'see?"

In self-revulsion and anger, shivering, I stood naked before the table. It was suddenly imperative that I should not faint. Unaccountably, a name was thrusting into my brain, that of Ina Crovenca, the wife of a young Yugoslavian partisan in the war. The Germans captured her, and after two days of torture she betrayed her husband's whereabouts; it cost his life and those of eight comrades. They found her hanging from the cistern of the lavatory by her brassière. I knew her with a sudden, vital affinity; I could hear my own breathing now, the faint scratching of the commander's pen and distant sobbing. He said, glancing up:

"You know we've got Fiddler, the finance clerk, back again?" I didn't reply.

"And Johanson of Intelligence? He made contact with Benedict you know." His eyes, unflickering, moved over me. "Even Anstruther wants to watch what he's up to."

I replied weakly, "I doubt if you've got Johanson; he's too important."

His eyes were amazingly blue in his tanned face, and I returned his stare.

Much of the horror of my situation was caused by this man's obvious intelligence and education; had he been an ordinary thug, like the two behind him, I could better have accepted him. He was, of course, the new product of the army cadres; an extremist of the new officer class, trained in the niceties of interrogation and cruelty, yet probably at home he had a wife and children. I remember once arguing with somebody—Benedict, I think—that Britain could never spawn such people; that this was a Germanic production awaiting the mad spark of Hitlerism: Benedict, for his part, claimed that they existed everywhere, irrespective of dictatorship or democracy; that it only needed a leap into extremism of any kind to bring them blinking into the light. This one suddenly said:

"Where were you born, Seaton?"

"You know it perfectly well."

"Yes, but I want to hear it from you."

"Beirut."

He nodded. "And your name before your father changed it by deed poll?"

"Mark Goldstein."

I had been waiting for this to come out publicly, of course; until recently, Brander had been careful to avoid a pogrom, but his publicity machine had more recently been building up a case against British Jewry. The commander said:

"Your mother died before your marriage. At her death your father left Britain and was a practising lawyer in Stuttgart. Where did he die?"

"In Belsen, but you know that, too."

He leaned back in the chair and tapped the pen against his teeth, his big face creased up: "Because he was a Jew?"

"He was in Belsen because he was a Jew," I said.

"And you're a Jew also, eh, Seaton?" He winked up at Flowers. "We can see he's a Jew now, can't we, Flowers?"

"Now he's got 'is trousers off," said Flowers jovially, "but it don't always follow, mind. I seen uncircumcised Jews down Mile End Road, 'aven't you?"

I closed my eyes. The commander said, "You're a dirty Jew, aren't you, Seaton?"

Flowers whispered, "You was asked a question, Mr. Seaton. You'd best reply, or you'll 'ave a terrible hidin'."

I nodded. "Yes."

"Oh, no, that isn't good enough. Repeat exactly what I said, please."

I whispered, "I'm a dirty Jew."

He nodded. "Well, that's better than the Kish Commission could do, isn't it?" He rose heavily. "And now, since you don't believe we've got Johanson, you'd better come and see him, hadn't you?" He prodded me playfully in the stomach with his fist.

It must have looked an incongruous procession—the big blackshirt leading the way, his steel-tipped jack-boots echoing on the concrete floor: I followed naked, with Flowers. Behind us came the two blackshirt guards. Pale faces watched us from tiny, barred windows in doors. A few hands tried to touch me as I passed; others called softly. In a few moments we came to a cul-de-sac in the passage: keys rattled and a cell door swung open. The guard commander said, "Well, there you are, Seaton—Johanson; remember him?"

Johanson was lying upon his back, also naked. He had been beaten. None stopped me as I knelt, raising his head. His eyes, moving slowly in his humped cheekbones, were vacant of expression; his nose was obviously broken and his chest was starched with blood. I said, staring up at them:

"You bastards."

For answer, Flowers reached down and hauled me to my feet. The commander said, "Now sign this." He pushed a piece of paper against me and held out a pen. I shoved it away. Flowers said, his hands out felicitously:

"Now don't be like that, Mr. Seaton. It's only to say you've seen Mr. Johanson."

"Sign it," said the blackshirt.

I took it from his hand, reading swiftly, and said, "It's nothing of the sort. It waives my charges against Cheriton and Harmsworth."

"Just sign it," said he, and nodded towards Johanson, "or we'll take you next door and do the same to you."

The paper trembled in my hands; all were watching me, intent.

"No," said Johanson, and his voice was clear; I turned to him. His eyes were suddenly bright in his swollen face. "*No!*"

I gave the paper back to the blackshirt. "No," I said.

"Right," said Flowers.

The two blackshirts began to pull on to their hands heavily padded gloves, and the commander said, "Now, I'm telling you again —this one's a public appearance. He's got to be able to stand, and keep away from his face."

In the cell next door Flowers said, twisting my arms behind me, "Well, no one can say you wasn't warned, Mr. Seaton. Right, me lucky lads, give him hell, for the quicker he changes his mind the better."

The beatings went on intermittently for two days.

Naked in the cell, without bed or blankets, I shivered in a corner of the concrete walls, in darkness. And three times next day the two blackshirts arrived; one held me, the other thumped his padded fists into my body until I screamed for it to stop, but it did not stop. They brought me neither food nor water. And these visits, coming every four hours, became sewn into my subconscious. I lay moaning on the floor, awaiting their footsteps in shivering terror, listening to the shouts and groans echoing down the passages as others were brought in and given the same treatment. Even Johanson, to my horror, was beaten again, presumably in revenge for trying to help me. On the evening of the third day Flowers came, and said:

"Dear me, Mr. Seaton, you're obstinate, you know. This could go on for weeks—all these gentlemen want is for you to sign that paper, it ain't much to ask. I'll 'ave to give you a goin' over meself before long if you come as stupid as this." He took off his coat. I cried:

"No, please, please . . . !" I crawled across the floor to his feet.

My body, from my chest to my thighs, was enormously swollen and heaped with contusions; my testicles so enlarged that I could not close my legs. Flowers said, "Just look at the state you're in, Mr. Seaton. Shall I call in the gentlemen again? Do you think one last do will help you change your mind?"

The saliva was pouring from my mouth; I caressed his feet, moaning unintelligibly, the last stages of degradation. Flowers sighed, as if dealing with a wayward child. "Then would you like to see Mr. Kish again? Would you like to speak to him?"

"Yes, yes, please!"

He wagged a finger down at me. "And no funny business—you'll do just as the gentleman says?"

"Oh yes!"

"And don't act awkward no more with Mr. Cheriton?"

"No, no!"

He brought his hands together. "Well now, it just shows yer, don't it—great minds think alike. That's why I've come, 'cause Mr. Kish wants to see you tomorrow . . . Shall we get you dressed?"

I was only semi-conscious, I remember, lolling in his arms, and one of the blackshirts had to come in to help him; they fed me, gave me brandy; brought in a bed and let me rest. In the morning they brought me a meal; it was the first real food I had eaten for three days. Flowers, hovering around, acted as waiter and was kindness itself. That afternoon the blackshirt guard commander came and gave me an injection for the pain. At four o'clock they helped me down the passage to a waiting car. A man was being horribly flogged, I remember; I could hear the sickening lash of the whip and his cries were terrifying; in my semi-conscious state I prayed that it wasn't Johanson, but later Flowers told me that his name was Maton, a man of French extraction, and that he had died, but he did not say why he was being flogged.

"Mind," said Flowers at the time, "we've got other ways and means. They're real wicked in here, Mr. Seaton, especially if you don't come clean when you meet Mr. Kish."

At five o'clock exactly by the clock on the wall, Flowers and one of the blackshirts helped me down the Treasury Hall and into the room where the tribunal was sitting. Kish said, kindly:

"Mr. Seaton, are you perfectly sure you feel all right for this interview? My Commission wishes to sympathise with you, you must be in very great pain. And we do appreciate your respect for our wishes."

It was as if no man had stirred from his seat; they were in exactly the same positions as when I had last appeared before them. Kish said, "You understand what I am saying, Mr. Seaton?"

"Yes."

"Well, statements made in the heat of a supposed discovery are often rashly conceived. This Commission admires your integrity —alas, I am only sorry there are not more men like you. But, now that you have had an opportunity to consider the case, wouldn't you like to abandon your allegations against your Minister and his P.A.? The case, you know, has caused embarrassment to all parties, and no little pain . . . but, you see, until the case is resolved and a withdrawal made, it stays open on the public account."

There was a silence, and he added, "You will be reinstated in office—your Minister actually wants you back in post. It can be done with grace, I assure you, Mr. Seaton."

I thought: all I have to do is bow my head. If I do this—just lower my face—they will let me go home to Hatherley. Even if I glance away in disassociation, as if I did not understand him, Kish will take this as assent. He is no fool: he will end the farce in seconds.

"Well, Mr. Seaton?"

I heard myself say, "I stand by my accusations against Mr. Cheriton and Mr. Harmsworth, and . . ."

Kish commanded, "Court usher, remove him, please. I'll not listen again to these slanderous accusations." He gathered his papers. "In due course you will tire of this, Seaton. For our part, we have plenty of time."

So they took me back to Army Interrogation and the blackshirts beat me again.

I do not know how long these beatings lasted. I only remember lying naked in the corner, watching the light under the door and waiting for the blackshirts. Pain, if you have enough of it, becomes a sort of guest; in retrospect I realised that I was losing my reason, of course, and I used to speculate on whether the footsteps I heard, day and night, were coming for me. And then, when I least expected it, I was removed to a small medical wing in the Centre and there put to bed. The nurses were male and better at nursing than women, and, as usual, more compassionate. It was an unreal

117

situation. And after four days Dr. Schreiber came into the little ward and stood at the end of my bed. "How are you feeling, Mr. Seaton?"

I did not reply.

"Would you like to go home?" he asked.

I nodded.

"In return for your release, then, are you prepared to make . . . ?"

"No."

Later he must have realised that it was a psychological mistake. Had he, instead, threatened just one more beating I would have wept, entreating him.

So they gave me up and drove me to Hatherley in official state.

CHAPTER 13

It was high summer over Hatherley and the woods were loaded with greenness, the wind perfumed with wild flowers. Down the yellow gravel drive the poplars stood in sentinel beauty, ringed with sunlight; doves murmured from the river where the big trout lazed in waving refractions of bindweed and light-flood; cattle drooped hang-head behind the five-barred gates of the Woking Lanes, their brown eyes heavily lidded, sated with bee-hum and heat. I came in slowly from the garden, distantly hearing the outside telephone bell, and Ezra cried from the porch in his stricken falsetto:

"Telephone for you, Mr. Mark!"

"Coming."

I took it in the hall. "Why, Hallie!"

"Darling, how are you?" Sincerity was in her voice.

"Another few days and I'll be back in harness," I said.

"Is Moira there? I mean, is it all right to talk?"

"Of course. In this house external lovers are a legitimate procedure."

"Oh, I've been so worried about you. As far as the office was concerned you'd just disappeared. Nobody seemed to know anything at all—either that, or they just wouldn't tell me. But Carrie said . . ."

I interjected, "Carrie's back?"

"Two days ago, she said—I started getting sense with her. You haven't been on to the office?"

"No, it's part of the therapy, apparently—no personal contacts."

"Does that include me?"

"Undoubtedly. You constitute sudden death, I would think. When can we meet?"

She said, "Oh, Mark, I've so missed you! Are you really all right?"

"At this precise moment, but I can't guarantee the future."

"Ring me the moment you come to London?"

"Of course."

Moira was arranging flowers as I came into the lounge, put down my sticks and eased myself into a chair. She said, "Who was that?"

"The baker. I told him to bring three." I picked up a newspaper.

There was a silence, then she said: "God, we've slipped, Mark. Can you tell me what happened?"

I did not reply. With Shearer an ever-present threat I didn't trust myself to engage with her in even superficial conversation; ironically, it didn't occur to me that my affair with Hallie was equally salacious. Perhaps this was because Moira could have had me back with a single gesture of affection: the root barrier between us was her affair with Shearer.

"How ye feelin' this morning?" She was very Irish.

"Better every day."

"I hope you keep it up—Joe's coming, you know." I ignored this, thumbing through the newspaper, and she said, "First the Mombara business, then suspension, now Joe. Next we'll be having Karl Marx parties." She examined the flowers, head on one side, a beautiful expression upon her face, and her fingers were exquisitely delicate on the long, green stems. I said:

"Don't blame me, I'm politically uncluttered, which is more than you are." I added, "Joe's the antithesis of everything you stand for."

"Are people usually hauled off and beaten black and blue for an accusation against a colleague?"

"They are today. It's a significant part of the system people like you have created."

"By God," she said, "trust me to get the blame for it." She smiled over her shoulder. "By the way, how's our darling Hallie?"

"As potent as your bloody Henry. He'll be here soon, shouldn't you go and change?"

The name of Shearer invariably silenced her, though, as far as

Moira was concerned, her lovers never entailed the scandal of divorce: nor did their demands seem to affect her beauty, I thought. She looked good in tweed, and knew it; and if she was a little fatter these days, this suited her well. Her hair, perfectly groomed, flattered the flawless perfection of her skin; even Kate Shearer couldn't compete with Moira for complexion. Suddenly she turned from the flowers and looked at me, and I lowered the paper. Then, with a gesture of emptiness, she turned, saying, "Oh, God, it's no use," and left the room.

I knew a vague but sudden emptiness; behind her was left only the perfume of the flowers. Sighing, I returned sightlessly to the paper.

Probably, I reflected, she was more bored by our bizarre existence than I, though she never lost the façade of the dutiful wife. Even before Shearer's betraying smile she managed to kiss me goodbye before he took her up to town. In a grotesque way I actually admired their discretion: the adultery was not taking place in front of the children, so to speak. And Shearer, schooled in the cult of the erotic, drank my whisky and discussed my suspension without a flicker of compassion, coming as he did from a line of roués who could have munched caviare before the starving of Bangladesh.

Su-len, I noticed, was wandering in the garden. She was dressed in a black and gold cheongsam split to the thigh, and it lent her a sensuality beyond her years. She had a white flower in her hair, I noticed, startlingly beautiful against its sheen of blackness. I stared relentlessly at the newspaper and a little while later Moira returned, looking mature and beautiful in a bright green dress. She said, tersely:

"That child's missed you, ye know. She walks around lost while you're away." She snapped open a tiny handbag and began rummaging within it. "She has to put up with the hostile Irish and I wouldn't wish that on an Irishman. Where's that bloody lipstick?"

"In your hand."

"Can't ye spare the child an hour? Take her out for a Chinese meal, or something?"

"Perhaps. Where are you going today?"

She shrugged. "Bridge this afternoon—with the Robinsons, then Covent Garden tonight—*Aida*."

It is a biological fact, I had heard, that women taken in adultery look their best. Moira's lips were red and petulant, her eyes sparkled, and her skin was like Cleopatra's must have been, though, as far as I knew, Moira didn't court immortality by crushing pearls into her wine. I looked at her, and the words beat in my head, 'And it came to pass in those days . . . there was a certain Levite sojourning on the side of Mount Ephraim, who took to himself a concubine out of Bethlehem-judah . . .'

Ezra suddenly appeared, saying, "Mr. Shearer's arrived, ma'am."

"Show him in."

Shearer came in with a rush, saying, "Good morning Mark, how're you feeling?"

"Marvellous." I rose, and we stood uncertainly, the three of us. I added, "Try hard not to boggle at the atmosphere, Henry. Joe's due home. When this happens the house adopts an unstable equilibrium—even Mamie Ez don't like it, do she, Mo?" I gave him a grin. "Drink?"

"Gin and Italian."

He got whisky and American; you have the edge on a man about to have intercourse with your wife. He said, uneasily, "What's wrong with Joe, anyway? He seems all right to me."

"In his rough, anarchistic way," replied Moira. "He spouts an offensive socialist gibberish. If we've got a counter-revolution in the offing, I'd rather it wasn't led by my Marxist shop steward."

"You produced him, remember," I said.

"Out of Moira by Mark," said Shearer. "He sounds like a racehorse."

"Which makes me out a mare," said Moira. "Ready, Henry?"

He actually bowed slightly to me on his way to the door; a blemish sprung to life. I called, "I take it you won't be back till morning?"

"No," he answered, "I thought we'd go on to one of Marsella's parties, and you know how long they last."

"Actually, I realised the Garden didn't run a continuous performance."

"Not the Garden," he said, and gazed at Moira like a schoolboy gazes at buttered crumpet. I thought:

'And his concubine played the whore against him, and went away from him . . .'

I followed them out to the drive and watched his big Daimler crunching away to the lodge in brilliant sunlight; it was the Hatherley of sensuous dreams. A voice said:

"So, they have gone without you."

I replied in Chinese, "How could I go? Joe is coming."

"They are away for the night, yet your son is coming?" asked Su-len.

"After the opera they're going to Marsella's party."

"And that will last all night? Tell me another."

I turned away, leaning on the sticks. "One day your nose will drop off with pry disease."

There was about her a faint perfume; diminutive, indeed, a woman in miniature, she was no longer Su-len, the child. With the likes of her the bald elders of Taipo village walk at dusk with their caged parakeets and other noisy little concubines.

"You like my new cheongsam?" She pirouetted. "Moira ordered it from Hong Kong, but I am not supposed to wear it, nor my wedding dress, until I come of age."

"Then why wear it now?"

"To please you." In Cantonese, she added, "In August I will be sixteen—it is not long."

I said, "In August you will be fifteen according to English law."

She opened wide, rebellious eyes. "How can this be? Chu Yang, the waiter is the same age as I. Is he only fifteen because he lives in Woking? *Shâp-lûk!*"

"Chu Yang?"

"The waiter at the Chinese restaurant."

"Chu Yang is a fool," I said. "This is England, not China; while here you live by the English calendar." I limped away and she followed, hands protesting.

"Yoi Yoi! You talk like the arse of a mule! In the Book of Rites . . ."

"In the Book of Rites it teaches children to keep clean mouths!"

"*Aiya!*" She groaned. "So now, if I read the Book of Rites in Peru, it speaks differently to China?"

"Read thoroughly the chapter on respect for parents."

Her eyes sparkled with pleasure. "I will also read that I am as old as the number of years I have lived through, not those I have been in existence." She danced along beside me into the lounge where I sat again, seeking oblivion in the newspaper. I said, unfolding it, "You claim consent for your body but do not know how to conduct your mouth." In English, I added, "Perhaps you should go away to an English school now, and learn some English manners."

"They are barbarians." She sniffed.

I added, "You have suggested a disgusting thing of your mother."

"She is not my mother and neither are you my father." She pouted, treading softly around me, sending side-long glances. "Nor are you Moira's husband, because you are in love with me."

Mamie came to the lounge door, calling, "Mr. Mark, sir, is that Joe fella comin' to dinner tonight, or not?"

Su-len said, "I am your woman, and you do not give me a glance."

Mamie shouted, "Mr. Mark, sir . . . !"

"In China it would not be like this," said Su-len.

"It was a great mistake, Su, and we are not in China now." I called to Mamie, "Serve it up, Mamie, he'll be here any minute."

"Anyway," said Su-len happily, "it is quite possible for you to have more than one wife."

I closed my eyes. "You are a pagan."

She went round the back of me and began to stroke my hair. "Perhaps, but it is good for you to have me here. If you continue with only one wife it will turn your brain. Do you remember Lu Pan who flew upon a wooden kite? It is said that he dreamed such flying because he only had one wife and had gone demented. You are asking for a serious illness."

"Multiple marriage, perhaps, but even the mandarins didn't subscribe to multiple fornication. Now leave me, for Joe is coming, I can hear him."

"Do not expect me to entertain him because Moira is away," said she, "for he is a man of little grace."

A word about Joe, for she wasn't far wrong.

Although I don't like Dickensian descriptions, you couldn't put your hand up the chimney of life and brush in Joe's characteristics, he was much too complicated for such treatment. Of the leonine type, he surely possessed affinity with an ancient Viking, unless, as Moira suggested once, they'd put the wrong tag on him in the hospital, for he wasn't at all our type. His flamboyant radicalism jarred on Moira's conservatism, his militancy jarred upon me. And he came at a rush, crying to Su-len in the hall, "Ah, there she is! My favourite product of the old Cultural Revolution!" and bowed low to her: she actually put her nose up.

Gripping my hand, he pumped it vigorously. "By God, it's good to see you, Dad!" Unkempt, apparently unwashed by the smell of him, his bright, untidy hair hung to his shoulders and his spade beard spouted obscenely over his torn, blue jersey. "Where's Mother?"

"Dining out—she sends her apologies."

"And she won't be home till morning—who's it this time?" He played with his big cherry-wood pipe, irony on his mouth.

"Claud and Marsella."

"Didn't Johnny Hampshire invite you?"

"Henry Shearer. Let's change the subject." I poured him beer.

He grimaced. "It's a wonder the Press allow it to pass—sponsored, censored. But I see they're still on your tail."

"It's less than I expected. They do have the grace to talk about courage."

"What good's that if they make you out a first-rate bastard?" He hesitated, adding, "I'm sorry about the inferences—Su-len and all that."

I shrugged: "You challenge an administration like this one, and you take the consequences—they did much the same to Sir Roger Casement in very much milder days."

Joe replied, "You didn't touch the girl, why should you care?"

I said quickly, "Cheriton is corrupt, and I shall continue to say so; in the end the public will vindicate me."

He said, taking the beer, "Don't go overboard for the great British public, mate; any time now it might arrive for a lynching."

"Is that all you've come to say?"

"No, but don't be too confident. The public's all right all the time it's got its beer and bingo, but it's going short now. I actually came to say 'well done!'"

"I can't believe it!" I turned my back on him; there was more to his arrival than this. He said, softly, "Your stand is making the right sort of impression in the right place, you know."

"Where might that be—the Kremlin?"

He grunted, adding facetiously, "Go on like this and the New Left will be proud of you."

At that moment Mamie put her head round the door, and Joe shouted, "There's me old black beauty—don't you love us any more, Mamie?"

"Dinner's ready, Mr. Mark," she said. "An' that Su-len's up in her bedroom with chop-sticks—she ain't in the mood for knife and fork eatin', she says."

Joe cried, "What's wrong with everybody?"

"The place is under the pickers now you're here, that's what's wrong," said Mamie.

We sat at the table and Mamie marched between us, her nose high, her mouth a little blue button, and Su-len did not come down. Joe said:

"It isn't a stable regime—governments like Brander's never are, especially in the early days. We've got the numbers, we're getting the arms. One good shove and they'd be over."

I replied, abstractedly, "That's what the Chartists thought."

He ate voraciously, snapping the food like a dog at flies, guzzling the wine. "What do you suggest, then, moral force?—the Chartists got their five points through agitation and violence."

I sighed. "You self-generated revolutionaries are all the same,

Joe. You take no account of sectional interests—the great middle class in this case—and your failures drive you into extremism."

"With that self-seeking, decadent lot we wouldn't get out of suburbia."

"They are the public, the average reasonable voter; you represent class in its most violent form."

He drank, watching me. "But they eat while others starve. The public you worship just doesn't exist."

"But it does, and this is your mistake. It may appear to be asleep, but it's watching, and when it acts everything rolls before it. The public, which you despise, Joe, plays the game and provides a referee; it forces politicians to look over their shoulders before they perpetrate the outrage—changes one fool prime minister for another because he's the fool it trusts. Jefferson said that the public will act wisely if it knows the facts, and since all the best brains lie outside Parliament, it always does."

He was suddenly intent, listening. I continued, "And by the public I don't mean the layabout in ermine, the unproductive executive, or the House of Lords' buffoon, I mean the ordinary man. Neo-Fascism may have the country by the throat now, but the people haven't spoken yet. Give them time and they'll speak for me."

"They didn't speak for Johanson; he's dead, you'll be sorry to hear."

I closed my eyes. Joe added, "Arrested on a breach of Intelligence charge—Defence of the Realm. He was shot yesterday while trying to escape. It isn't in *The Times*, of course. Don't you take the underground Press?"

A vacuum was forming in my head; caused, perhaps, by the shock. Also, although I found it hard to accept, Moira was now playing a major role in the approaching chaos of my mind—this and the recent beatings. Now it seemed that her adultery was a sensuous rhythm to the thudding fists—her soprano gasps with Shearer an accompaniment to my shouts of pain. I heard myself say to Joe, "I knew a Johanson just after the war. He wasn't a complete idiot, although he looked like one."

Joe peered. "I beg your pardon."

I said, "Actually, it was before I joined the unit, for he was bomb-busting during the war—according to Vidor he worked the most delightful racket—based on the premise, of course, that if he was blown to bits a grateful government would make quite certain that his dependents starved."

Joe said, "What are you talking about?"

"Well, they'd dig out a bomb, defuse it, steam it, and put in it a ten-bob alarm clock like the one I collected in Malaya. Then they'd stand the bomb against the wall of the nearest house and make a clatter with shovels and things till the householder came out. According to Vidor the conversation went like this:

'God Almighty, what's that?'

'A bomb, sir.'

'What are you doing to it?'

'Trying to defuse it, sir.'

'Supposing it explodes?'

'That's our bad luck, sir.'

'But, do you have to do it here?'

'As good as any other place, sir.'

'Is it a live one?'

'Listen to it ticking, sir.'

'But can't you take it away?'

'Truck's run out of petrol, sir.' "

Joe's face was pale, I remember, and I added, "Vidor said they averaged seven pounds a night for six weeks, but none of them lived to spend it. Sapper Johanson and five of them were killed on Hackney marshes by a double-boobied Mark IV 500 kilo just after I took them over. They were a grand lot."

"Dad," said Joe quietly, "are you all right?"

It seemed grotesquely unfair that Johanson should be dead—people shouldn't be allowed to find release so easily—the pull of the trigger, the buoyant ride into oblivion; still, on reflection, he did stick it out. Joe said:

"You're ill, Dad. Don't you realise it?"

"Don't you start." I got up, walking about.

There was building within me a new warmth for him; I saw him suddenly as a bright contribution to courage amid these miserable deaths—Stan Waters, for instance, hanging there with his trousers down; there was no honour in it. Sibelius, I suspected, discovered such warmth in his artist friend Akseli Gallen-Gallela, within the conception of his glorious music: the drunken mood, the arm-in-arm stagger home with a comrade, when they looked over their shoulders at their plodding imprints in the snow that sat in semibreves concisely within the moon's reflection of the telegraph wires, a stave of music miraculously caught. *Finlandia!* A single chord of sound began to grow in my head. *Vidor . . . of guilt* accompanied the phenomena; after all, it was just possible he *had* gone to one of Marsella's parties and even if she was a minor here, she was, by Chinese law, of the age of consent. I stared into my glass, seeing the slits of Johanson's eyes, the humped, bloody cheeks in the golden slat of the whisky, and a nose bulbous and broken. Su-len said, 'Do you like my new cheongsam?' and Joe interjected:

"I wouldn't drink any more tonight if I were you."

"Don't you tell me to stop drinking!" I glared belligerently. "We never see each other from one year's end to another, and then you come in here with your stupid, bloody rhetoric! Just because I take a stand against Brander's lot, it doesn't automatically mean that I support your New Trotsky Left or whatever you call yourselves."

He replied, "I came to say I'm proud to be your son—that the working class needs men like you, Johanson, Waring. But you can't sit on your middle-class fence and fight them alone—they'll pick you off one by one. Dolfuss was no good to Austria dead."

I sipped my whisky and got up, wandering about. "You really mean to go, don't you!"

"We've no option."

"You'll take a rabble against the officer class—picks and shovels against the Army's S.A.S. and the Brander blackshirts?"

He said, "The East End is armed, the patrials are with us. We've got a Fifth Column waiting to rise in every city. Within a week we'd have London. All the union squabbles are over, all the factions are moving collectively—the Dock Apprentices, the New Deal Left and the Liberal Approach; the Maoists and Lenin Communists—there's not politics in it any more, we're just going to shift Brander . . ."

"Within a week you'll be dead."

He shouted suddenly, "Christ! Then what did your generation die for in two world wars—a Fascist future?"

"You don't need to go into revolution! One organised, massive demonstration . . ."

"Demonstration? *Balls!* What has it gained? Peaceful demonstration is an excuse for your inaction—please go quietly with the policeman and he'll knock your bloody head off when he gets you to the station. Don't you realise this is your fault? For years you've been shouting patriotism and don't rock the boat; you've been making individual stands, like yours, that lead to nothing, and begging for justice from people in the pay of Government. You can't fight thugs like Brander with a half-baked Whitleyism!" He was furious now, shouting into my face.

I said, turning away, "My God, I don't know what's happening to your generation."

"Then I'll tell you. We've got to die now because you didn't bloody care. You've watched people like Macmillan and Wilson, Heath and Powell take us to the Right in a world that's going Left: we've watched you sell us to the Branders—couldn't you see him coming?—we could, a mile off. Now you won't even let us fight for you. When we sit down in the street we're a bunch of long-haired weirdies; we're agitators when we march and hand in petitions, and we're commies when we fight the police. Couldn't you hear the little Hitlers of the officers' messes? Didn't you read the warnings men like Chalfont gave you in the 'seventies? You're *responsible* for Brander, and the only language he understands comes out of the wrong end of a gun."

"I wonder where I've heard that before?"

He came closer, saying into my face, "Oh, no, you don't, you're not pulling that. We're not Stalinites or Trotskyites; we want no truck with Mao, Castro, Che Guevara, Nixoncide or Greek colonels. You'd put a label on us, the same old game, but we know nothing about communes, presidiums or politburos. We're just the young of this country working one day a week for the tax man and two for the moneylenders, and whom you and your kind have always despised, although we make your wealth. The old union boys might have failed, but we haven't, and we're going after the things your generation lost—whether you're with us or not."

"The standard of oratory isn't very high, Joe."

"But the intention is—we're going to fight. Your middle class did nothing about Heath's Rent Act, the stopping of school milk and meals, the means tests for men on the dole, the hire purchase rackets: the man in the street is on his bloody uppers under the mortgage rates. And don't talk to me of demonstrations until you've lived in slums, where they toss the rats out of the windows before they eat the meal. Decent men know when to pick up a gun, and that's how we're paying for your sodding moderation."

I said calmly, "You'll regret it. Nobody who attacks an established government can claim he's right, because that's the law of the jungle."

He was at the door. "So you're against us?"

"Yes."

I listened to his footsteps echoing down the hall and the slam of the front door. Almost immediately Mamie appeared, crying:

"Now, who's goin' out this time o' night? Ain't that Joe staying?"

"No."

"Well, God Almighty, this is one hell of a house."

A massive understatement.

I was a little surprised to hear Su-len talking in Chinese on the phone.

At the time I thought it was to a Chinese waiter.

CHAPTER 14

After Joe had gone I went to my room and undressed slowly, staring down at the drive.

It was what, in younger, happier days, my Moira would have called a Hatherley night, one of baying moonlight and faint screams, for stoats were hunting in the thickets and little things were dying, and this increased my depression. People like Claud and Marsella, Moira and Henry Shearer possessed the wand of oblivion, I reflected. They did not live their lives, but celebrated them; and although philosophy was not my strongest point, I thought, I would have liked to put back the clock of my existence, come face to face with myself and accept that it simply wasn't good enough. Perhaps Joe was right; perhaps I had allowed myself to be canalised by misplaced moral principles into a blind acceptance of the law. Even my challenge to Cheriton's corruption was not dictated by honour so much as by a blind acceptance of the ethos of the public service, my master. Benedict once said that an outsize dog can urinate against the carriage of the Queen, leaving to his intellectual betters an interpretation of freedom; he is unimpressed by the theological rubbish propounded by Canterbury and Rome, the fiddling of the Bank Rate, the puritanical revivalists who do it for gain, the cupidity of the workers who voted for the Industrial Relations Bill that proved their downfall, or the avarice of their comrades given half a chance. He cares nothing about the real pornography—that of the Stock Exchange; that the dangers of smoking are advertised to increase tobacco sales; the cost of food, the suicide rate among young married couples who couldn't get a mortgage from the building societies until they bred a son who could eventually take it on . . .

Benedict's dog was some bloody dog, I reflected; he certainly put things into a truer perspective. But he is unaware that the Russians now control the Mediterranean and are ringing our coasts with their war-ships; that, in crucified but unified Ireland, we now have an enemy State on our door-step; that South Vietnam is now Communist-controlled after one of the bloodiest reprisal slaughters in the history of Man: that an all-black government rules in Rhodesia, and South Africa is ringed with native insurgents. Nor does Benedict's happy dog know that Taiwan has been liberated, King Hussein assassinated; that France is neo-Communist; or that America, compared with China, is a third-rate power—a ripe plum, like Britain, ready for the picking by a passing aggressor.

I took off my underclothes, examining my bruised body in the moonlight. Perhaps Joe was right, I thought; it needed not one, but the mass, to make the stand.

This depression was not mainly alcoholic; I had realised that Joe and his revolutionaries were about to give their lives because of the apathy of my generation. During the unhappy days of Heath a cohesive T.U.C. might effectively have opposed the growth of militarists like Brander, but so many union leaders, cajoled by flattery and weakened by power, had retreated from conflict in the name of Tory peace, instead of unifying for war under its old cloth cap.

I went downstairs and got a bottle of whisky, then I locked the bedroom door so Su-len couldn't get in.

"You awake, Mr. Mark?"

Getting out of bed, I opened the door.

It was Ezra. In the light of the landing I saw his white, rolling eyes first, like dull disembodied onyx; then his purple face made shape. He said, soprano, "Mister, me and Mamie Ez, we thought you was dead. Ah've been knockin' and knockin'. There's police downstairs."

"Police?"

"Well, one is, and the other don't look healthy. Best you come down."

I wasn't surprised to see Mr. Flowers standing in the hall, but the *Vaporiser* blackshirt pushed past him, saying, "Mark Andrew Seaton?"

"Yes."

"I arrest you on suspicion of the murder of Bolo Mombara, the Minister of Patrials, in this house on June the second."

I said, "Well, I suppose you've got to have something to go on, but that's ridiculous."

Flowers said, with a winning smile, "We ain't ridiculous, Mr. Seaton. We wasn't ridiculous last time, was we? Now you get your clothes on, sir, for we don't want no trouble with a very nice gentleman."

"You're a bastard, Flowers."

He rocked on his heels. "You don't know what a bastard I can be, sir."

"I'll go and dress."

"Don't make a meal of it."

The *Vaporiser* man followed me with his tommy-gun, watching while I dressed, then, probably believing I was going to the lavatory, he followed me to Su-len's door.

Su-len stirred in sleep as the light from the landing touched her face—a dark profile staining the white pillow and I smiled at its beauty. I think it was Emerson who said that on the debris of our despair we build our characters: certainly, in the midst of my fear, I saw Su-len as a daughter asleep, not a forbidden obligato on a theme of love. In Cantonese, I said softly:

"Goodbye, Su."

The blackshirt glanced at me. "That the adopted daughter the newspapers talk about?"

I nodded.

"Very sad."

I pushed past him. "Don't compound the injury, mate, just keep your finger on the trigger."

Hearing this, Flowers said on the stairs, "You talk too much, Seaton—get into the car."

I was not at all surprised when we took the road to London. Inconceivably, I was becoming important again.

Political internment camps had sprung up during Brander's rule, but the one on the site of the old Hounslow Barracks usually received the more dedicated activists who, probably as disillusioned as I, held no strong political views. These, according to Brander, were the most dangerous of all.

We swung through the barrack gate and on to the square.

Here was a hamlet of semi-permanent hutting surrounded by the usual unclimbable fence, with fire-control towers at every corner manned by blackshirts; I had seen it all before. We got out of the car and Flowers pushed me before him into a hut.

Around the edges of the square the New Army recruits were being trained in bayonet fighting, and their vicious yells of *"In! Out! On guard!"* sullied the coming dawn. And I think I realised for the first time that it was from such places, the legendary homes of the army, that military extremism had projected itself upon a civil population used to paying respect to the officer class. In such places the sabre-rattling against the unions had begun: here, almost unwittingly, a pyramid of military violence had been built by reactionary elements who despised the Government's weakness in suppressing the workers. Brander had been born in such an establishment, the logical leader of the new bachelor army. I stared around at the neo-Prussian elegance and the camp's drooping inmates; heard barked commands, the yells, the stamping boots.

"Mark Seaton?" A young lieutenant glanced up at me with effete charm, then ran his finger down a list of names, adding, "Security Block; hut fifteen, cubicle one." He tossed an identity tag towards me. "Hang that round your neck—number two hundred and seven."

I asked, "Have you a warrant for this arrest?"

"Search him." It was as if he hadn't heard me. Two young paratroopers did so, taking all my possessions. The dawn was breaking,

I remember, as Flowers and the two soldiers took me into my hut, and here a man was lying.

"Good morning," he said, and slowly sat up.

Flowers, pushing me into the middle of the floor, cried, "There you are, mate—a real live bishop—ain't you lucky? Now you can tell him all about that little Chinese daughter." The door slammed and was locked behind him.

The man on the bed rose, standing before me in a long, grey gown. His body was that of a starved ghost, but his voice was strong and beautiful.

"Mark Seaton?"

I recognised him instantly, despite the poor light; it was Bishop Forsward. His face and hands were bruised, I noticed.

I asked, "You were expecting me?"

"According to the underground Press you were due here yesterday—we get the pamphlets at a pound a time—the New Army is corrupt, I fear. My name is Forsward, still a bishop, but scarcely an activist." He gestured to me to sit beside him on the bed. "Ah, well, we've got the Church and the Civil Service now—given the Navy and the R.A.F. we could have a rubber of bridge." He peered at my face. "You are surprisingly unmarked for a man just interrogated."

"I had mine weeks ago."

"A belated arrest? You shouldn't have persisted!"

"I was expecting it."

"The nature of the crime?"

"It seems that I murdered Bolo Mombara."

"Ah, yes—the Minister of Patrials—an excellent man in many respects." He stared upwards, rubbing his thin face. His eyes, I noticed, were unusually bright: he added, "Really, they do change their minds, don't they? I understood you were coming in for an offence against a minor: I wouldn't have thought that very seditious."

"It was mainly paper talk," I said, and got up, moving about the tiny room. Ironically, I reflected, Carrie would have been able to supply the vocabulary number and erection manual for the Minis-

136

try's central dump at Blackheath—our running contract for Nissen and M.O.W. huts, long since out-moded. Once they were there for a conscription overload—defence of the Realm; now they provided accommodation for Brander's internment programme; later, perhaps, his gas chambers. I said:

"Have you been here long?"

"About six weeks, though I'm expecting release this morning—doubtless you are here in order to be impressed."

"You'll be glad to be out of it."

"Oh, certainly. Young soldiers do make such a terrible noise, you know—it puts a strain on one's personal faith."

"You surprise me," I said, uninterestedly.

"Well . . ." he moved testily, "I'm getting old. Can't bear noise these days. Incidentally, you didn't kill Mombara, did you?"

I shook my head, and he added, "If I remember correctly, wasn't there some newspaper talk of a similarity between your case and that of Lord Wentorth?"

"I'm surprised that you give credit to the newspapers."

"Well, we all make this mistake, but you have to read something in here. Wentorth, too, if I recall, was accused of an offence against a minor; luckily, the child was not his adopted daughter." He looked at me.

"They hanged him for treason, not that," I said, "though he was innocent of both."

"Of course—it's general knowledge. However, in these days it is necessary for the public to agree with military justice."

"They're doing the same to me," I said.

"So you're not guilty of this offensive allegation—intimacy with a minor?"

"No."

He pondered this. "Count yourself fortunate, then, if you die for Mombara's murder—even if innocent. The other thing's too appalling."

I was tiring of him. Had I had the choice of a cell companion, I wouldn't have chosen a bishop, though I admired Forsward's indictment of Brander and the Triumvirate, not to mention his stand against racism.

Beyond the barred window I saw a sand-bagged firing-butt and its grassy slope; beyond this was clattering a denimed snake of sleepy recruits clutching breakfast mugs and plates, and I remembered the war of my youth. My companion, when I turned to him, was sitting like a wraith from the rack, his large eyes glowing unnaturally in the folds of a shattered face, and he said, "Actually, I've been following your case quite closely. Apart from the moral lapse in respect of your adopted Chinese daughter, you came out of it well—and don't tell me nothing happened to the child because I won't believe it." He smiled at me. "These little minxes can play havoc with a middle-aged man . . ."

"Believe what you like."

"Yes, you did well in the Kish investigations, even if it was an orgy of self-destruction."

"What do you mean by that?"

He spread his bony hands. "Your forthcoming punishment is a balm to your conscience, isn't it?" He added, "But anybody can help the executioner stoke the fire. Whatever your sins, Seaton, it would be best to stay free. You can serve your country well by staying alive."

I said, wearily, "What do you want of me?"

"Recant."

I stared at him. "Let Cheriton off the hook? You're as bad as he is. The man's corrupt!"

He shrugged. "We're all venal in one way or another. How can we hope for forgiveness if we aren't prepared to forgive? Cheriton himself might one day serve his country, which he undoubtedly loves. Come, man—bend! Confess your sin to me, the offence against the child."

"Oh, yes," I said, "the usual theological cant: as long as the soul is purified the body can burn. Or is absolute morality confined to bishops?"

"Not entirely. I'm Anglican, and therefore not celibate. As Ben

138

Johnson said, 'there's no fun without it,' though to date I've restricted my activities to those above the age of consent."

"For God's sake leave me alone."

"I might, but I doubt if He will." Reaching out, he caught my arm and drew me nearer, and his serenity disarmed me. "There's not much time left to me, and because you're the only human being within reach, I find you important. Individuals can't change things, Seaton; we can only contribute, with others, to the downfall of evil. We've both done our best in facing life, but now we're facing death. Be generous to Cheriton."

I said, "You're an astounding bishop."

A sudden clamour came from the square outside. The dawn light sworded the hut floor as the door burst open and soldiers crowded in.

"Right, Bishop, your turn now," said a corporal, and they tied his hands behind him while he looked over his shoulder at me, smiling. It was as if he were resigned to death, but he suddenly shouted as they pulled him to the door:

"*Wait!*"

The authority in him silenced them, and they stood dejectedly.

Forsward said to me, "You have nothing to bargain with, Seaton, except your soul. Recant and forgive Cheriton. You can serve your country best by staying alive."

I watched them as they marched him to the firing-butt. There can be a majesty in a man prepared to die; I had seen this before, after the military trials in Germany. In his long, grey gown he went, inches above the marching soldiers. He looked hard and long at the sky, I remember, as they tied him to the post, and turned away his head as they offered to bandage his eyes. The bullets of the firing squad cracked raggedly through the red dawn, manipulating his thin limbs like those of a disjointed puppet in a cacophony of ricochets, and he slowly sagged forward, his head on his chest, then dropped to his knees, and died.

It was a significant contribution to humanity, I reflected: to date, even in South Africa, they hadn't executed a bishop.

I was still gripping the bars of the window when the door came open again and Flowers, smiling, said:

"Well, Mr. Seaton, that was put on especially for you—and it's the sixty-seventh this week. If they can do that to a bishop, old son, can you guess what they'll do to you?"

"Get out."

"Just as you like." He nodded towards the window. "Meanwhile, you've got a grandstand view as they knock 'em off—unless you'd like to make a statement about Mr. Cheriton to the guard commander?"

They were cutting down the body of Forsward; now they laid it out on the grass. My throat was dry and my heart began to thump; already I could feel the shuddering impact of the bullets. I took a deep breath.

"Go on, get out."

"Be seeing you then," said he. "Same time tomorrow."

I began desperately to long for Moira.

CHAPTER 15

The counter-revolution, beginning peacefully against the Brander Triumvirate, was in motion within hours of the murder of Bishop Forsward, whom the people, for want of a man of heroic stature, immediately built into a martyr. Brander, with a typical military lack of diplomacy, had provided the perfect specimen, and during the interminable days of my detention in Hounslow Internment, the rebellion against his authority grew.

It was a necessity. During this time over a hundred more men and women were executed: it was a daily carnage, and my cell reeked with the tang of cordite.

They came singly, mostly; sometimes in batches. Some walked, bantering with their guards or cheering their comrades who were in terror.

The tiny window from where I could see the firing-point had a savage magnetism: out of a sense of duty I always watched their dying.

Many had to be carried to their execution, others fainted at the sight of the bloodstained posts to which the blackshirts bound them. A few went with arrogance, spitting at the feet of their executioners, whom, I noticed, were mainly recruits—this being Brander's baptism of death. Many shouted their messages in the moments before the bullets raked them, mainly of patriotism. And their sacrifice, for me, was a feed of courage to the people who were free; their comrades of the streets who were now on the move.

A sense of outrage at Bishop Forsward's death was sweeping the country, promoted by underground radio stations and the secret pamphleteering. Effigies of the martyred bishop, hitherto practically unknown before his defiance of the racists, were now being carried in silent torchlight processions in the towns and cities, and the blackshirts watched and dared not move.

Portraits of Forsward were everywhere with astonishing suddenness—pasted on buses and railway carriages, bridges, telegraph poles. Private presses were commissioned for their mass production. Paper boys, milkmen, office boys, bakers and other roundsmen carried stocks of his picture free of charge: the people seized them, handing them away in the streets, taking them to the offices and factories, sticking them to passing cars, wearing them in their hats.

And the Church, until now suborned by Brander, saw in this great national liberation movement the opportunity to turn its coat with comparative safety. Ministers of every denomination now flouted Brander's authority, denouncing not only the martyrdom of their companion but the militarists they once unofficially supported.

The Royal Family, safe on the race-tracks of the Continent, issued proclamations calling on the people for loyalty to the Crown. The Queen's broadcasts from private continental stations were repeated for home consumption as the fight for power among the new revolutionaries grew: equally, out of the backwoods of political obscurity the career politicians moved in safety back into the open for their usual buccaneering speeches. Uncensored articles appeared in *The Times* and even the *Telegraph*. The *Guardian*, its presses smashed since the advent of Brander, returned slowly to life. Criticism, slight but effectual, began to grow in pace and power. Pop idols, made courageous by the mass support of the young, composed new songs, hits overnight, debunking the stupidity of the neo-Fascists for only shooting one bishop when they could have shot the lot. Even the official comedians of the government-controlled television began to titillate the new public taste by sly innuendo about Brander's mistresses and Boland's transvestite tastes; careful rhymes were composed about Whiting-Jones and the beautiful Countess Devernon, forty years his junior. Phallic symbols appeared on the walls of public places depicting Brander's last stand: even the schoolboys were at it, said Benedict later.

Then the effigy of Forsward was followed by other respected national figures. The torchlight processions grew around the country, and on the banners of the outlawed Unions the pictures of Feather, Jones and Scanlon appeared—all of whom were spirited away by the Triumvirate at the outset of the coup: an outrageous act of revenge, for all had ceased active Unionism.

But it was the murder of Forsward that the people took as their emblem of national protest; a martyr had appeared on the horizon of public discontent, inflaming it to anger. Rocketing food prices since entry into the Common Market, landlord-ism, and the creation of a usurer's paradise within the rigid discipline of junta control—all crystallised into a national explosion, of which Forsward was the detonator.

The people had taken to the streets.

Overnight, although apparently without purpose or organisation, they moved in concert, their internal dissents forgotten. In the first week of August a slow but growing exodus began from the towns and cities from every corner of Britain; straggling black snakes of people moving on to London. These early migrants did not carry banners, nor did they march to the beating of drums, as later protestors did; but they were the vanguard of a general stampede that eventually assumed majestic proportions. They made no protests when scattered by the batons of Brander's blackshirts; they stood obediently aside when brushed by the New Army's half-tracks and their soldiers. At night they camped in the fields, lighting fires for communal feeding. Many were young and brought their guitars, but they did not sing on the march: only around their camp fires did they sing at night—the soft, slow chant that was to become the theme-song of their growing revolt—the *Goodbye Brander* song, a parody of that reserved for De Gaulle by the students of the Sorbonne.

As the days went on their numbers grew.

Towards the end of that first week they came to London in cars, on motor-cycles and bicycles; singly, at first, later in groups from the shut-down factories of the north and south: but these were not the hard-core revolutionaries, like Joe, my son; they were the ordinary people bound on a peaceful protest against the Brander Triumvirate.

They came in hordes from the East End slums, Notting Hill Gate and the Elephant and Castle: and these gathered in the moving masses of Poplar and Houndsditch, from Woolwich and Catford to Hackney and the Isle of Dogs. Banging on their tambourines, singing now, the Londoners swarmed out to the suburbs to meet the masses streaming in.

They came from Bristol and Southampton; also from Cardiff, with the more distant contingent from Swansea and the Gower coast swarming in by train. In packed coaches and commandeered buses they came from the east—Hastings to Colchester. As the factories of the Midlands began to close, they came down from Birmingham, Coventry and Leicester in growing contingents of noise, clamouring into the restaurants for food.

From Liverpool to Newcastle, Aberdeen to Glasgow they crowded the night trains, running special excursions for the march on London. The Welsh came, carrying the emblem of the dragon; the Scots marched from the railway stations to the skirl of the pipes. In the second week they arrived ceremoniously, the Pembrokeshire contingents with their women in national dress; the clog-dancers of the north revived the old dances; the Scots wore their kilts, the gipsies their bodices and scarlet skirts. And they marched in ranks fifty deep along the motorways, halting the traffic, demanding lifts, sitting on the bonnets of cars, hanging from the tail-boards of trucks and lorries amid the high whining of the ambulance sirens—a growing mass of accidents. But mainly, they marched in a gigantic, initially unplanned, untidy jamboree, asserting their instincts for the mass meetings of their ancestors, and their pride in protest.

They grew noisier and more confident with their growing numbers; on their way to the city they picketed factories, bringing out the workers in support, with marshals running amongst them and pleading for moderation. The docks of London closed after a massive show of hands and the dockers streamed in their thousands towards Hyde Park, this the first rally-point of the peaceful demonstration. The Underground stopped at midnight during the second week, the bus depots closed throughout the country, and the buses were used to ferry thousands more from remote towns and villages. A black wedge of traffic was converging on London; the North and South Circular roads were hopelessly jammed. As vehicles broke down, impeding the flow, they were dragged on to the side streets, and still the numbers grew.

The railways came to a stop through cuts in electricity, and the migrants swarmed out of the carriages across the moonlit fields; vehicles ran out of petrol and were abandoned where they stood, and the roads were blocked. Four million people (unofficial estimates put it at double this number) were thronging into London's suburbs in six enormous columns—one from east and west, one from the south and three from the north; straggling without direction at times, retracing their steps in the sudden urges of the mob sensation.

Panic began, and the old and young were crushed underfoot; lost children wailed for frantic mothers; the old clung to the strong in the crush of the human tide; prams were overturned and babies spilled out; the injured were dragged over the doorsteps of those too old to join the exodus: doctors abandoned their cars and fought among the milling people, tending the fainting in halls and back yards, telephoning near-by hospitals for drugs. And still the people poured in, climbing over the hedgerows and garden walls, running through the traffic jams, crawling between the wheels of standstill trains.

And into this frightened, disorganised mass came the revolutionaries.

The Maoists and the followers of Che Guevara were there, the New Deal Labourites and the International Socialists: the disciples of Kindan came, the new cult of the Indian Left, as did the Trotskyites, the anti-Fascists, and the Anti-Branderites, to which Joe, my son, belonged. And they came cohesive, one; for the first time since the advent of Brander they were unified in the common cause —revolution against the State, and they were organised.

They came with portable loudspeakers and public hailers—with banners proclaiming the martyrdom of Bishop Forsward, for whom they now cared nothing. Arm-in-arm the revolutionaries came at first, then dispersed, spreading like fingers through the people, shouting for order, calling for calm and silence, and the crowd, seeking leaders, responded. In the beginning of the third week of the demonstration the contingents were organised. Following instructions, they split into sections; some were told to stand and await, others to move. With a central movement headquarters installed in Hyde Park, the multitude discharging its millions on to London, slowly began to decentralise. With their banners sagging on their shoulders and their pictures of Bishop Forsward held high, they began to converge on Hyde Park and Regent's Park. Those travelling in from the east packed into Southwark Park and Deptford, Victoria Park and Hackney marshes; those from the north took Hampstead Heath; Kensington Gardens, already crammed, took the overspill from Battersea Gardens: significantly, St. James's Park was tented, and here the organisers settled, guarded on all fronts by the new revolutionaries.

And at the weekend of the third week there came a massive column of two million unemployed. With brass bands at their head they marched down Whitehall, through Trafalgar Square and into Pall Mall. A hundred abreast they went, carrying their lodge banners and pennants of the outlawed Unions, with their uniformed bands thumping and the Scottish contingents skirling their bagpipes in the rear. The *Goodbye Song* thundered from their ranks and the crowds that lined their route. And they marched on Buckingham Palace with their leaders in the van, the outlawed Unionists wanted by Brander. These climbed on to the shoulders of their comrades and addressed them in turn, while the blackshirts watched, doing nothing. The mounted policemen, batons drawn, waited for a signal from the army, but it did not come; secret agents tried to take photographs of the leaders, but their cameras were seized and they were savagely beaten. Some police fought to keep back the mob, but the cordon was broken and the palace yard invaded. Strangely, once inside, the crowd appeared placated. With Brander, Boland and Whiting-Jones cooped up within, the demonstration sat, as a man, and there camped, and this was on the evening of the third day in the London suburbs, and all was strangely calm.

For the revolutionaries were waiting until the people grew hungry; this hunger had grown into a heady sickness on the second day in London: on the third day into anguished quiet. But on the evening of the fourth day of the peaceful demonstration, with four million people shouting for food, the leaders led them in search of it. With guns out in the vanguard now, sweeping aside the mounted police, they concerted the crowd movement into four enormous prongs—from Victoria Park in the east and Park Lane in the west, Euston in the north and Lambeth in the south. Trampling underfoot the portraits of Forsward and the dead heroes of the Unions, an armed multitude began the march on Central London.

Behind the sand-bagged façades of the high buildings the machine-gunners of the Civilian Riot Control and the blackshirt élite waited, their gun-sights trained on to the streets below.

The revolution of the working class had begun.

CHAPTER 16

According to later reports, the violence began slowly; at first only small cafés were entered by the rebels, and, though ransacked, the food was paid for. But later the big restaurants fell to the hungry crowds, and protesting proprietors were roughly handled. In diverging fingers the crowds thrust into Central London, combing through the little eating places, entering the big hotels in force, sweeping down to the kitchens. When the Cumberland and Dorchester were attacked, the S.A.S. reacted, supported by blackshirts. Moving in behind mounted police they split the milling people into groups, creating narrow swathes in their ranks with their flailing truncheons, and when a company of black patrials fought back with knives, the guns came out; buck-shot at first, fired indiscriminately into the attacking mob, spraying black and white alike, and the violence escalated.

House-to-house fighting developed first in Knightsbridge, the barrack headquarters of the London S.A.S., and the gun-carriers were called out, charging into the throngs surging down Brompton Road to Kensington Palace, and the revolutionaries moved in counter-violence, firing from the roofs of buildings, sniping from side streets. These isolated incidents, flaring up in the midst of an organised protest, began slowly to merge into a general conflagration that spread across London.

Mayfair and Park Lane were the early casualties of the coming battle; here the pavements were littered with dead and wounded. A patrial regiment had occupied the Dorchester, and blackshirts were emptied out of the high windows. The Army brought up a six-pounder mobile gun, its high explosive shells battering the apartments, and the slaughter began. This initial fighting, within an arc from Kensington to Marble Arch, was the signal for the pitched battles of Hyde Park and Mayfair. The sky was dulled with the smoke of burning buildings; individual fires began which spread down Park Lane in a glowing incineration fed by arson; ineffective fire-engines, sirens blaring, were trapped in the streets. And the new revolutionaries, now fighting in isolated groups, sniped remorselessly from the trees of the Park, bringing down the S.A.S. commanders from their tank turrets, toppling the mounted policemen out of their saddles. Arms, appearing from nowhere, were handed into the crowds.

The battle for London was on.

In the suburbs special insurgent squads were fighting for key points; Heathrow Airport was under fire by the morning of London's fifth day of the counter-revolution; Gatwick was captured by an organised, fast assault of Civilian Militia infantry: by the afternoon of that day Knightsbridge Barracks, the very home of the S.A.S., was invaded: the B.B.C. television studios at Lime Grove were taken at almost fatal cost, for here the blackshirt companies were defenders, and the Civilian Militia, faces blackened for night-fighting, were shooting their way from house to house from Chelsea to Oxford Street, ferreting out and executing small groups of army patrols, infuriated by the slaughters of Park Lane and Mayfair.

Within hours the pressure groups of the counter-revolution became apparent, spilling out of the cellars of Notting Hill—a Black Patrial Brigade formed from countless small squads racing in from the suburbs to assemble in the parks. Selfridges, made a bastion by the army, was attacked on the afternoon of the sixth day, and was fought for, floor by floor, its departments a scene of carnage where New Army soldiers and insurgents lay together in grotesque attitudes of battle. And still the mob poured in, running from the exits with looted goods, carrying out furniture for bonfires in the street below. And into these bonfires, around which the patrials were dancing, Brander's tanks charged, guns blazing. A smoke-pall began to grow over London: the dusking sky tinged red; the city was rocked to the growing concussion of the guns.

That evening, the sixth day of London's siege, the attack on Hounslow Barracks began and the boy called Willie, from the Civilian Militia came for me.

The fighting for Hounslow Internment and its internees went on intermittently for five hours. I measured its progress in growing degrees of faintness, for the guards, defending their lives, had brought us no food after the first two weeks. Now, lying on the floor of the cubicle, I watched bullet holes miraculously appearing in the curved corrugated iron around me; heard them ricocheting off the Nissen tee-irons and standards, filling the place with choking cordite fumes. Cries came from adjoining huts as prisoners were hit, one after another. The camp siren that signalled escapes was wailing like a banshee; the crashing hand-grenades of the fighting for the perimeter wire detonated in concussive blasts, for the black-shirt defenders knew what awaited them, and they fought with the desperation of men condemned. Nearer, nearer came the battle in ferocious hand-to-hand fighting; and I assessed its vicinity by the groans of the wounded. After midnight, when there came a sudden lull, a man shouted outside my window:

"How many in there?"

"Only one," I cried.

"Stand to the right of the door!"

I did so and bullets shattered the lock; two men shoulder-charged the door and darted in, wheeling, automatics at the ready. One was very young, with blood pouring from a head wound; his companion was older, his chest festooned with slung bandoliers. "Where's Mark Seaton?"

"I'm Mark Seaton."

"Joe Seaton's father—the man in the Cheriton case?"

"That's right." I picked myself up, facing them.

"Who brought you in?"

I said, "Blackshirts. I've been here weeks."

They moved uncertainly, gasping for breath, staring at each

other. The boy called Willie said, "We collect the wrong one and there'll be a bloody row." He looked at me. "Got any papers?"

"Don't be ridiculous—in here? You go and fetch Joe," I said.

The older man said, "Your son's dead, Mr. Seaton." He watched me carefully. I leaned back against the wall, eyes closed.

"Killed at Paddington station this morning," said Willie.

I whispered, "Oh, God!"

His companion said, "But he was all right when we left him this afternoon," and grinned.

Grief, I had discovered, is a statement of identity. Willie added, "Got to get going, sir—you're wanted in the city."

"Who by?" I was recovering from the speed of things.

"Don't ask us—they just said fetch you. Your son's a power in the Revolutionary Committee, and we're keeping on the right side of him."

Vaguely, I wondered if Moira would be proud. Willie said, jerking his head at the door, "Check if it's clear outside, Ben. They'll knock off the pair of us if we lose him now."

It was my first insight into the counter-revolution.

A scene of carnage met me within the internment wire.

The heaped bodies of slaughtered blackshirts and National Guards were piled down the hutment lanes; a toll out of accord with the period of the fighting, and I realised that the Civilian Militia had taken no prisoners; that much of the volleying I had heard must have been executions, akin to Brander's practice. Massed near the barrack gate were crowds of gaunt prisoners, the internees, their flimsy clothes tented by their drum-stick limbs, and they moved with the lethargy of men already dead. Many of these were intellectuals imprisoned since the days of Whiting-Jones, a testimony to the Rightism which Brander had changed to Fascism: we gently pushed through their ranks to the exit, still barred and locked.

Here women and girls were handing bread and milk through the railings, and the internees were clawing at it in wolfing hunger. I remembered such scenes from an earlier generation.

A car was awaiting us a little down the road and I got into its back seat with Willie, while Ben, the older man, acted as driver;

slowly we edged through the tearful women. Willie said suddenly, "Christ, what a mess." He was staunching the flow of blood down his face. "Better a quick machine-gun, and put them out of their misery."

I glanced swiftly at him, realising that this was the new generation of Brander's practicality: an era funnelled into despotism, professionalised in the 'seventies. Cutting through side streets, the car gained speed along the Great West Road towards the city.

Once, as a child, I had lived here amid blossom-tree suburbia and the thundering jets of growing Heathrow. I remembered again the traffic jams on Derby Day, and the faces of sleepy, home-going children at steamed windows after a day's outing at the sea. Now Willie, who was of this generation, sat beside me with blood on his face and his finger itching on a gun trigger. It was men like Willie, once lolling at coach windows, sucking ice-cream cornets, now freedom fighters, who were the victims of the Macmillan burlesque of *Never had it so good;* the Left Wing socialist reforms which so magically swung to the Right, the electioneering promises of price cuts by Heath which ballooned into towering rises—all this, together with a communication media of half-truths, selected interviewees and slanted opinions, had lulled their youth into a sense of quiet, and given birth to Brander.

"The people are on the move," said Willie, now.

They were.

They were spilling from the massed semi-detached estates of Shepherds Bush and Ealing. Freed from the interrogation cellars of Hammersmith and Chiswick, men and women came in fluttering rags. From the execution yards, still under sentence, they came from Nine Elms, the dreaded prison of the S.A.S. Raked from Wormwood Scrubs by the shock attacks of the Civilian Militia, political prisoners and hardened criminals, they came cock-a-hoop, dressed in gay colours looted on the way. They came drunken and on the wrong side of the road in captured half-tracks they did not know how to drive, blowing on hunting horns and bugles, leaping across the verges to loot and fire, making for London, and Brander.

Armed civilians were swarming around Hammersmith Broadway when we reached there, the fulcrum of the Militia attack. Here, in the Underground, a blackshirt company had made a last stand, before being driven into the tunnel and the oncoming rebel-driven trains. Here, through the sealed exits drifted the bonfire smoke that finally suffocated them.

Machine-gun fire was spurting intermittently from the shattered buildings, many already ablaze from the house-to-house attacks, their windows gaping at the jam-packed traffic below. Mortar-fire was coming from Ravenscourt Park, still in New Army hands, and here the last remnants of the Scots Guards were fighting desperately, surrounded by the First Black Patrial Mombara Brigade, once based on Notting Hill. And above us, as we slowly edged forward, the vanguard fighters of the French Air Force were machine-gunning rebel contingents making for Central London. Now, clear of the Broadway, we entered a thin line of honking traffic and overtook a great parade massing outside Olympia.

Gay with banners and fluttering pennants came this parade; with fine military precision it was marching towards Kensington with its gold and gilt union banners, emblems of the revived Lodges. It was an army on the march, the tattered remnants of the Dorchester Militia which the blackshirts had nearly cut to pieces on the roads from the west. Bloodstained, grey with old wounds and fatigue, they yet marched with verve, these men, held together in common purpose, unused to war but comrades in defeat. To the beat of a single drum they marched, many with bloodstained bandages, their rifles sagging across their shoulders. And around them, weaving through their ranks, danced the children and wives of the riverside houses, garlanding them with summer flowers. Old men waved their sticks from the pavements, cheering weakly, remembering their own defeats; white-faced urchins did cartwheels and handsprings along the gutters beside them.

Leading this ravaged army of insurgents was the main body of the southern cadres; the loping, raw recruits of the factories of Slough and Staines; three thousand hands trained secretly and now led by the old Emergency Reserve, the grizzled experts of Normandy and Cyrenaica. Spear-heading these rumbled six heavy tanks, prizes taken from the Wiltshire School of Infantry which had been submerged by high intensity operations. . . .

"Take the pavements!" shouted Willie. Horn blasting, Ben did, scattering the pedestrians, sending children in a wave before us. Belaboured with sticks and rifles at the outrage, we sped past the marching column, gaining the fore momentarily—only to crawl again behind a company of Home Defence veterans, and these were shouldering sporting guns. With these twelve-bore and four-tens they had defeated the Brander blackshirts at Esher and prevented the mass execution of militant tradesmen in Surrey. And they went with pride, this small company, men of the old bayonet charges of Arras, with horsed out-riders on their flanks and a captured mobile twelve-pounder at their head. Fifty yards in front of them were union silver bands, marching to the rally of armed workers in Hyde Park, ever the central point of agitation. But few lived to reach it, I later learned, for the National Third, Brander shock-troops, were awaiting them in the side streets and shredded them with cross-fire. Slow to react, the old men died in scores.

"I don't give that lot more than an hour," said Willie, for cowering outside Knightsbridge Barracks sat the remnants of the Brander guard: trapped without arms, in their beds, they sat in hundreds with their hands locked upon their heads, while among them strolled the boy-soldiers of the Apprentices Battalion, the anti-coup survivors of the massacre of Leicester Square. Soup kitchens from the Dorchester and New Imperial had been set up on the edge of Hyde Park, and around these were crowded the new patrial revolutionaries; free of the slums, they were dancing in groups in the road, firing without command or discipline, raucous in different tongues, drunk with power.

"Look," shouted Ben, and pointed.

On every lamp-standard lining the road a body was hanging: children were pelting the corpses with stones.

"They're only blackshirts," said Willie, glancing up.

"Doesn't that make you as bad as Brander?" I shouted.

"Summary justice doesn't belong to him," said Ben.

"Summary justice doesn't belong to anybody," I replied.

Willie shrugged. "Kill or be killed, eat or be eaten. Belief in toleration died when your generation made a bloody mess of it—just thank God we're still in one piece."

The bodies were circling on the ropes; the children were shouting with joy.

"And those?" I asked, nodding upward.

"That's their bad luck."

Outside the entrance to the underground car park the traffic halted again.

Here bomb-shocked civilians, lost in the fury of the battle, added their misery to a blaring cry funnelling out of the exit, a strident loud-speaker. For beneath us, in place of cars, were three thousand stretcher-wounded, brought in from the hand-to-hand fighting of Barn Elms, and doctors were operating without anæsthetic. In the park surrounding this area hundreds more wounded were lying on the grass, twisting and turning, begging for drugs. The traffic moved; we jerked on amid fire-engines and ambulances, mobile guns, despatch riders and commandeered buses, all vying with each other for passage towards the Arch-pennanted tanks, their R/T blaring, their furious commanders shoving vehicles aside by side-swinging, were frantically trying to reach a Brander anti-tank regiment still dominating the side streets of Maida Vale. Above us rebel helicopters were machine-gunning targets deep within the park: the ground was shaking with gunfire from a Brander anti-aircraft battery situated on top of Peter Jones, now gutted after days of burning. The only government bombing so far, according to Willie, had come from the French Air Force based on Channel port stations, for Boland's military landing grounds had long since been over-run by the workers.

Said Ben, as we crawled along, "God, who'd be a blackshirt at a time like this?"

Along the railings of the park men were being tortured: these, the Second Echelon of Brander's paratroopers had been caught on the ground at Luton Airport and sent south to the summary revolutionary courts: accused of civilian massacres, they had been

155

convicted and sentenced, after surrendering without a fight: this had earned them the nickname 'Cold Feet'. Now, manacled together, they were being hoisted on to the railings and petrol poured into their jack-boots. I saw the pluming flames and I heard, too, the cheers of the crowds as group after group of the Brander élite exploded into dull red glows. Willie was idly checking his Ku Passa automatic, a smile on his mouth. I said:

"And I suppose you approve of that, too?"

"It's part of the obscenity."

"It's a descent into anarchy!"

Ben swung the wheel. "Based on revenge, like the Nuremberg trials. Christ, Mr. Seaton, you're in no position to talk. My father was in the court-rooms. Hundreds of Germans got little more than a token defence—U-boat commander or tea-boy, they hanged you just the same, within half an hour of sentence."

"But we didn't set them on fire."

"Yes you did," said Willie, "at Hiroshima."

Ben said, "And you doubled it up at Nagasaki before they could take a breath—one day history will put Churchill and Truman in the right bloody category."

"And don't talk to us about Hitler, either," said Willie, "for you landed us with Brander."

Walking wounded were crowding in around Speakers' Corner, coming from the barricade fighting of Oxford Street and the Edgware Road—all union men by their arm-bands, mainly reformed lodges of the dock workers. They stood in pathetic groups, heads bowed or leaning on their comrades, a little army of broken limbs and grimy bandages, silent. Here, too, was gathered half the nursing staff of University College and Bart's, their hospitals burned out by indiscriminate French bombing. Blue-coated nurses were working swiftly, their young faces white with sweat and shock. Ben said:

"I'm going on the grass—we'll never make it through this lot."

Willie stood guard as I got out.

"This way," said Ben, and pushed through the crowd.

Incongruously, on the very edge of Speakers' Corner the bodies of Whiting-Jones and Countess Devernon, his young mistress, were hanging; an ironic repetition of history. Guarded by Apprentice Boy Militia, they were hanging by the feet in the manner of Mussolini and his lover, and disembowelled. The old man rigid in death, had his arm protectively about her. The crowds gawked up: the road beneath them was still slippery with blood.

I thought, the revolutionaries of today are the oppressors of tomorrow: this, the workers' cause, a sacred egotism. Predictably, their crusade, initially based on idealism, had degenerated into a fundamental hysteria. Willie tried to pull me away.

"So this is your Workers' Democracy," I said.

"They got less than they deserved."

A Black Patrial regiment marched past us down Park Lane to take up residence in the Dorchester; followed by their camp followers they went, going to the beat of tribal drums. And their black followers danced about them in gay colours, their crimson headdresses and yellow sarongs flowing in the red glare of the fires. They took the middle of the road, for the Grosvenor was already occupied by Pakistani troops, and bedding and furniture were being thrown out of the windows for bonfires; incendiary bullets were making steep arcs of red and gold in the night sky, incredibly beautiful.

A mob of demented East Enders flooded up Oxford Street to meet us; waving burning torches they came, bawling abuse at bystanders, dragging in their midst scores of aged men more dead than alive, the frail residents of London society clubs too late to escape. Many of these were nearly naked, their clothes torn from their bodies: some, the infirm, were carried like sacks on the shoulders of the crowd, others were shielding their heads from blows. They came booted and reviled, heading for the execution grounds of the Bayswater Road where the blackshirts were dying. Willie and Ben led the way, flinging people aside, dragging me through the crowds, and one man I will always remember: in the middle of the mob, his face streaming blood, he went with dignity, his head high amid the threatening fists.

New Bond Street was burning from end to end, and I feared for Hallie, but Monsieur Courval's salon and the shops either side of it were miraculously intact. Scattered bodies were lying over the pavements near Piccadilly; the vivid dresses of the afternoon shop girls, caught in the cross-fire, were splashes of colour upon which we stumbled through the rolling smoke. Twisted beneath the hind legs of a wounded police horse a young man was dying, beating his fists on the road. Overturned taxis, blown-up cars and abandoned luggage were piled amid the road blocks of furniture, for here the Third S.A.S. had made a stand against the Patrial X; the broken plate glass of the once-ornate shops gaped at us as we swerved through machine-gun fire; tracer from upper windows spattered along the walls beside us. Firing now were the dropouts of the revolution, neither Brander's blackshirts or workers, but those drunk on looted whisky. Boots up on the windowsills they were shooting at nothing while the building burned about them.

"God Almighty," shouted Ben, flattening against a wall. "Look what's coming!"

Although we did not know it then, Buckingham Palace had been taken and Brander and Boland captured. Coming now in their ceremonial parade around London was the flamboyant procession of the new Workers' Democracy, exhibiting its captives.

At the entrance to Piccadilly was evidence of the final rout: here the Patrial Fourth had trapped a relieving blackshirt regiment in one of the decisive battles of the rebellion. Outnumbered, the Nationals had called for reinforcements, and Boland had sent in paratroopers. These, with his personal bodyguard, had fought to the death in the dropping zones of St. James's and Battersea Park, already rebel occupied, and scores lost their lives as they swung against the sky. But they regrouped and made contact with the National Guard, fighting to release Brander and Boland, now in the hands of the Civilian Militia. But the Workers' Third, spear-headed by captured armoured cars, had taken them in the rear, and the Nationals' last stand was made between Regent Street and the new Underpass. Here the blackshirts were butchered: the suicidal charges of the patrial companies isolating them into groups. Now the victorious rebels of the Notting Hill Internment were cock-a-hoop despite their dreadful casualties, a rabble flying its bloodstained banners of Black Power, brushing aside the commands of the organised Civilian Militia, intent only on revenge.

"Get against the wall," yelled Willie, and pushed me into a door-way.

They were bringing Colonel Brander and Air Chief Marshal Boland through; Whiting-Jones had already been butchered.

They came twenty deep under their sagging banners, the Black Patrials yelling their tribal chants.

In the van they carried an effigy of Bolo Mombara in straw, the man they said had betrayed them. Behind this, carried ham-strung like a carcass, was Georges Hildane Denist, Brander's young assist-ant Foreign Secretary—captured in his office, devoted to Brander to the last. Now he swung on a pole by his hands and knees. Be-hind him came one I actually knew—Jonathan Speels of Environ-ment, a Fascist trained in Spain: half naked was he, swinging like a dead stag, his face sunk on to his matted chest, his large stomach bulging above the stretch of his buttocks. From his left side his en-trails were extruding; he had been cruelly flogged. Behind Speels came six others, one being Dovid, the old Minister of Trade, they said, but I could not identify him in the jubilant crowd. Another was Kerrigan, the Chancellor of the 'eighties—never a Fascist—and he, I thought, was dead. At the end of the procession came Torbin, the Minister of Power under the Whiting-Jones clique; earlier selling his birthright to the blandishments of the Heath government. Now he hung on the pole, stained with his own defecation. Only young Denist, slow to die under the torture gave way to panic; al-ternatively howling threats or begging for release.

A score more men were being carried on the poles—Celtic em-blem of reprisal in an earlier century, and around them jigged and jogged the victorious white and black Militia. Pistols fired into the air, flaring torches red on the faces of the marching men, told of the coming of Brander and Boland.

These came naked, their outstretched arms and legs pegged to hurdles: one end of each hurdle was fixed to a horse, the other trailed the road in bumpy progress.

They went like Tudor traitors going to the Tower for treason in another age. Both were bleeding from minor wounds, sweating with the cruelty of the hurdles, and caked with mud and dust. Boland was crying in a strange falsetto, his femininity exposed; but Brander made no sound. With his massive head lolling, he went, eyes closed; the weals of his beatings bright across his chest. Later, they were handed over to patrial butchers, taken to Smithfield, and there put to death by the slicing process.

Behind this procession came a hubbub of madly excited people, mainly unarmed. These, white and black, were the freed political prisoners from the Whiting-Jones regime. Once the cowed citizens of the Third Class zones, they were now top dogs: a great wall of the under-privileged pitched into insanity by the battle for freedom.

With the total defeat of the National Fascists, the sluice gates were flooding out the old class hatreds. Private scores were being paid off in alleys, gang warfare renewed with ferocity. The democracy of centuries went overboard, deserted by those who had fashioned them for gain. Successive governments since the war of 1914 had mistaken the people's inaction for timidity, and stolen too much. Now the ruling class knew the fury of the people in resentment. Overnight, the middle class had merged with the workers' revolt for self-preservation, committing its own atrocities to ally itself with the workers' cause. The rich and powerful were now on the run, blocking the streets with their furniture vans, crowding the airports, invading the beaches in hope of escape. And the 'Workers' Democracy trapped them, stripped them of their money and jewels, and executed them in batches.

I stood in the doorway and listened.

The detonation of the patrials, as Enoch Powell had prophesied, was the logical effect of the Rightist regime begun by Heath. Simmering on the edge of revolt, watching the demolition of their Unions, the workers had hardened into action. This, beginning with national ridicule and the abuse of career politicians, had changed to violence through desperation, for there was no Press outlet. The economic grievances of the Fair Rent Act, soaring food prices, the manipulation of the pound by government financiers had joined with public hatred of the building societies and others serving the rentier class. The isolationist attitude of a horsey Royalty, the parcelling out of the country to American and continental speculators, all was a pageant of stupidity that had destroyed democracy. It was a time of gambling and horse-riding—always a sign of national decadence—when it could have been a call to brotherhood.

It was an almost nomadic simplicity that the people would one day take the streets.

The mob following Brander and Boland was thinning.

In growing exhaustion, I followed the two men at a run, climbing the road blocks of Jermyn Street into Norris Street and the clearer area of the Haymarket.

It is awesome to me how dead horses balloon. Their pumped up bellies and glossy coats, their stiffened legs raking the red glare was an apt contribution to the Haymarket dead who lay in grotesque isolation.

Here were being penned the city businessmen of the great banking houses: the brokers, tellers, even the clerks of the Stock Exchange; trapped in London for want of transport, they were now being herded in groups for summary execution. Although the fighting had ceased here, we had often to duck or lie flat to the chattering of automatic fire as the city men were gunned down; later it was said that more than two thousand died in the first three days of the counter-revolution. One group, I remember, knelt and prayed before the entrance of New Zealand House, an incongruous sight in their pin-stripes. The patrials blazed their guns at them, sending them toppling in a mad gyration of arms and legs. We ran quickly through Trafalgar Square to Whitehall. Here a road block manned by the Second Civilian Militia, the Old Revolutionaries, barred our way. Ben led us to the top of the shivering queue, for the wind was cold away from the fires.

"Government representative, Mr. Mark Seaton."

An old sergeant said, "Where's his papers?"

"Got none. Hounslow Internment."

The old Militiaman grunted, waving us through.

As the road-block wire shut behind us we walked swiftly past

Old Scotland Yard. Here eight men were hanging on a rough scaffold along the pavements—three I recognised despite their blackened faces: Smython, the new back-bencher of the Woodford constituency—a Rightist if ever there was one; Pelhim-Hannets of Pendletowns and Wirdle of Bristol Fore. And then, as his body turned in the wind, I saw poor old Gunnins of Llander East; never popular with the Tories because of his obsession that Welsh should be the language of the Welsh. Others were hanging in the Yard, said Willie later—men such as Winterton, the Halden member, whose sole claim to fame was his membership of the Bath Club. With him died Pam, aged three, who, with the family, had been forced to watch his execution, but her mother had snatched her up and ran; both were caught in cross-fire. The P.A. of the Minister of Sport died, too, trying to shield them: also Aveling, the brilliant young Minister of Economics, who died of wounds in mistake for another; the electric bomb that shattered his car was meant for Charnes-Anderson, from whom he had borrowed it that day. Harmsworth, it was rumoured, was killed while trying to escape arrest, but Cheriton, my Minister of Building, was said to be under guard in the country.

Before the Cenotaph white-surpliced priests were haranguing a crowd of Civilian Militia—a forest of waving fists and crosses: here the crowds were dense again, and behind the railings of Parliament Square some two hundred Tory Members were being thumped into workers' lorries for Hounslow Internment . . . together with Labour Members, whose politics had moved to the Right.

Outside my Ministry entrance ambulances were hopelessly trapped as they tried to get up Westminster to the House of Commons, for fighting had been bitter there—Brander's blackshirts actually retreating into the Chamber behind a screen of hand-grenades, and many Members, loyally returning in the hope of regaining control of the disorder, had been shot down at their benches. Nollison was killed early on, for he refused to leave the bench; also Penhearros and Claveeton, Roy Bleckie and Davidsin: the three socialist brothers died, too—John, Robert and James Mantan-Preston, being shot on sight by the blackshirts; also Richard Carn and Manning, by the Civilian Militia, unwittingly, as they tried to enter the House. Many died here who were not recorded, their bodies being taken away by friends and relatives: many died who should not have died, for the innocent were executed with the guilty, like four of the kitchen staff who ran to save their Members, the comrades of years. But Big Ben, indestructible, relentlessly boomed the hour of five as Willie and Security Jones, still bulging and blue, pushed me up the steps of the Ministry to the hall.

"Well, if it ain't Mr. Seaton!"

Willie instantly said, "You recognise this man, porter?"

"He's the Director of Contracts!"

"Sign for him."

Jones did so, and Willie and Ben left without a backward glance. It was an ironic change in the affairs of the Department, I reflected, that I was now being signed for by the hall porter. Benedict, doubtless, would have had a word for it.

Now Jones said, "They're comin' in thick and fast, sir—all upstairs —Room 303."

"Who's upstairs?"

"Mr. Anstruther, Mr. Benedict, Hargreaves—Dr. Leyton—you remember Dr. Leyton; Simms and Davies, Mr. Redpath . . ."

"All right, all right."

"And Miss Carrington."

It turned me. "Is she, indeed?"

He screwed his big, red hands as I stared around the shattered hall: patrials had been billetted here, by the look of it; gone were the lovely teak handrails and oak panelling—probably for cooking-fires.

"The lift ain't working, sir."

"I can manage."

He spoke more, but I did not hear him: I was thinking about Moira. Until now I had not realised the danger to her safety, for Shearer was now a wanted man. Caught together, they could finish up like Whiting-Jones and his mistress on Speakers' Corner: the revolutionary militia didn't often stop to discriminate. No doubt they were trying to get out of the country; I knew with certainty that she was with him, though, thank God, Mamie and Ez would stay in Hatherley, so Su-len would not be alone in the house.

The memory of Su-len brought me to a new vigour and I walked to the staircase. Jones was still chattering, telling of what had happened to whom, but I ignored him.

On the first floor I paused to listen to the emptiness of the long corridors after the strident confusion of the streets; allowing my disordered mind to be contained by the very solitude.

Here, once, was the bell-pushing clamour of the Secretariat, the clash of the typing pool; here, on the first floor, was the beating pulse of Conditions of Contract where specifications, codes and standards grew to Bible proportions amid paper-shoving aides. Here, the non-costed administrator wrote to his opposite number, and got a reply (copy to you) by post, and the financial heart-beat of the nation raced to live up to the estimates—spend it, for Christ's sake, or we won't get it next year, and this could mean redundancy. Here public money went down the drain in abortive design and faulty construction in a world of rigged promotion boards, wire-pulling, and for God's sake see that old George gets it, because Alice can do with the money. And here, in the Architectural Division, was the apex of the folly, perpetuated by people who knew all about Cubes and Clasps, but had little interest in building construction.

To me, standing there in the emptiness, it was a vacuum within a classical nightmare, where the only true public service was rendered by the cleaners.

I heard myself say, "By God, if only the public knew. If I'm back with any power at all, I'm changing you."

Cheriton's office door was ajar and I pushed it open, staring into its emptiness: from here, I reflected, Harmsworth had taken the telephone call when I had first protested about the Severnside Power Project; it seemed an age since he and Cheriton had tried to defraud the public. In retrospect, I considered, it might have been better to let them get away with it. On the fifth floor, to which I climbed with unresigned impatience, I heard the bass grumble of men, and as I approached Stan's old room in Finance, the door opened magically, as if expecting me. I saw Anstruther first; behind him was Hargreaves, still impeccably dressed, though what he was doing there was anybody's bet: others were there, people like Willie Beese of the Foreign International, big John Shrivenham of the Legal Department, the constant opponent of the Public Prosecutor and his assistant. Arthur and Henry Redpath, the Q.S. stalwart twins grinned a wholesome greeting, and Michael Curzon, the only architect I would have paid in anything but washers, approached me, his hand out. Hargreaves said:

"Well, well, well! You really can't kill them off, can you?"

"You should try harder," I replied, and Anstruther said with charm:

"We're delighted to see you safe and well, Mark."

They all spoke at once then, but not Hargreaves. With Hallie sleeping between us, as it were, we just glared at each other, and I heard Anstruther say:

"Treat the latest survivor with the respect he deserves; if there's any justice at all in the world he's likely to be our next Minister."

"Not while administrators abound," I said, and closed the door behind me.

Carrie, I noticed, was still wearing her red dress and her hair was still untidy. But she flung me a fleeting joyful expression of greeting, before remembering, and bowing her head.

"How's your mother?" I asked.

She lowered her face. "Euthanasia," she said.

"I'm sorry."

She said, "I should have known better. I'm sorry, too, Mr. Seaton."

"Have you been through to Hatherley?" The normality of it steadied her.

"Not yet, sir."

"Please do it now, if it is possible," I said.

She straightened, smiling brilliantly. "Of course, Mr. Seaton."

For the first time I think I knew the beauty of her face.

CHAPTER 17

I stayed in London for about a fortnight, telephoning Hallie every night and morning, never managing to contact her, and I hesitated to phone Monsieur Courval to ask where she was. But Su-len was always at home, her excitement at the sound of me ringing down the line in its cadent Cantonese.

To be needed in this life is unbelievable wealth.

When I had reformed the Design and Contract section of the Ministry and the Provisional Government of the Workers' Democracy had opened Parliament, I returned to Hatherley.

Mamie and Ez were awaiting me on the drive; Mamie with her apron up to her blubbering face. "May God forgive Mrs. Moira for treatin' you this way, sir," said she. "May she be struck with the holy fire."

This before I was scarcely out of the taxi. I replied, "With Satan in charge of affairs, Mamie, she'll probably get away with it. Where's Su-len?"

Ezra replied, going purple, "Now, don't you talk to us about that Chinese back-chat, for she ain't human, Mr. Mark."

"What's she been up to now?"

"She's been out half the night in that black cheongsam thing, showin' enough leg to murder a bishop—that kid is trouble."

"She's found a friend?" Strangely, I was not perturbed.

"Reckon she's found a tribe o' Chinese waiters."

"You've seen her with one?"

"Mister," said Mamie, "I ain't talking about that child 'cause she don't need me—she got a host of friends." She added, "People keep

166

ringing her an' she's always phoning." She awaited my reaction, hands folded on her stomach. Ezra took my suitcase and followed me into the lounge. I said, "No messages from Mrs. Moira, Ez?"

"Neither hide nor hair, sir."

Shearer was no fool, I reflected; like as not they were somewhere in America where pornography paid even better than on the continent. Ezra continued, standing at the door, "It don't seem right, pestering you so early, sir, but me and Mamie ain't been sleeping proper since you left."

"You're not the only one." Pouring a whisky I wondered if Joe had survived. Ezra scrubbed his white palms together, saying, "Things are changing pretty rapid since this Workers' Democracy took charge, an' us servant blacks just don't know the way the wind's blowing. You reckon they'll keep us out o' the rain?"

Through the lounge window I saw the poplars waving in the wind, caught in rings of evening sunlight. I replied, "As a black man you're on the right side of the blanket, aren't you? What's wrong?"

Ezra shifted uneasily. "Well, with ole Bolo Mombara up at the top we was all right, for he kept riotin' niggers in their place. But now those goddam workers are in charge, people like Mamie and me're living from minute to minute." He stared at me. "You remember that Jamaican boy who worked for the Shearers?"

I nodded, and he said, "He don't do now, for he's cleanin' sewers up in Birmingham—he wrote an' told me. And Sarban and Coko, the Besford cookie and boy? The Patrial Militia come down here and pitched 'em out in the street. You ain't waiting on white trash no more, they said. Ever since the Besfords were took, Sarban and Coko been lost."

I turned. "Ever since the Besfords were taken? What do you mean?"

"They been took, Mr. Mark. Don't you know?" His white eyes rolled. "Took last week by the Civilian Militiamen. And they pitched Mrs. Shearer into the same police van."

I put down my whisky. "Kate? Arrested? On what charge?"

He emptied his hands at me, "Ah don't know, sir. The Besfords' daughters, too—those houses are empty."

"Good God!"

"An' they treated those girls somethin' terrible. The big one, Miss Portia, she got off 'cause she's ugly, but the two little twins, they got rudenessed, Mr. Mark."

I left him and went into the garden, appalled by the treatment of Kate Shearer, whose sole crime was that she was wife to Henry: the only guilt of Claud and Marsella Besford was that they were rich. If this was the yardstick for arrest, then half the population of inner London would finish behind bars.

Su-len showed little excitement as she waved to me coming down the drive, but she knelt momentarily, then rose, her face glowing with pleasure. I kissed her cheek, and she said:

"Moira is not here, you know this?"

I nodded, and she added:

"Do not miss her, for she is nothing—a woman who mates beyond her kind. In China we would feed her with the reins of a mule. You are going to stay with me now?"

I did not reply. The silver cheongsam she was wearing, her hair piled upon her head in Moira's chignon style, lent her a frightening maturity.

At dinner that night, sitting in Moira's place at the top of the table, she shot Ezra a glance of tempered incomprehension, her tongue in her cheek.

"Thank you, Mr. Ez."

He put her noodle soup before her and backed away.

For all her delicate beauty she ate like a Tangar sea-wife, in gasps and shovelling chop-sticks, using her hands when in doubt, sucking up the noodles in dangling streams, oblivious to everything but her stomach. In this mood she was not of Hatherley but the packed red-mud streets where the street-criers bawl their wares, and the snake-feeders jam the cobras in the art of the skinning alive.

I was one with her in the spittled alleys where babies roll on naked breasts. The horney life of the sea-junks came to me in flashing colours where the Pearl River flows to the sea. Nodding at my plate, she paused with wet fingers, smiling at me. "You like that?"

"You know I like smoked salmon."

"That Ez is an arse, and he says cook something different, but I buy it for you—me, Su-len."

I saw her as a sand-rat of the Hong Kong front, squatting on her haunches in the Peking Road, eyes switching up at the tourists who waddled about her like great coloured ducks; and she was there, not in Hatherley, sucking the rice through her strong, white teeth, pausing for a shouted insult at a passing friend; strangely virtuous, then the harlot, when she would cost little more than a Hong Kong dollar; but if her mood was wrong money couldn't buy her. Now she raised her face. "You are displeased with me?"

"No."

"Then why are you silent?"

I pushed away my plate. "Because I see you at the head of the table and you are not the woman of the house." I indicated a chair to my right. "Your place is here."

In Cantonese she replied, "I did this to charm you, for your wife is gone. Also, the Book of Rites makes it clear. When First Wife is absent from the table then First Concubine takes her place. But first she must wash her body and perfume her mouth: also, she will leave immediately First Wife returns. Page sixty-four. You want more smoked salmon?"

I said, sipping my wine, "You presume too much; this has always been your trouble—there is nothing worse than a presumptuous child. Tomorrow, at breakfast, you will sit where you belong."

She grinned at me, chewing over the top of a chicken leg. When Ezra came in with a savoury for me and almond soup for her, I said:

"Ez, you've laid the places wrongly. The top of the table belongs to Mrs. Moira, and will be hers until she returns. Su-len sits on the side."

His eyes bulged in his purpling face. Encouraged, he said, "See now, didn't I damn tell you?" He bent to me. "Me and Mamie Ez, we told her, and all we got was cursing and swearing and she loosed a pot at me. Mr. Mark, you never seen such tantrums!"

She winked at him, wiping her hands on his tablecloth: his eyes bulged with horror.

"Leave it, Ez," I said.

Su-len and I did not speak again at the meal, but every time I glanced at her she enlisted an inner merriment, as if handling the pique of a wayward child. I was quite glad when Anstruther telephoned.

"You take it in the hall, Mr. Mark," said Ez, glowering, "you got a bit more privacy there." He shot a look to kill at Su-len and she replied by sweeting her lips at him. I reflected that they must have had a hell of a time while I was away. And I recognised her mood—it was rarely constant. Later, if things didn't suit her, she would become an arm-waving Chinese virago. Anstruther said on the phone:

"Mark, I happen to be in your area—can I drop in?"

"At this time of night?"

"It's important. Are you alone?"

I glanced through the dining-room door. Su-len was into the grapes, head back, eyes closed, dropping them into her mouth from a height, savouring them with accentuated relish. It was scarcely the time for Anstruther.

I sighed. "Practically."

"See you in half an hour."

I wandered back to the dining-room, saying, "Su-len, I've an important guest coming, and it's getting late. Also, it is business talking, so it is best you go to bed."

"Of course." She picked up the rest of the grapes. "May I take these to my room?"

I did not entirely trust her. At the door she bowed to me. "You look tired, Mark. Please soon come to bed."

I began to long for Moira; it was a penetrating self-analysis, a mood of bizarre extremes.

I went out to meet James when I heard his car in the drive. "You're a bit adrift for a Londoner, aren't you?"

"God," he breathed, slamming the car door, "you don't have to be a Londoner—have you missed any of your friends?"

"Missed any? It's an evacuation. Half Woking's behind the wire —this is worse than Brander—even he didn't subscribe to rape."

"Rape?"

"The Besfords' daughters. Luckily Portia got away by the skin of her teeth."

He said, reflectively, "Portia? That's the big one, isn't it? She'll be sorry about that."

"James, it's important!"

"I've never been partial to Portia." In the lounge he took the brandy I offered, adding, "Where's all the ideals of anarchy? I hear they burned the Stock Exchange last night."

"That's a step in the right direction."

He glanced at me. "Isn't that cynical? It has started a run on the banks; foreign investment will be affected, you know."

I sat opposite him. "It's time we had confidence in people, not money. Is there any diplomatic activity anywhere? The usual jockeying for jobs?"

He made a wry face. "John Drover's been asked to form a workers' government with Nigel Kinson's son as deputy—there's even talk of a General Election. He's standing for the New Left."

"He wants to watch that," I said. "The greatest mistake the Socialists made was to ask a snob middle class to vote Labour."

"You're in a naïve mood tonight, aren't you?"

"It's a naïve situation." I drank my whisky, looking into the empty glass. "Let's have a class system based on merit for a change, then the meek shall inherit the earth, even if they die doing it."

"Well, well—you're certainly not at your best, are you?"

"I'm not. Where the hell was Drover and his friends when the chips were down? If people like him had watched Heath and Powell we'd never have smelled Brander and the Workers' Democracy." I filled my glass and sat down again. "Now perhaps you'll tell me why you're here at this hour?"

"You're drinking too much again, you know."

"I've some firm excuses."

"Then here's another. Drover wants you to take the post of Minister of Building."

I managed to conceal my surprise despite the fumes of the drink; not even in the epic moments of my life had I considered ministerial rank. Faintly I heard Su-len singing; a strange, sad song that I had heard before.

I said, "Who the hell assumes I'm Left anyway? Surely they can find a city financier—after all, in a technical department he won't have to know the size of a brick, will he?"

"Will you take it?" He ignored the cynicism.

"If Drover asks me himself."

He smiled disarmingly. "It's scarcely the sensitive reply taught at Eton, old chap."

"I don't trust the bastards," I said. "Tell him that, too."

Su-len entered with a tray of coffee, and I was astonished. She was dressed in a child's party frock that was six inches above her knees; her hair was down her back, tied with white ribbons; she looked thirteen, and said:

"Papa, Ezra was tired, so he asked me to bring this in."

In Cantonese, I replied, "What the devil are you doing dressed up like that?"

"Because I'm a child."

I said to Anstruther, "James, this is our Su—you'll recall the Kish report and the newspaper accounts?"

He whispered, "God, she's only a baby . . . !"

Su-len gave him an adolescent smile, and said in English, "Shall I pour the coffee, Papa?"

I replied in Cantonese, "Yes, and after that go to bed."

"Isn't it wise to show him I'm only a little girl? When he leaves here he'll send it around." She smiled into his face.

"Su-len, for God's sake leave us in peace."

"How charming," remarked Anstruther, "conversing in Chinese . . ."

She said, as she poured the coffee, "For weeks you have been away—I never have you to myself. When you get rid of him I'll be waiting upstairs."

"Get going."

She took a backward step, bowing to Anstruther. "Good night, sir, you stringy old moke."

I called after her in Chinese, "And don't come down again."

"What a charming little creature," said Anstruther, after she had gone. "How low can people sink? Those newspaper suggestions were absolutely libellous."

I didn't reply, and he added, "I think you should know that Hargreaves is in on this Drover suggestion—indeed, he suggested you."

"That political animal? I'm flattered. When the time's ripe he'll cut the throat of his grandmother, let alone mine."

"But you'll take the post, Mark? Come now!"

"More than likely."

Out on the drive, he said, "Naturally, the workers will want to know a bit more about you—this you realise?"

"Not another Kish-style investigation, I hope?"

After James had gone I went back into the lounge and drank a lot more whisky, trying to obliterate my thoughts of Su-len.

The lounge clock was striking midnight when I got into bed; the house was silent save for Ezra's faint snoring. I was on the edge of sleep when, again, I heard Su-len's song, and tensed, listening.

Before the Feast of Excited Insects I am come of age.
From the womb of my mother I arrived at the autumn moon.
See, upon my wrists I am wearing golden bangles
Which are the emblems of the sorceress Tang
Who lived in the palace of the Ming Emperor.
Beaten silver of the Tangar I am wearing at my throat.
Within my loins is green jade from Shansi.
With cinnamon I have decorated my breasts.
My mouth I have perfumed with the scent of musk.
And painted my lips with berry wine.
But now the wild goose is calling from the village
So I shall untie my hair to please my lord,
Standing at the foot of his couch, that I might please him.
And he, who knows of women, will remember that I am young

And have not been used before.
Tomorrow, while the world still sleeps, I shall be married
And acquainted with the joys of love.

Hearing this song, I remembered Lei Tao-sung, who first sang these words: a fierce little piece of eighteen was she, with black hair down to her waist.

Sold into Mui-tsai at the age of twelve—the barbarous child-selling still practised in Hong Kong, she had graduated through concubinage to a rich man's house, and then, because she produced no sons, to the brothels of Wanchai, and you could have her for three dollars, which was all I could afford at the time. Jardines, the old opium runners, didn't pay a lot to a boy come East, aged twenty.

Verse after verse, Su-len sang in her bedroom.

So I remembered the small-boned women with curved lips and painted faces, who brought amorous night to a youthful reveller. Their bodies were dark, like Su-len's, their skin was oiled, their hands and feet tiny—miniatures in love-making, expert in the trade. And their brazen laughter came from the Mist and Flower bawdy houses of Macao under gorgeous Chinese sunsets, dry-swimming the mahjongg tablets into the night.

I first met Lei Tao-sung in Wanchai, and took her to Macao in the cabin of the old *Fatshan;* there she would play to me the music of her childhood and read passages from *The Dream of the Red Chamber,* her favourite novel. Later, with the old ferry rolling down the China coast, she would gollop noodles and rice, enough to sink a navvy. Lithe and quick was she, cleaving to me in gasps and reviling me in Cantonese curses; bemoaning her stupidity for collecting half a man.

On the sands of Big Wave Bay, in moonlight, I first made love to her; brine was on her lips, I remembered, I *slept . . . sand* trickling through my fingers beside her head and the disarming mechanism of the mine was red with rust on a beach in England. I begged its spigot to turn, for I didn't want to be mutilated like Joey Tyler, who died through loss of blood. Land mines have a warped sense of compassion and I talked to this one, taking a deep breath in the bed of Hatherley and heaved on the helve, and the spigot clicked into safety-cock; I should really have been blown to pieces. But the sun burned down on the beach, gulls sang; the wind fanned my sweating face, and I sat up staring across the room, amazed that I was still alive in the moment of waking.

Su-len was standing at the bedroom door.

Upon her wrists were gold bangles; pinned to the high collar of her mandarin gown were emblems of longevity. Her face was heavily powdered, her lips scarlet. She was perfectly attired in the red and gold gown of a Tangar bride.

It was her sixteenth birthday under Chinese law, I remembered. "Mark!"

I did not reply.

She whispered, peering, "You are awake?"

Again, I did not reply and she came to the bed, saying, softly, "You have been expecting me? See, I will untie my hair as did Hsiang Fei, the Fragrant Concubine before the eyes of Khan—she who came to Peking from Asku." She pulled a slide from her hair, shaking its blackness over her shoulders; removed the bracelets and dropped them to the floor. Slowly she undressed, whispering as she folded each garment.

It was the incantation of the marriage ceremony; the same unreal water-painted world of celestial beliefs in which the Taoist Popes lay in their cellars a horde of bottled souls, one day to unleash them into the camps of the western world. Now she said, following the custom, "Remember that I cannot live on air, so feed me; that linen is better than cotton to keep out the cold; remember, also, that I will prove more obedient in a silken bed than in one of straw."

Reaching out she took my hands and put them against her lips. "Lie still," she commanded.

In retrospect I realised that I had no chance; but mine, not hers, was the responsibility. And, if she knew the tumult of my mind she made no sign of it, since she was now engaged in the pressing business of love; but careful, too, to retain my dignity, this being the ancient duty of a very young wife.

And so, as First Concubine of her lord Mark, and according to the Book of Rites, page eighty-four (which she apparently assumed was my age) she unified us in the consummation of marriage, rule by rule, in the standard courtship of age by youth according to the mandarins: kissing my face, my hair, my hands, but never my lips . . . it being necessary to ensure that what breath I still possessed be not restricted; and that the old, if ambitious lover, be not unnecessarily wearied.

In a rift of her hair I saw patterns of moonlight playing on the ceiling.

It was an astonishing expertise, and very considerate, but scarcely flattering at my age of maturity.

Indeed, I found it difficult to restrain her enthusiasm: Lei Tao-sung, my first lover of the old *Fatshan* ferry, without the assistance of the Book of Rites, was a dolt compared with her: Hallie didn't come into it.

Moira, for once, was a replaceable dream.

CHAPTER 18

I was becoming increasingly worried about Hallie's whereabouts. Even a month ago, at the time of Moira's disappearance with Shearer, I would not have been able to identify the reason for such concern, because it was mainly the dangers to Moira that kept me awake at night, despite my attempt to reject her.

Once, I knew quite simply, it was the flattery of Hallie's youth that was her attraction to me—a balm to my fading pride at the loss of Moira. But now I realised that, beyond the physical relief she brought me, Hallie had become in her youngness, the substitute for my wife; her comparative immaturity revived in me the joys of my early days with Moira: I had created in her an attainable ghost of one who once was mine, before the coming of Henry Shearer; a gay, lovable shadow whose name I once called in the flat above the Courval Salon . . . in the midst of Hallie's breathing.

But I was certain that Hargreaves knew where Hallie was, and I began to wonder if the situation between the two of us was now reversed, and she had gone back to him.

When passing me in the corridors of the Ministry, Hargreaves always had one eyebrow slightly raised as if in silent comprehension of my loss, and was grieved about it. I wished him to the devil.

I continued to ring her flat; I wrote to her many times.

It was as if she had been spirited away, and I wondered, too, if Commissioner Kish knew anything about her . . .

On the very day that I decided to visit Monsieur Courval himself, I was called before the tribunal of the new Workers' Democracy for confirmation in the post of Minister of Building in succession to Cheriton, whom, they said, was still in the country awaiting trial. Mr. Drover having officially appointed me, I yet needed the blessing of the Revolutionary Committee before I could be confirmed in the post: it was a patent example of the power of the new Workers' Democracy—particularly as Drover was himself awaiting his confirmation as Prime Minister as well.

But the greatest affront, for my part, was that Joe, my son, should be especially called by the tribunal to sit in assessment of me. To this was added the frightening coincidence that the room in the Treasury Hall chosen for this new examination was the one in which I had three times sat before the Kish Commission.

Anstruther said carelessly, "You realise, of course, Mark, that it is pure formality?"

"Of course."

"I mean the whole thing's really cut and dried."

My life, I reflected, was entering the realms of sublime absurdity.

"Your name's Seaton?" The ragged Civilian Militia guard rose as I approached the door where he sat.

"It is."

He slouched away, his rifle trailing the floor, and I followed.

Entering the room I knew so well, I sat before the same semi-circular mahogany table; the same clock was ticking on the wall behind me; the same smoke pall was hanging over London in the window behind the chairman's head.

Of the six men sitting at the table, Joe was on my left, easily the youngest there; he was slightly removed from the others, I noticed, as one of junior rank. On his left was a man with a bandaged face. The chairman, broad and jovial Irish, said:

"Ah, Seaton, it was good of you to come." He smiled at his companions. "And a joy to meet up with your son, as well, no doubt. My name's McNamara, and I'm head of the Workers' Appointment Committee—ye realise this is only to confirm you in the Drover post?"

I nodded, glancing at Joe. His eyes were steady on mine but gave no hint of recognition: with a bandolier of bullets over his chest and his Ku Passa repeater on the table before him, he could have been the Committee guard. McNamara said, "I take it you're prepared to answer a few simple questions, Seaton—it's only procedure; with a record like yours the appointment's automatic."

"Then why have it at all?" I asked.

"Mainly to give you the congratulations of the people on the way you handled the Cheriton corruption, and the Kish Commission in particular." He tapped his pencil against his teeth: heavily jowled, unshaven, his great size dominated the room. "I've been reading the findings and recommendations made by Kish—weren't they a bunch of unspeakable sods!" He grinned affably. "But you'll be happy to hear that a few heads rolled—Schreiber's, for instance—we got him early. And Kish himself's in the company of a gent called Flowers, who now works for us." He paused, then added, "Or perhaps, as an extreme moderate, you don't subscribe to the violence?"

I gathered myself. "I don't. There's been too much already."

He grinned wider, showing fine white teeth. "Aye, well you're entitled to an opinion, but when you're running a revolution there's no time for niceties. Did you hear we captured Cheriton?"

"Yes."

"And his wee stooge, Harmsworth."

"I heard Harmsworth was dead."

"Give it time."

There was a silence and the men before me raised their faces to mine. They were a typical cross-section of the workers—artisans, labourers, I heard later; two were members of the reformed T.U.C. Council. McNamara said:

"You're not forthcoming, Mr. Seaton."

"What do you mean?"

"I mean you don't approve of us, do ye—it's written on your face. If you don't believe in summary justice you shouldn't have sat on your arse when times were better—it's people like you who've brought the need for violence." He stiffened. "God alive, man, we've got to destroy the dross! It's the elemental need of a revised institution."

"You're making too much of it," I said.

"Thanks. But we've just finished dying for one politburo, and unless we rub them out we'll soon be dying for another."

"It isn't the doctrine of Marx."

"But it'll make a better Britain."

"I wouldn't have thought so. People like Cheriton and Harmsworth are innocent until proved guilty."

His hand went up. "Wait, wait, man—didn't you yourself prove the guilt of Cheriton and Harmsworth beyond all reasonable doubt?"

"That's for a judge to answer."

He regarded me, rubbing his chin. "You know, for a man of action ye tend a bit to the established order when it comes to the crunch. But you'll approve of the standard methods in one case—we've got your wife and Shearer."

I got to my feet. "Where is she?"

"Sit down, man—all in good time, for she's well enough. Can we stick to the case in hand? What do you know about Shearer, for instance?"

"Very little." I scarcely heard him: Moira was safe!

"Is that a fact? And him a constant visitor to your house?"

"He was nothing to do with me."

"But you knew his political colour."

"Of course."

"And you tolerated it?"

"Yes, as I'm tolerating yours."

His eyes, bright blue in his tanned face, opened wide. "Indeed to God! And what's my political colour?"

"On the evidence I've seen I expect you're an anarchist."

"You'd not pay me the respect of being a Socialist?"

I said, "Socialism died in the 1970s, McNamara."

"I'm pleased to be informed. And what might be your political convictions, since we're on the subject?"

"I haven't any."

The man with the bandaged face said, "Then you can't agree with the parliamentary system?"

I sighed, saying, "I can't think what all this has to do with my confirmation in a ministerial post. Secret ballot is the essence of democracy; personally, though, I don't vote for anybody."

McNamara said, "So you waste your vote?"

"Oh, no. I vote for them all."

"The attitude's cynical."

"It isn't. Up to the polling booth we've got democracy; after it we've got the parliamentary system—the whips come out, the M.P.s change their ground, representation is lost and democracy's destroyed."

They stared at me. McNamara said, "Good God! It's an enlightening observation for a prospective government minister, Seaton. Can't you do us better than that?"

"I can tell you how many trades there are in the building industry."

He smiled, "Have you views on the subject of your father's politics, Joe?" He leaned forward, looking to his right, and Joe's eyes were expressionless in his bearded face. He replied:

"My father's qualified to take the post of Minister of Building. He's a Fellow of the R.I.C.S.—he has worked on building sites, learning the trades on the ground; he's a fine administrator, but he isn't our man."

"Is that a fact?" asked McNamara. "Why not?"

"Because he isn't one of us," said Joe. "The Workers' Democracy is of the Left. People who aren't with us are against us, they can't sit and watch."

I replied, "I'm a civil servant, not a politician. If a new government comes to power, I'll serve it."

"As you served the Brander set, for instance?"

"Until I discovered Cheriton's corruption; that's the criteria of the good civil servant."

"Christ!" ejaculated McNamara, "that's a new one!"

There was a silence, and I said, "This is worse than the Kish Commission—what the hell do you want of me?"

Joe answered softly, "Political loyalty, but the job's too messy for you middle-class reactionaries. You're always on the fence like the great British public, taking the easy line and never a political stand. You let Hitler come and you waved bits of paper, and it cost you thirty million dead. You supported, by idleness, the rape of Abyssinia and the bombing of Suez; you watched Callaghan send troops into Ireland because you never believed the slaughters of Cromwell. Do you know the massacres by Lake at Wexford, for instance? For three hundred years you've stood apart while others did your dying. You've supported governments of financiers and fools, and you're still at it today." He took a deep breath. "From a technical stand-point you get my vote, but you lose it by your criminal apathy."

McNamara said, "God bless the Pope, man, I enjoyed that! There's some interesting asides comin' up, isn't there? Are you pro-Soviet, Seaton?"

"No more than I'm anti-Chinese."

"Then you agree with the Chinese conquest of India?"

"Of course I do—India's eating at last."

"But India was a democracy and now she's Marxist."

"Good enough. If democracy doesn't work then democracy must go."

"So you're a Communist?" said a man.

"No, a humanist; it's important to me that people get their share."

"And the black immigrants? It's claimed that ten years from now they'll be thirty per cent of the community—you approve of this?"

"Of course. Our wealth was founded on their blood—the slave trade; this is supposed to be the Mother Country, so it's as much their heritage as ours."

"And Bolo Mombara?" asked Joe. "Did you approve of him?"

"He was a brave man."

"Was that why he was in your house?"

"No, your mother invited him."

"And the charge the Brander police arrested you on—his murder —was false?"

182

"Of course."

"It must have been false, for you weren't anywhere near the house, if my memory serves me."

"No, I wasn't."

"You were down at the river with Su-len, I believe . . ."

I interjected, "The Kish Commission brought in the business of Su-len to blackmail me away from my charge against Cheriton: I didn't expect this from your Workers' Democracy."

"But the Workers' Democracy has the right to expect morality in its ministers," said Joe.

For the first time I heard the clock ticking on the wall behind me.

These men, I thought, could just as easily be the Kish Fascists, for nothing had changed except the name of the regime: it was the same old interrogations, brutality and slaughter. The deaths of men like Stan Waters and Waring were proving an idiotic futility; the thousands who had died to overthrow Brander had made empty sacrifices. McNamara said, playing with his pen:

"How old is the Chinese girl Joe mentioned, Seaton?"

"Sixteen."

Joe, I noticed, glanced up at this, and McNamara continued, "You've had some off-beat people living in your house, and the visitors come worse, that Johnny Hampshire, for instance—there's a ponce—to say nothing of Shearer. There are good reasons why new brooms sweep up the social pornography that always grows under the Right with its hunting, shooting and chandelier brawls, but what the hell were you up to with Shearer and his dirty *Act of Love?*"

"I hated Shearer and all he stood for—hadn't I reason?"

"Right, Seaton, but I could be happier about the company you kept nevertheless—your wife was Shearer's mistress, and you tolerated this. The Besfords, too, aren't quite the proletariat; Marsella's a whore and he's a community parasite."

"The worst of us have qualities," I said.

"No doubt." McNamara straightened, breathing heavily. "You manage a mistress, I understand?"

"Yes."

"Her name, please." His pen was poised.

"Oh, no you don't."

He sighed, rubbing his face heavily. "Would it be Su-len the Chinese kid?"

"It is not."

Joe said, "Her name is Hallie—I don't know her surname; she's a model at the Courval Salon in Bond Street. Before she met my father she was living with Hargreaves of the Moral Guidance Council."

"Dear me," said McNamara, and whistled softly. "There's one good thing about this lot, Joe, they're handy below the waist. *Hargreaves!* No wonder the Prime Minister loves him!" He clasped his big hands. "Now, one last question, Mr. Seaton, before we confirm you in post. I've a wee thing to ask you about the Chinese measurement of time. Is it true that a Chinese child born on the last day of the last month of the year could be two years old at birth?"

The sweat was cold on my face. "Yes."

He nodded. "This has no bearing at all on the subject, of course, but as a point of interest—I understand the Chinese girl had a birthday recently—is that correct?"

"Yes."

"And she was a year old at birth—right?"

I nodded, and he said, "This being so it makes her fifteen years old in Woking—never mind about sixteen in China?"

"Yes."

"And under the age of consent in Britain?"

"Yes."

He said, drily, "I expect I'm right, for I checked with the Chinese Embassy. Would you consider her in need of care and protection, then, since you agree she's a minor?"

There was a degree of humour in it; he could be forgiven, of course, for he didn't know Su-len. "No," I replied, "I wouldn't."

He got up from the table. "Opinions differ, Seaton, for at the age of fifteen she's not entitled to professionalism. Holy Heaven, man, I'd not trust you with me pet tom cat, let alone a child-woman. Which is not to say you shouldn't be the new Minister of Building, for there's some randy bureaucrats sitting in Whitehall in the shape of public servants, and everybody's howling for Cheriton's blood." He glanced at me, breathing heavily, and added, "Make yourself available at half-past ten tomorrow morning, for we're not quite finished with you yet."

The door slammed behind them like the lid of a coffin, leaving a brooding male violence, and Joe was the last to leave, without a backward look.

I crossed the room and opened the door, shouting after him down the polished Treasury Hall:

"Joe!"

He did not turn to me; it was as if he had not heard.

Disconsolate, I returned to my office.

Seeking escape from the growing sense of disaster that pervaded the room, I left the office despite Carrie's protests about the mounting work. Returning the salute of Security Jones in the hall, I walked down Whitehall in warm sunshine; it was a truly beautiful day.

One had to give credit to the new Workers' Democracy when it came to civil organisation, I reflected: although it had been in power for just under three weeks, things were rapidly returning to something like normality.

Clusters of people were in Trafalgar Square, I noticed—ever the rendezvous of Londoners in times of crisis, anxiety, indecision, and festivity. Some were actually feeding Nelson's pigeons: these, less in number through poaching, and thinner through lack of tourists, flapped around the monument to an earlier tyranny, one glorified by the lie of history. Since childhood I had eminently preferred Emma Hamilton to her sadistic lover—he was surely unworthy of her as the epitome of Establishment violence, and scarcely beloved of his working-class tars with his dreaded keel-hauling and "Flogging around the Fleet".

Of abstract mind, I wandered, dolefully considering the era of violence in which I lived: a violence constantly denounced by the unholy liaison of Church and State, which existed on the fringe of violence, ever ready to indulge in an orgy of it, should its precepts, or profit, be threatened: using as its emblem of benevolent dictatorship the public exposure of a man crucified, bleeding from a dozen wounds before the eyes of the adolescents of a hundred generations. And in the shadow of such sadism they protested about violence.

The hypocrisy was appalling, I reflected, when one comes to consider it. It was the accepted violence of government after government, irrespective of political colour, which had brought us to this.

But London, like China, has the strength and character to contain, absorb and destroy such enemies after the initial shock of their conquest. Now she was in the process, after digesting the governments of Wilson, Heath, Powell, Whiting-Jones and Bull Brander, of masticating the new Workers' Democracy.

Presumably the trains had started to run again—lately I had been using the car—and Charing Cross station was boasting in her forecourt her usual jam of honking geese, the taxis, and a few drab London buses were edging a nervous path across traffic lights of smashed signs and overturned beacons. Even the office girls, the coloured birds of London, were scurrying again, eating their sandwiches on the street this time, for lack of restaurants. Most of them had gone into bright summer dresses, too; some working on the ageless principle that the tighter the sweater the looser was the girl.

Anstruther, I recalled, held the academic opinion that, far from reflecting the peace that always follows violence, the dress of the female actually instigates war: that the transient changes in fashion are an elemental process, designed by Nature, the mistress of fashion, to control the size of the population. But, with the dress of Eastern women unchanged for a thousand years, I was content to speculate on its healing of the wounds. A youngster about Su-len's age smiled brilliantly at me; I raised my hat to her.

Down on the Embankment, I looked at the river. Significantly, the Royal Yacht and Boland's ocean barge were moored together: both, it was said, were now occupied by high-level revolutionaries of the Workers' Democracy: I was not in the least surprised. . . . Only the government had changed, not the ethics.

The tramping of feet turned me here.

Street-cleaning squads were returning to their wired Internment Camps, coming off their shift from the areas of Millbank and County Hall.

They were marching in a clanking of pails, these people; a forest of drooping labourers carrying brooms and pulling refuse carts. And beside them, guns at the ready, went the coloured patrials, the vainglorious victors who had brought men like McNamara to power. In the van, heavily guarded, were some who did not escape: politicians from the time of Heath and Wilson, pale well-remembered faces from the late 'sixties and the 'seventies, caught up in the long-awaited revenge of the people; carrying buckets and brooms, they were chained together with scores of others, including peers of the now untenanted House of Lords, dressed in the ridiculous finery of their office.

Next came the aristocratic and rich, the pin-striped battalions of city big business, and many wore dunce's caps: financiers, barristers, solicitors and artists were there; priests and Quisling patrials were roped together, and behind them trundled the night-soil carts from the slums of Notting Hill: these were pulled by younger prisoners, and drunken harridans were standing on the footboards behind them shouting obscenities and threatening them with clubs. I saw the broken spirits of the new slaves, the tattered, hair-down, defeated women and girls, a few of whom were in riding habit, and one of these was of Royal blood, captured at a gymkhana during the fighting.

I knew the failure of a revolution that exchanged one class hatred for another. Nothing had been gained: the ideals of freedom had been fought for and lost. Now was beginning the purification process—labour was good for the soul; the thought-revisionist cures of the New Left.

"Mark!"

I had turned away, appalled; Moira's voice spun me.

"Mark!"

I saw Marsella first. Moira, roped by the waist, was beside her, and she raised skinny, naked arms to me. "Mark, Mark!"

It was unbelievable; I just stared. Kate Shearer I saw next, but

187

she did not call. With her bright hair down to her waist, she went with pride; her legs were bare and she wore no shoes. In one hand she carried a bucket, with the other she held together the rags at her breast, and she was smiling. Marsella, suddenly seeing me, called for help, and a patrial went into the ranks and struck her with a stick.

"Moira!"

I ran through the column to the other flank, darted in and grabbed Moira's arms, trying to pull her away. But she was roped to the woman next to her, and both tripped and fell. Shouting, I set my feet and hauled at them and other women tumbled in a heap. People were shouting; Moira was clasping me about the legs, and the guards came in, striking down everybody within range. One, a big black patrial, raised the butt of his rifle and jabbed it down, but I avoided the blow, stood square, and hooked him hard to the face. Yelling with anger, he fell, clawing me down among the feet of the prisoners. Somehow I got hold of Moira's rope, heaving her out of the ranks. Then I heard running footsteps: other watchers were joining me; a pitched battle began that spilled across the pavement. The road was now covered with threshing bodies, the air filled with cries; whistles were being blown as guard after guard was brought down, attacked by the furious onlookers. But then came the Civilian Riot Militia. They came in a baton charge, brutally felling some, hauling others to their feet, tightening ropes, threatening with their pistols. Lost in the confusion, I rolled away, still hauling at Moira's rope, bringing her down on top of me. Momentarily, we were together, unseen by the guards. With her face against mine, she gasped, "Oh, Mark. Oh, God! Mark . . . !"

I held her. For a moment I held her, kissing her face, her hair; and when the guards lifted her to her feet, they raised me, too—as one with her. Then two men grasped me and flung me headlong. On the pavement I watched as they pulled her back. The attacking crowd was now being pitched out of the street-cleaning ranks. Eyes clenched, I listened to Moira's cries as they beat her.

I leaned on the wall of the Embankment and watched them go and some were my friends: mainly together, these, seeking in degradation the old companionships. Claud Besford was there, his face heavily bruised, and he went like Kate Shearer, his head high: nor did he turn to me, though I repeatedly shouted his name. Beside him was Johnny Hampshire; there, perhaps, because his father was rich; stripped to the waist, he had been badly flogged. The daughters of Marsella—Alicia and Gertrude of the Hunt Club were behind him; Portia, their sister, shuffled along, as did Genevive Dolan and her little jockey husband. And the last one I recognised was Henry Shearer; manacled to him were Sarban and Coko, Ezra's African friends, the servants of the Besfords.

A big cockney woman, unkempt and blowzy, was leaning against the Embankment wall, weeping in frustrated grief.

Turning her into my arms, I held her, and she wept against me.

After Moira and the street-cleaners were gone, I sought whisky; my usual alcoholic drown.

In the Strand, at Mick's Tavern, I drank hard, subsiding by late afternoon into a tipsy, morose relief. Unaccountably, I could not remove from my mind the picture of Stan Waters's face, the first casualty in the dull pantomime of my life. Perhaps, indeed, it was the Civil Service mind that took me back to the office a few minutes before signing time and Carrie regarded me with faint disapproval, shaking away the friendly arm of Security Jones who had escorted me up.

"You're in a bit of a state, aren't you?" said she.

"You go to hell."

"Ought to be ashamed of yourself, Mr. Seaton. You really did!"

I sat down in my chair and swallowed the aspirin she brought me.

She said, "I suppose it was the Workers' Democracy that did it —did they confirm you in post?"

I didn't reply; I was listening to the cries of Moira. Then I heard Carrie say, "The Prime Minister's secretary has been trying to contact you since lunch, you know. Shall I get him?"

"Not yet."

"Also, there's a gentleman in the waiting-room I've seen before —Mr. Flowers."

I got to my feet instantly, but she had turned, not noticing my agitation.

At the door, she said, "And Miss Hallie telephoned . . ."

"Hallie?"

She added, flatly, "It appeared to be important."

It sobered me. "Did she leave a number?"

She nodded.

"Get her at once." I began to pace about.

"But the Prime Minister . . . ?"

"Get Hallie."

She sighed in matriarchal disapproval: a bottle and napkin for the wayward child, and said, wearily, "Mr. Seaton . . ."

"*Get her!*"

She slammed the door behind her.

I thought of Flowers in the waiting-room, felt the thudding fists: not even the executioners had changed. Shaking now I snatched up the receiver when Hallie came through.

"Hallie!"

"Why, Mark, how lovely to hear you!" Joy was in her voice.

"Where've you been? I've been worried to death about you."

"Why, you poor old thing! Can't a girl take a holiday? Who wants stuffy old London during a workers' revolution? Are you still in one piece?"

"I am." The monitor clicked in and I cursed it silently. "Where are you speaking from?"

"Is it wise to tell you on the phone?"

Thank heaven somebody was sober, I thought, and answered, "Perhaps not . . ."

"Listen, then—do you remember where I used to go on holiday? Now, think."

I peered my memory through the haze of the whisky, and re-called it—the old climbing hotel, the Pen-y-Gwryd, near Llanberis in Snowdonia. Hallie cried, "Surely you remember it Mark!"

"Yes, I do now, but really, you might have told me you were going!"

She ignored this. "I've another three days here—it's glorious at this time of year—would you like to join me?"

"I'll be there tonight!"

"Then I'll book you a room."

"Try it," I said.

A new excitement seized me that hazed the astonishing clarity of Moira's face. And there came to me then a need to put as much distance as possible between me and the Workers' Democracy, the new junta that had replaced Brander; one pig in exchange for another, as Benedict once said, but this time an uneducated pig. Pressing the intercom, I said to Carrie, "I'm . . . I'm just slipping out for a couple of minutes. Tell Mr. Flowers that I'll receive him the moment I'm back, and give apologies for delay to Drover's secretary."

"But Mr. Seaton, I've got him on the line . . ."

"All right, then, I'll take him," I said.

But I did not, and it was cool in the street.

I could have got Sam, my taxi, for he was haunting in his usual place, I noticed, but I chose the safety of a bus to the underground car park in Park Lane.

There, I got into the Jaguar and took the road to the west, to Wales, and Hallie.

Moira's cries followed me relentlessly through the London traffic surging down the Cromwell Road. Here, brown-shirted soldiers of the Workers' Civilian Militia were patrolling the pavements, batons drawn: others, with sub-machine-guns, were standing at the open doors of houses being searched for suspected Tories and Liberals, a new purge. A group of ragged, dejected blackshirts, recently prised from a cellar, apparently, were being herded into a lorry for Hounslow Internment: one, a girl, had fainted on the pavement and her long, fair hair was flowing over the kerb, directly in the path of my nearside wheels. I edged away, trying to avoid it, but was instantly pressed back again by hooting, furious traffic. Bile rose in my throat, and I swallowed it down. In a rising discord of car horns, I stopped the car, slid over into the passenger seat and opened the door. I had a foot on the pavement when a brownshirt stooped, gathered the girl into his arms and tumbled her into the back of the lorry.

It was a patent example of the new, working-class democracy, and I never forgot it.

Now, on the premise that I could do nothing to help anyone, least of all Moira, whose vision continued to follow me, I got on to the M4 and put my foot down, embarking on a process of her total obliteration.

CHAPTER 19

Perhaps in my blood there exists the spirit of the ancient Iberian, the nomadic Welsh tribe who inhabited the rolling land of Gwent. Certainly, there is an affinity between me and Wales—matured, perhaps, from my youth, when Moira and I, with a car tied up with string, roamed the mountains from Plinlimmon to Cader Idris with no money in the bank—long before the betrayal by Henry Shearer. Now, in late afternoon, I motored in a gigantic landscape of mountains and sky, with the sun blazing behind clouds of a windy world, a halo of light around the peak of Siabod. Within this aurora I seemed to hear the pealing and clashing of bells.

Here the gullies and gulches reared about me around the Llanberis Pass, bringing me to insignificance: the skeleton chimneys of the old slate workers were pinned with slanting light.

Hallie, timing my arrival, walked a mile out of the Pen-y-Gwyrd Hotel to meet the car: she looked like Hiawatha with her Indian tan and her long hair in plaits either side of her face; her red shawl was a splash of blood on the deserted road. She said, getting in beside me, "My name is Mrs. Seaton and you are my husband. Please make sure you include me in the conversation."

I kissed her. "Isn't it a little prim in these loose times?"

"It is not a loose hotel. When I said I was expecting you and wanted to change to a double bedroom, the landlord looked at me twice."

"Don't blame the landlord."

"Also, there's an eighty-year-old shower in the bathroom. You stand up in it and the water spurts out of the sides."

"I hope there's room for two. How long are we staying?"

I heard Moira's screams as they beat her and thrust the sounds away.

"Until Sunday."

"And I'm supposed to be back on Monday for another investigation by the Revolutionary Committee."

"What for this time?"

"For the post of Minister of Building, though it's hard to believe it. This time tomorrow there'll be a hue and cry."

"You've run away?"

"You could call it that."

"Because I asked you to come? Oh, Mark!"

"It was an opportune time. I've had just about enough of their Workers' Democracy."

"But they'll look for you—won't there be trouble?"

"Perhaps, but they'll scarcely find me here."

A happy thing happened when we got out of the car. As I locked it and turned towards the hotel entrance, Hallie reached out, turning me to her. Momentarily, she stood there, her eyes moving over my face in silent assessment, then she deliberately put her arms about me and kissed me on the mouth, saying,

"Is it so terrible to ask for a man to come? I love you."

I held her against me and did not reply; sadly, I wished she was Moira.

In the little bar where Tensing and Hillary had signed their names on the ceiling, we drank beer amid the chattering guests, mainly mountaineers, and Hallie said, "Standing in the hall is a woman watching the back of your head."

"I hope she's enjoying it."

"Do you think you have been missed already?"

"Possibly. Let's hope she's not a T.V. addict."

"So early?"

"A vanished Minister of Building under investigation could make the screen within hours."

Hallie said, "Now she has turned away."

"Probably your imagination. After all, the men in here have been watching you for the past half-hour; it'll confirm their worst fears if I take you into dinner."

I followed her into the dining-room, and thought she looked delightful in her white mini-dress and her black plaits down to her waist; indeed, the darkness in her, her small, high-boned face gave her kinship—if a slightly larger version—with Su-len.

The dining-room filled rapidly; we ate in silence. For me it was pleasing that our very quietness might be proof of the growing bond between us—one of affection that would eventually obliterate Moira—growing out of the romantic fury of our earlier relationship. Moira, if momentarily, was forgotten.

Hallie said, softly:

"That woman's come in, you know. She's sitting in the far corner, and she's staring again."

"Perhaps, after all, I haven't lost my touch."

A party of young climbers entered, marvellously boisterous; the men angular and brown-faced, their heavy boots clumping as they found their chairs; the girls were bright-eyed and tousled: they brought with them the smell of the mountains. One, I noticed, was very like Moira at the same age; her charming Irish lilt reached out to me over the years, a sweet nostalgia. But I had forgotten Moira again by the time Hallie was combing out her hair in Glyder Fawr, our bedroom.

Lying in the bed, I watched her; Lockwood's Lake, I remember, was a shattered mirror of silver under the moon, flashing beyond the window.

To have spoken would have banished the phenomenon. Enchanted, I watched her bare arms moving in the moonlight, the astonishing glow of the comb, and static electricity was running along her fingers, a glow of a myriad sparks that trickled like frozen water down the long, black strands. It suddenly seemed an appalling affront that I had betrayed her by my intimacy with Su-len. She asked, as if reading my thoughts, "Is Su-len still at Hatherley?"

"Yes."

"And Moira's away with Henry Shearer?"

I decided not to recount the horror of the street-cleaners. "Yes."
She lowered the comb, turned and faced me. "Did you make love
to Su-len?"

It would be an expiation of the offence to tell the truth, I decided.
"Yes," I said.

The effect was greater than I had assumed. She said, "But, how
could you, Mark? She's a child."

I didn't reply, and she added, "So all that the newspapers say is
true?"

"It is."

She put the tip of one finger in her mouth and looked at the
moon.

I was a little surprised when she came into the bed and put her
arms about me; amazed when she made no mention of the betrayal.
She merely said, "You men are all the same, you expect too much
forgiveness. There's not so much love about that women should give
it free, you know."

Her lips when I kissed them were dark in the moonlight flooding
the bedroom; it could have been the mouth of Su-len. Her hand
on my arm was a black stain, and it could have been the hand of
Su-len. My head was aching, I remember, for a leaf had begun to
tap on the window-pane with monotonous regularity. Hallie said
against my face:

"Don't make love to her again. If you do, I'll kill her."

The leaf began to tap louder, now more quickly in a little wind.
The body of Hallie, lying against mine, was suddenly cold, like the
ice-coldness of the bomb casing when you're fighting to get the
nose-cone off, and the tap-tap-tap continued, like the ticking of a
clock suspended from the heavens, but I knew in my heart that it
was a bomb. The ammonal *weight* . . .

. . . *imagined* the brain igniting within the tenement of the skull
in that infinite second between life and death: the face then dis-
integrates—an appalling ugliness, as in a distorting mirror, when
the features are perverted into shapelessness within a light-blaze of
detonation . . . now exploding into immensity, seen by a slow-
motion camera, in jerks, frame by frame. First the eyes protrude,

extend and melt before the bulleting teeth that fly as the jaws blow apart, darting with the little bones of the hands in rocketing trajectory; the cheeks puff up and expand, the hair singes to baldness and the vertebrae of the neck lift slowly.

I said, "Have you ever been to Bath, Hallie?"

"Bath?" She opened her eyes. "What are you talking about?"

"It's a lovely Georgian place."

Antiquity has to be protected, according to Colonel Vidor. We owe it to posterity, Corporal Evans, so get down that hole and short this bastard out—no, Seaton, let him alone, this is his first. Bombs, Evans, are referred to as bastards because bastards invent them, other bastards manufacture them, bloody bastards drop them and silly bastards like us defuse them. But Corporal Evans (atomised in Bath) didn't know how to short out this particular bastard, which was probably why he was only a corporal, but he got down the hole just the same while Colonel Vidor (then a captain) sat in another, safe, hole and said into the intercom, "What is she, Corporal Evans?"

"A 600 kilo, I think—standard Mark II, sir."

"Have you got the cover-plate off?"

"Yes, sir."

"And you can see the terminals?"

"Yes, sir."

"And you're sure there's no anti-handling device?"

"Quite sure, sir."

"Do you want me to come and check, Evans?"

"No, sir."

"Right. Short out, then report."

"Wilco," said Evans.

But he shorted a pair of brass casing studs which were nowhere near the terminals and there was a report right enough. Hallie said, shaking me:

"Mark, wake up, you're having a nightmare!"

I said to her, "It was a low-capacity circuit, of course, and he was so scared that his hands must have been sweating. When he touched the terminals, everything went up. The only thing we found

197

of Corporal Evans was an ear—his right one. Ears are astonishing things, they seem impervious to blast—the things actually take off. But we do have something to bury, thank God, said his sister: she was a pretty little thing, they were twins."

Hallie said, getting out of bed, "Now you stay here, I'm going for a doctor."

I heard from below stairs the bass shouts of men and the laughter of women, and Moira screaming as they beat her, and I sat up in bed, staring at the leaf still tapping at the window. My body was wet with sweat. I said, dragging at Hallie, "I am all right—I tell you, I'm all right—please don't make a scene."

We did not make love.

Next morning, leaving the hotel for the car park, the woman followed us.

"It's her again," said Hallie.

"Surely she won't have the neck to follow us up Snowdon," I replied as we got into the car.

"She must have seen you somewhere—the newspapers, perhaps. The police might be waiting when we get back."

"We'll make it a calculated risk. In any case, I'm not ducking out in perpetuity. Shall we give her a run for her money?"

"She's a bitch."

So was Hallie a little later.

With the idea of taking the little mountain railway to the summit of Snowdon, we drove carefully through the tourists crowding the High Street in Llanberis and savoured the placid beauty of the morning, betwitched by the enormity of the country about us. For my part I was aware, despite the sense of isolation and safety, that the net of my life was tightening about me. The ticking of the bombs of my youth, the icy touch of the nose-caps and the chatter of the intercom now crystallised into a bitter neurosis.

Now, with the car left in the park, we fought for seats in the little railway carriage, barged by climbers' rucksacks and scrambling children; a hubbub of excitement. Hallie said, "Don't look now, Mark, but that woman's sitting behind you."

"Then we'll give her something to listen to," I replied. "Are you aware that the Welsh name for Snowdon is Snawdune, a mistaken translation of the derivative being *The Rock of Eagles*?"

"No, but I do know that the lake up there is the home of a monster. Is she still looking?"

I said, "Yes, I can see her reflection—her chin is practically on my shoulder. And this monster caused flooding in the Conway Valley, so the townspeople chained it to a team of oxen and towed it up the Miners' Track—Welsh monsters of the fifth century expired at high altitudes, apparently."

Hallie said, "She's listening to every word."

"To escape its tormentors it dived into the blue lake and was never seen again."

As the train started and the carriage assumed the angle of the Cresta Run, I could, by glancing at the window, clearly see the woman's reflection; she could be an agent of the Workers' Democracy, I thought, but I couldn't understand why she was following me up Snowdon. Below us now loomed the parachute drop into the valley. In a whine of the cogged drive the little Swiss puffer took us up into the clouds and the passing stations of Hebron, Halfway and Clogwyn. I reflected that the expectation of life for one rejecting the new regime was about fifteen hours; the banishment of major names in the Ministries was thick and heavy. The woman behind me leaned forward, smiling into my face.

"Excuse me, sir, can I have a word with you?"

"No," I said.

Now, standing on the platform of the little station near the summit of the mountain, we were consumed with the beauty of the scene below us—seeing clearly, for the air was clean, the vista of Glogwyn du'r Arddu and the Portmadoc estuary knifing its bright country; even the mountains of Ireland and the Lake District. Hallie said:

"Look, I've got a call to make—I'll join you on the summit and we'll have the highest kiss in Wales."

I replied, "That woman's vanished, you know. If you see her in the ladies' toilet ignore her."

Here, I recalled, as I trudged up to the summit amid the excited children, lay the bones of Rhita Fawr, the giant ogre who wove his cloak from the beards of slain kings. The winds of myth and legend seemed to banish the harsh realities of my present, for within hours, after the woman had telephoned, I would be back before the Workers' Democracy. The coquetry and tragedy of Moira, the death of Stan Waters, the betrayal by my son—all was suddenly an inconsequential phase of my life. My intimacy with Su-len, the child of my trust, encompassed me with a sudden shame in this place of purity. I thought, as the children raced about me and the summit approached: were I to lay my bones up here with Rhita Fawr, who would be the greater monster? A bottle of brandy and sleeping tablets . . . ? If I could sleep with him in this place, would not this be the eternal life for which fools prayed? Where did idealism lie, I wondered—in life, or death? And where was truth? In the vicious beatings of the new political soldiers or the bullet-spattered bodies of the Workers' Democracy?

When I reached the bench mark on the top of Snowdon two men were standing there. It did not surprise me in the least when one of them asked:

"Mark Seaton?"

I glanced around; there was no escape other than the long drop down the mountain. The elder of the two said:

"We've come from Sean McNamara, Seaton. We're armed, so don't cause trouble."

I looked down at the railway terminus for a sign of Hallie, then turned back to them: she could not help me, and I did not want her involved.

The first man said, "Just follow, my friend, and I will walk behind. It's steep down the Zig-Zags, but I expect you can manage."

"Mr. Seaton!"

We had just started off when the woman from the Pen-y-Grwyd

called me; in her hand were a notebook and pen. One of the men, turning, said, "You've made a mistake, lady, there's no Mr. Seaton here."

"Oh, yes there is!" She approached me, her eyes bright with expectation. "The moment I saw your picture in the evening newspaper I knew it was you—the lost Minister of Building."

"Congratulations," I said.

"So please can I have your autograph?"

I grinned at the two men. "If you take a message to my friend—she's down in the ladies' toilet—just give her my love."

"Are you going without her, then?"

The men were relaxed, staring about them. "It would appear so," I said. "Tell her I'll see her in London."

I went with them down the Zig-Zags, the shortest route to the Pyg Track and the curtained car which was awaiting us in the car park at Gorphwsfa. Vaguely, I recognised this car, so I was not totally surprised to find Mr. Flowers sitting in the back of it.

"Well now, Mr. Seaton, if it ain't me old friend."

I envied his ability to please everybody.

My arrest was inevitable, I suppose. Nobody had yet succeeded in raising two fingers at an idealistic Workers' Democracy.

CHAPTER 20

I was a little surprised when the car headed north-west instead of south, for the road to London; and more surprised still when Flowers pulled the window curtains going through Llanrug, taking a second-class road to the sea a mile or so below Caernarvon, in whose castle, I heard later, the Prince of Wales was then incarcerated by the Welsh Nationalists. Mr. Flowers ignored my agitated questions, even when we walked through the shallows of the incoming tide to where a little cabin cruiser was anchored. I began to wonder what they told Bill Waring before he was found dead in the sea off Sidmouth. . . .

"This is ridiculous. I demand to know where you're taking me!"

One can drown equally well under Fascism or Democracy, and Flowers said in his politest tone, "Just do as you're told, Mr. Seaton, and you won't 'ave a going over."

On board the little boat they locked me in its cabin, and I realised my predicament as the engine started. If another boat came and took Flowers and the others ashore, they'd only have to knock out the bungs for this to be another boating accident. Through the cabin window I watched the shores of Wales recede, and calculated that we were somewhere outside the Menai Strait when the engine stopped; the anchor chain dropped; we rolled and heaved in the hiss and slap of water. I slept, awaking almost instantly to darkness and the activity of running footsteps: then a yellow beam of light swept the sea, and I heard the unmistakable clatter of a big ship in the vicinity. The cabin door came open, and Flowers said:

"It's the end of the road, Mr. Seaton."

Now, on the deck, I stared up at the tarred hull of the ship above me: a rope-ladder descended, swinging against the evening stars. Distantly I heard the drone of heavy aeroplanes; from the shore came the incessant explosions of guns; searchlights swept the sky.

"Good evening, Mr. Seaton."

To be sitting in the state-room of a ship before the inquiring stares of three strangers enlisted in me no apprehension. Investigation, inquiry, confrontation had become so much of my daily round that it was now approaching realms of unreality. Yet the atmosphere, in this case, was almost benign. One of the men was young, though his hair was almost white: he was of immense size in his grey jersey and sea-boots; the other two were nondescript, rather like drab city clerks; probably lawyers, I reflected. The chairman said, "Mr. Seaton, I apologise for the manner of your capture, but time is short—there is no alternative to haste. . . ."

I interrupted, "I demand to know who you are and why you've brought me here!"

He nodded understandingly. "I'll be brief, sir. We are the legal representatives of the government in exile, and we're interviewing high-level civil servants with a view to ministerial appointments."

"Not again! I'm already a minister under the Workers' Democracy."

"By this time tomorrow, Mr. Seaton, that administration won't be in existence. Two hours ago European Community paratroopers began seizing key points in our major cities—it was inconceivable, surely, that our European partners would allow such anarchy to exist!"

"So we're going back to Fascism, are we?"

He smiled benevolently, "No, Mr. Seaton—a Coalition—Socialism and Conservatism working together for the common good."

"By God," I said, "it isn't before time. If they do it this way they can both share the profits—nepotism and usury on both sides of the fence."

"It means cohesion for the first time in years, sir. Surely you approve of unity of purpose?"

"Not the way the politicians serve it up. You're as bad as Brander's Triumvirate and the Workers' Democracy, because you brought them about. Now you listen to me. In your time, Labour or Tory, you wasted your efforts in class wars and served your careers instead of the people. Just how long would it be, with a Coalition in power, before you started your party politics all over again?"

He nodded forgivingly. "You have another alternative, Mr. Seaton—Communism."

"And I'm likely to give it a try."

"Come, come, as a member of a free society you can't mean that!"

I took the cigarette he offered me, and Flowers, hovering near, lit it ingratiatingly. "I don't know, the thought's beginning to intrigue me. It couldn't be worse than Socialism as a diluted brand of Conservatism or Tory benevolence as the prerogative of the rich. Communism isn't coming, man—it's here."

"Then you refuse to be employed?"

"Of course I don't—I'm bound to serve."

"As Minister of Building under our administration?"

"As long as I see the end of Fascism and this Workers' Democracy!"

He brought his hands together. "Excellent; we have agreement in principle—bring in the first witness, Mr. Flowers, and, at this stage, stay outside the door." He turned to me. "You have no objection to hearing the testimony of our agents, sir?"

"I've had it all before, man—wheel them in."

"Mr. Hargreaves, gentlemen."

"Christ," I said.

I stared at Hargreaves. Indeed, he was extraordinarily handsome; a political hyena, as Benedict once called him, soliciting at the doors of personal advantage. Now he actually winked at me as he sat down beside me. The chairman said, "Are you quite sure you wouldn't like to wait outside, Mr. Seaton—this could be embarrassing."

"Let him talk," I said, "I'm an expert in this," and Hargreaves said:

"Mr. Seaton is naturally upset, sir—I ask you to remember his earlier interrogations, but I'm sure he'll find this one rewarding as far as I'm concerned. I have no hesitation at all in recommending him for the post of Minister of Building."

I swung to him. "*You* recommend! That's a good one!"

Ignoring this, Hargreaves said, "He's a man of high professional qualification in the new era of the technocrat. His very flight from the Workers' Democracy proves his detestation of public disorder —though he can be a trifle intolerant, as you observe."

"It's a qualification in some instances," said the chairman, drily.

Hargreaves continued, "This candidate is politically uncluttered, as you know—nobody has earned his vote—this came out in the Kish Commission inquiry. Would you like to see the transcript?"

The chairman replied, "It isn't necessary." He turned to me. "You are married, of course, Mr. Seaton?"

"Until my wife ran away with a Fascist."

He nodded, expressionless. "And I see that you have a son."

"I had."

"You live by yourself near Woking, it appears."

"Actually, no. I have an adopted daughter below the age of consent—in times of stress we sleep together. If I don't tell you, Hargreaves will."

"Need you be facetious?"

"It's a rewarding exercise in the face of these juvenile questions. You know damned well there's been a scandal about my daughter."

The chairman looked surprised.

Hargreaves said, "If every professional man I bring before you has to be morally sound, Mr. Chairman, I suggest you look to the theologians for your technocrats. Are you to be influenced by the slanderous attacks of the Kish Commission, and the lies they spread about Mr. Seaton and his adopted Chinese daughter?"

"That is for me to decide," came the reply. "Mr. Flowers, bring in the next agent, please." To me the chairman said, "It would save a lot of valuable time and considerable unofficial explanation, if you were prepared to hear these official reports—time is the very essence of this appointment."

"Anything you wish," I answered, and Hargreaves said at the door:

"I've got good news for you, Mark—Shearer's dead, but Moira's safe—I've taken her into the country. . . ."

The surging relief and the following joy paralysed my movements. He again winked at me, adding, "And more—she wants to come back to you."

Hargreaves went out and Hallie came in.

The very substance of the room became insubstantial; a stage of nullity where the actors were phantoms, their dialogue unreal. Only the opening and closing of Hallie's mouth was actuality. The chairman said, "I am delighted that we managed to find your wife, Mr. Seaton. Now please sit down—this won't take long." To Hallie, he said, "Please make your report as brief as possible, ma'am," and Hallie, without even a glance in my direction, read from a paper:

" 'It became clear to me, on meeting Mr. Seaton in his house—we were introduced by Mr. Hargreaves, as you know—that he was soon to be very important in his Ministry: more, I learned that he rigorously opposed Brander's Triumvirate. His opposition to militarism crystallised when he exposed the Cheriton fraud. Resultant Kish publicity, though denouncing Mr. Seaton's morals, at least proved his utter incorruptibility—even in the face of torture he maintained his allegations in the public interest. . . .' "

The chairman interjected, "Mr. Seaton, I didn't realise the private nature of this agent's report. I ask you again—would you like to retire, to save yourself embarrassment?"

I said, "On the contrary; the eulogy is fascinating; I only hope it continues."

Hallie smiled faintly and replied, "It doesn't: I was asked to observe on your personality, and I will do so." She read, " 'Mr. Seaton is, I consider, the complete technician; a man in service to the public, the only master he respects. He is intolerant of politicians; he sees Royalty as a sop that chains the people, the Church a blasphemy which keeps the Queen in power, the aristocrat a parasite and the rich corrupt. His view of the working class is no less derisive

—the vote of the average British housewife, he considers, can be bought by a promise—this, he says, is how Heath came to power.'" She looked at the chairman, adding, "You wish me to continue, sir? What comes next is very personal. . . ."

I said, "Don't spare me; you haven't done so far." The chairman nodded, and Hallie read, " 'The Kish Commission tried to prove Mr. Seaton's mental instability, and did so, I believe, with some success. As a result of bomb-disposal experiences, he endures frightening hallucinations, depression, actual mental vacuums. Nor do his morals stand examination—we became lovers, as you know, so I speak with authority. Mr. Seaton is incapable of loyalty—except to the public: he has few personal standards.' Shall I go on, sir?"

"Please do," I said. "It's enlightening."

" 'In my opinion,' " read Hallie, " 'official integrity is not enough for ministerial rank, nor are professional qualifications—we can get those anywhere. The fact is that Mr. Seaton is morally unstable—he has actually confessed to me his offence against a minor. And if political enemies of a Coalition could substantiate this, the repercussions could be damaging to a new administration.' " Hallie took a deep breath, adding, "This report, sir, is based on months of inquiry: the last day of which has been spent in the area of Snowdonia, in order to allow me to detain him before the agents of the Workers' Democracy made his arrest: this would have been disastrous."

The chairman did not look up. "And your findings, ma'am?"

Hallie replied, "I don't recommend this unstable man for a post in the Coalition government."

"Thank you, you may go," said the chairman.

"Congratulations!" I called after her.

She bowed almost imperceptibly.

The chairman said, "I hope you didn't find that too hurtful, Mr. Seaton—in such urgent times there is little opportunity for diplomacy."

"I'm full of admiration," I replied. "Hargreaves and Hallie—they make a marvellous pair."

He warmed to me. "Yes, don't they?—irony apart. Political consultants can name their own price these days, you know—and these were trained in the finest schools."

"Without doubt."

He leaned forward confidentially. "The man Hargreaves is a pupil of the Conservative Central Office, you know. The woman's a product of Transport House; an excellent actress."

"They're a credit to each other," I said. "Do I get the job or not?"

"Of course; Mr. Cheriton's insistent that you become his Minister of Building."

I stared at him. "Mr. Cheriton . . . ?"

"Of course."

"You can't mean it!" I rose from the chair. "*Cheriton?*"

"Oh, yes I do, Seaton—it lays all the ghosts, you see. Actually, you're not the best candidate: I mean—personally, I wouldn't recommend you. But Cheriton, our prospective Prime Minister, needs you so badly—it would have the effect of shooting all our opponents in their political ankles, though you'll have to cut out the Chinese girl, of course. Have a drink?"

The two men at the table rose and drifted away; one was carrying a tape-recorder, the other held the microphone.

"Cheriton . . ." I said aloud, dully. "Prime Minister? God!"

The chairman put his arm around my shoulder. "Oh no, God doesn't come into it. I mean—no prayers rise from the House of Commons, do they? That is performed by the professionals in the Abbey next door." Going to a cocktail cabinet, he poured two whiskies. "Brander's gone in bits and pieces, so has the Workers' Democracy—or will have, within a day or two. So the intelligent politico moves with the times; the people simply must have palliatives . . . and Cheriton knows how to dispense them."

I cried, "But the man's a criminal!"

He drank. "Yes, but who really cares?" He moved his big hands. "Look, Cheriton loves you and you must learn to love Cheriton—everybody pees in the same pot for a good Coalition—for a time, anyway. You can't flounder about in a mess of idealism, Seaton: too much of that and you become inconsequential."

I shook my head, staring into the whisky.

So they took me ashore and motored me back to Hatherley as the official Minister of Building in the coming Cheriton government. Mr. Flowers, sitting with me at the back of the car, looked quite morose.

"Mr. Seaton . . ." he began.

I gave him a cheerful wink. "Don't worry, mate, I'll bloody see to you."

But in my head were beating the words, Moira is safe, *Moira is safe*. The relief, the growing realisation, and the joy, were sweeping over me in waves of intensity.

Nothing else mattered now, nothing at all.

It was just conceivable, with Shearer dead, that she might even return to Hatherley.

I shut my eyes, rejecting the nearness of Flowers, trying to recapture the symmetry of her, the beauty of her face.

CHAPTER 21

Actually, I went back to Hatherley with V.I.P. status—armed motor-cycle police escorting my Jaguar fore and aft. This was necessary, I was told, because disturbing reports were coming in. The Irish Republican Army, for instance, had landed parachutists on the Welsh coast and were spear-heading for Cardiff in light motorised columns, exercising reprisal for the old Black and Tans, and the more modern refinements of Long Kesh. To avoid those we took a more easterly route, but north of Birmingham ran into fierce fighting between a Workers' Democracy regiment and two French companies trying to capture the airport. Banbury, of all places, was being heavily bombed by German reconnaissance helicopters who were searching for the workers' arms dump at the Ordnance Depot there, and great plumes of fire were rising above the spires of Oxford—probably the worst bombing of an open city by Common Market forces during the whole insurgency. Light infantry tanks with Community markings stopped us at the M4 fork to Reading, and these were Dutch troops, but it wasn't dramatic: indeed, there was some light-hearted banter between these and my guards. According to them the workers' grip on the military situation was already faltering, for London had been saturated with Community airborne troops, and all key points of administration were in Community hands.

We drove through diversions to a sleepy Bagshot where blacks from Martinique were lounging on the pavements, waiting for a dawn push, armed to the teeth; these were the out-guards of Aldershot and Camberley where the army and Officer Cadet Force had answered the call from Paris and handed in their weapons. Only in the London East End was strong resistance being encountered, we heard, and this, strangely was from the great patrial regiments. Bloody street-fighting raged through Islington and Bethnal Green, and it took a battalion of German parachutists supported by gunships and river bombardment, before they surrendered.

But the Woking area was quiet, with no sign at all of the pressured events that were bringing about yet another change of government, though I suspected that it would only be a matter of days before the countryside was swarming with troops from the European Community centre of operations, based on France.

It was an ironic turn of events, I reflected, as the little procession reached the lane to Hatherley, that all the freedoms fought for, and lost, in the processes of inter-party, class squabbling, should reach finality by a foreign occupation.

For six years of the last war the country, unified and cohesive in the face of the onslaught had fought in brotherhood, and kept the enemy beyond the cliffs of Dover. Now, abdicating all rights to national success in the tracks of the personal vendettas, the greeds, the racial suppression and class hatreds, we had succeeded in opening the flood-gates to European conquest: French and German troops who, for centuries, had been kept from our shores at the cost of generations of death and sacrifice, were now strolling into a land they never would have gained by conflict. And their presence now, formally requested, would mean servitude, not liberation, despite the pompous phraseology of the Council of Europe. All the diverse aspects of the British soul could never have expected such a descent into the abyss: we, who never had been slaves, were at last enslaved by racism, political adventuring and personal avarice.

The traditional enemies had become the traditional masters.

"Leave me here, please," I said at the gates of Hatherley. "I'll take my own car up, I don't want to wake the house."

But I had to knock up Ezra because I hadn't got a key.

"Why, Mr. Mark!" His large eyes bulged white in the faint light of the coming dawn. "Oh, Mr. Mark, thank God! . . ."

"It's all right, Ez, it's all right. Go back to bed."

"But that telephone, sir—it ain't ever stopped ringing. We had to take it off the hook. Where you been . . . ?"

I went into the hall and switched the telephone up to my room.

Undressing swiftly, flinging my clothes away haphazardly, I put on my dressing-gown and slipped into the cool, welcoming sheets, to awake almost instantly, it seemed, to the clanging of the bedside bell. Sleepily, I lifted the receiver, and Anstruther said:

"Mark, is that you?"

"Not at this time of the morning," I replied. "Don't you Fleet Street people ever sleep at all?"

"Not for the next month or two, the way things look. I suppose you know that the French president is in Whitehall?"

"He must have moved faster than Napoleon."

"It's a provisional arrangement, of course—until your old friend Cheriton gets going with his Coalition."

"Do you really believe he'll get the chance?"

He said, "What's that supposed to mean?"

"If it comes to a choice between the French president and Cheriton, I'll take Cheriton, complete with corruption. For God's sake, James, don't tell me your political reportage is as naïve as that. If the French get their feet in Whitehall, nothing under an atom bomb is going to ease them out."

"You can't honestly believe that—they're the Community leaders!"

I swung my legs out and sat on the edge of the bed, lowering my voice in fear of waking Su-len, and said, "Exactly. But unfortunately, reporters of the calibre of James Cameron are dead, so you're not getting sound advice. Now's the time for your banner headlines. 'Out with the French'—because, unless we shift them in the next ten days they'll be here for the next hundred years. Are you still there?"

"I've never heard that one before, it's a new brand of scare-mongering. Are you taking your Ministry under Cheriton? We heard on the tape this morning . . ."

"Unless somebody shoots me before I get to the office."

"You sound depressed." His voice was faint now, and there was a lot of disturbance on the line, with the monitors clicking in and out, and in the midst of the cacophony of foreign chatter, I distinctly heard a sudden, harsh flow of Chinese; then the line cleared a bit, and I replied, "It's a depressing situation, Anstruther. What's this about an American task force coming in by sea?"

"Understandably, the White House doesn't like the idea of a Continental take-over. They also, like you, say that once the French get London it'll be a job to move them. A lot of American business interests are involved, you know."

"A lot? They've got half the bloody country sewn up in investment. Well, thank God we'll have a super financier like Cheriton to auction us in the next few weeks—if the French freeze American money the Pentagon will incinerate us—another Vietnam."

Anstruther said, "And you want to watch what you're doing at ministerial rank, because it doesn't end with the Americans. The Russian Sixth Fleet is sailing up from the Mediterranean; Russian agents—paratroop signallers—community liaison officers have already been seen in the south coast towns."

"Jesus."

Anstruther spoke again, but the line went dead in my hand; I replaced the receiver and went to the window. The first rays of dawn were splitting the sky like a hatchet and the poplars down the Hatherley drive were being filled, as usual, with a dull, rosy light. Continuous, dull booming of gunfire was coming from the east: the London suburbs were catching it, apparently; later I learned that vicious fighting had broken out there between American and French troops for the prize of London, with the poorly armed Workers' Democracy militia and the old Brander blackshirts fighting side by side, now, trying to contain them, welded by patriotism.

It was an appalling absurdity: one of the richest countries in the world had flung away its heritage by internal squabbling in peacetime, yet in war it was invincible. Now it lay, this Britain, as a glittering trophy; a dying fox with its legs in the mouth of the Americans, its mask in the maw of the Russians and its belly in the claws of the French.

The telephone rang again and I took the receiver. Anstruther said, "Hot news, Mark—you really must cut all links with Cheriton. Ministers of government will be first in the line of fire—he has already begun negotiation for a take-over by the French—the ticker-tape's going mad here. Are you there?"

"Yes, go on."

He said, "Everything's happening now. American paratroopers are dropping on London; there's fighting between Dover and Felixstowe: the Workers' Democracy is a dead duck. Resign, for God's sake, while there's still time, and . . ." The line cut out again and I heard the unmistakable clatter of radio morse.

I stood there, thinking. Strangely, despite Anstruther's obvious panic, I was ice-calm. On the face of it I had the choice of flight, the tender mercies of the C.I.A., or the dubious hands of French Intelligence. And if the remnants of the Workers' Democracy found me in either camp, I'd renew acquaintance with people like Flowers.

Flight, in more senses than one, appeared the wisest course: with my present ministerial papers and diplomatic immunity, it might be possible to get a plane to Scandinavia—anywhere for a start. From there it would be a short step to China, the only safe place.

With Su-len?

Such was the race of recent events that I had completely forgotten Su-len. At any cost to myself I would have to protect the child . . .

But before I moved to go to her room the telephone rang again, and a voice said, "Ah, Seaton—I'm glad I caught you in. This is Hargreaves. I expect you've heard that the Americans and French are hoping for a partition—the idea being to share us out between them. Now, my consultants have just had a call from the Russian embassy —apparently the Russian ambassador has been trying to get hold of you: naturally, they have interests in Europe—a foreign occupation of Britain is quite against their external policy. Would you be interested in a post with a Russian caretaker government? Their airborne forces have got most of the south coast towns between Eastbourne and Plymouth . . ."

I closed my eyes, replacing the receiver, and, as I did so the thing rang again in the moment Su-len, in her nightdress, came wandering through the door. Amazingly, she did not run into my arms, but just leaned against the wall, smiling at me. As I lifted the receiver I heard Hargreaves say, "Apparently we were cut off, Mark. Look, I must have your answer—Benedict's going along with it, so is Adam Steen and Anstruther—these are men you like and trust. So, with your open-ended politics it surely proves attractive—obviously the Russians won't be here long. . . ."

I put down the receiver again, then changed my mind and left it off the hook. Su-len, unspeaking at first, slowly approached me and kissed me gently on the mouth; she said:

"Now everything's going wrong for my poor Mark; I am sorry. But you have me. You will always have Su-len. You wait a moment?"

Picking up the telephone receiver she dialled a number while I blandly watched.

"What the devil are you doing?"

She said, "You leave it to me and everything will be all right." Then, into the phone she said in rapid Cantonese, "Yes, he has returned, as I expected. Please put the Ambassador on." And she handed me the receiver. A voice asked:

"Is that Mr. Seaton?"

I looked long and hard at Su-len. "Go on, answer him," she said.

"Seaton here," I said into the phone, and the reply was instant:

"Good morning, sir, this is the Chinese Ambassador. Our contact has reported your love of China and your devotion to your own country. In the interests of Britain, the Peking Government would be very happy to receive such an important man with a view to . . ."

He got no further, for I had depressed the receiver. To Su-len, I said:

"My God, you didn't waste much time. How long has it been going on?"

"Since I was fifteen—by the Chinese calendar." She added, "Nobody here is any good to you, you know—you'd be much better off in the East. And with Chinese influence spreading over here, you'd even be able to bring me back on holiday—I know how much you love Hatherley. Moira does not care . . ."

"Leave your mother out of it!"

She pouted, eyeing me.

I looked her up and down. "Our contact . . ." I said, nodding at her, "our contact . . ."

"It is for your own good, Mark." Her arms went about me but I levered her away, going to the window. The sky was bright above the trees of the river; somewhere in the woods a bird was singing with enchanting clarity, and I reflected that once, when young, I sat under a tree and watched a nightingale; saliva bubbles from its throat were drifting up against the night sky. Then I heard the rumble of the guns and the clouds reflected vicious redness.

By God, I thought, everything was going mad in the very midst of Hatherley's beauty—even Benedict and Anstruther had changed now, and I would have staked my life on their opinions.

Presumably, with Moira in the offing, it was safest to conform, and go mad as well. But it was an ironic reflection that, at a time of such national insanity, I should possess three certificates stating I was sane, which was a damned sight more than George Orwell had. . . .

Indeed, I thought, so much for the Orwell box-office bonanza of the failed Socialist that so delighted the Right—the prophecy of a dictatorship of the Left. Nothing, *nothing* Orwell had predicted had yet come to pass, and there were but a few years left to 1984. And now, with the only Big Brothers loose serving in the New Army, it would have been an affront to predict anything save national obliteration via the new political soldiers, who continued, undaunted, to make more violent plans for us in the nation's officers' messes. . . .

I turned to Su-len. "Yes, we'll get away from here. Ring your Ambassador again and ask him to send an official car. If I can get you to your Embassy at least you'll receive care and protection, which is more than you've got now."

She gripped her hands and her eyes became alive with excitement, and she cried, "We are going to China? At last? To China?"

"You are," I said, "I'm going to find Moira."

But I didn't, because Joe and Mr. Flowers were waiting on the stairs.